To Nancy Farndon. Thank you.
Thank you for opening your fabulous bookshop Press Books and Coffee in Market Street, Hednesford, Staffordshire. For letting me swan around in your shop as if I own it. For allowing me to have fabulous book parties and events in "our bookshop" and for always letting me sit in one of the best chairs in the window.
But mainly, thank you for being brave enough to follow your dream. What an amazing inspiration you are.

THE BOOKSHOP AT THE CORNISH COVE

KIM NASH

B

Boldwood

First published in Great Britain in 2024 by Boldwood Books Ltd.

Copyright © Kim Nash, 2024

Cover Design by Alexandra Allden

Cover Images: Shutterstock

The moral right of Kim Nash to be identified as the author of this work has been asserted in accordance with the Copyright, Designs and Patents Act 1988.

All rights reserved. No part of this book may be reproduced in any form or by any electronic or mechanical means, including information storage and retrieval systems, without written permission from the author, except for the use of brief quotations in a book review. This book is a work of fiction and, except in the case of historical fact, any resemblance to actual persons, living or dead, is purely coincidental.

Every effort has been made to obtain the necessary permissions with reference to copyright material, both illustrative and quoted. We apologise for any omissions in this respect and will be pleased to make the appropriate acknowledgements in any future edition.

A CIP catalogue record for this book is available from the British Library.

Paperback ISBN 978-1-83561-370-2

Large Print ISBN 978-1-83561-369-6

Hardback ISBN 978-1-83561-368-9

Ebook ISBN 978-1-83561-371-9

Kindle ISBN 978-1-83561-372-6

Audio CD ISBN 978-1-83561-363-4

MP3 CD ISBN 978-1-83561-364-1

Digital audio download ISBN 978-1-83561-367-2

This book is printed on certified sustainable paper. Boldwood Books is dedicated to putting sustainability at the heart of our business. For more information please visit https://www.boldwoodbooks.com/about-us/sustainability/

Boldwood Books Ltd, 23 Bowerdean Street, London, SW6 3TN

www.boldwoodbooks.com

1

I knew I should have been paying more attention to the box I was carrying, rather than staring at the amazing sunrise over the sandy golden beach of Driftwood Bay. The box felt so much lighter when I left home than it did when I got to the harbour front on my way to Books In The Bay. And when it wobbled precariously, because I was too busy looking at the sun which had just peeked its head out, the thud, thud, thud of the books hitting the ground along with the 'ooomph' noise which came from the person I'd walked into was the only sign that I wasn't alone.

I yelled out my apology. 'I'm so sorry! I wasn't looking where I was going.'

'Clearly! You could have knocked me over.' An abrupt deep male voice literally talked down to me. I grabbed at the books that were scattered around me on the floor. This was brand-new stock and I couldn't afford for it to be ruined. That was the last thing I needed. Every penny in the till counted when you had your own business.

I looked up, still annoyed with myself, but even though I knew it was probably mostly my fault, surely I couldn't take all the blame.

'Well, you must have seen me coming. Couldn't you have stepped out of my way?' Luckily there were a number of benches around the harbour so I started to pile the books onto the nearest one.

'You're right and I'm sorry too. I was too busy looking at the sunrise. It's an absolute cracker this morning. Here, let me help.'

Ah, a kindred spirit. Someone else who appreciated Mother Nature's handiwork. Maybe I should forgive them for that alone. I straightened myself up, stretching my spine out, and moved my head from left to right as I looked at a mop of messy dark brown hair, and an arm reaching for a book that was teetering dangerously close to the edge.

'There you go, last one. At least none of them ended up in the water.'

He popped the final book onto the top of the pile and straightened up. Blimey. If I wasn't mistaken, the most handsome man I'd ever met was standing before me. He looked like a Hollywood movie star and was dressed like one too in a pair of dark denim jeans, a crisp white open-necked shirt and a pair of Ray-Bans perched on the top of his head. I'd say they were the real McCoy too, not some dodgy knock-off ones that you're sold by a lucky-lucky man on the beach in Spain. Typical that on that very morning I had made a decision to chuck a fleece over my leggings and vest top and head down to my bookshop, before even washing my face, combing my hair and brushing my teeth. It was so early, I wasn't planning to bump into anyone. Let alone literally.

I tilted my head at him. He looked familiar but I couldn't quite place him. I didn't think I'd seen him around before. I'm sure I would have noticed. Obviously.

'Have you got far to go? Do you need a hand?'

I waved my arm behind me towards the shop.

'Only there, it's fine, thank you. I can make a couple of journeys.'

'Come on, I'll help, it's the least I can do as our little collision was probably half my fault. And it'll save you another trip or two. You grab that pile and I'll grab this one.'

'Thank you. That's very kind.'

'No problem. I'm waiting for my nan to get up. I've popped down to visit but it's a bit early. I anticipated more traffic on the roads. What time does that bistro over there open? Do you know? I'm gagging for a coffee. And to be honest, I could do with the loo too.'

'Ah not till eight.' I glanced at my watch. 'Most of the people in Driftwood Bay will still be asleep. I thought it was only me that got up at the crack of a sparrow's fart to see the sunrise.'

We said the next sentence at the exact same time.

'My favourite time of the day.'

We both laughed.

Gosh! He had a gorgeous laugh and I couldn't help but notice that his eyes crinkled up when he smiled. It wasn't every day that you bumped into someone who got you in a bit of tizzy first thing in the morning. Maybe today was going to be a good day.

The handsome stranger followed me to the shop and I put the pile of books on the step as I turned the key in the lock and pushed the door, propping it open with the cute little doorstopper that my friend Meredith had made me in the shape of a pile of books, before picking the pile of books up again. He followed me in and copied me as I placed the books on the wooden counter. It felt strange having someone come into the shop with me. This was normally my sacred time. The realisation of my dream come true.

Never being the most spontaneous of people, I don't know

what made me do it but the next words came out of my mouth before I'd even really thought about it.

'I don't suppose you... oh never mind.'

'No, go on...' He raised an eyebrow in anticipation.

'Well, I was going to make myself a coffee. I don't suppose you'd like to join me, would you?' I could have kicked myself. Why on earth did I just invite him to join me? What was wrong with me?

'That's very kind of you. Do you normally offer random strangers drinks in the morning?'

'Only on a Wednesday.'

He grinned back at me. 'Well in that case, I'd better make the most of the day and I'd love to accept and perhaps if I tell you that my name is Dennis, and my nan is Vi, then I won't be so much of a stranger.'

I spun around. 'Oh, so *you're* Dennis. Vi's grandson. She talks about you all the time. It's nice to meet you. I'm Nancy.'

'So I gathered. Nan has talked about a bookshop coming to the village non-stop for weeks now. Invited me along to a launch day.'

'Bless her. And yes, the more the merrier. I'll just go and get some mugs and get that coffee machine on the go. The loo is that door over there.'

Heading into the kitchen, and swilling the mugs that I'd used the day before, I wondered what on earth had made me just invite someone I'd never met before to join me for a coffee. I didn't do things like that. Not my style at all. But then, he wasn't really a stranger if he was a relative of someone I knew. And Vi too. One of the loveliest people who has ever lived in Driftwood Bay. Most of the village would describe her as a real character, even if she called herself a daft old bag most of the time.

As I came out of the back room, he was back in the main area browsing the non-fiction shelves and I smiled when I saw him reaching out and touching the spines.

'Ah, so you're a book toucher, are you, Dennis?'

'Caught red-handed. Though, I suppose, better than a book sniffer.'

'Absolutely nothing wrong with a person who loves the smell of a good book I'll have you know.'

'Ah, so *you're* a book sniffer then, Nancy?'

'I couldn't possibly confirm or deny.' We both grinned at each other as I handed him a plate with one of my sacred almond croissants. 'Coffee won't be long.'

'Thanks. So what do people around here do for fun? It's always seemed like a little sleepy village with not much life in it.'

Insulted on behalf of Driftwood Bay, I was a little surprised at the turn of mood.

'I can't speak for everyone but I'm all for doing everything I can to save the environment.'

I couldn't be one hundred per cent sure, but he may have started to roll his eyes at me and then stopped himself.

'Yet you sell books, which are made from paper, and paper is damaging to the environment. Interesting!' I knew that Vi didn't mince her words. Maybe her grandson had inherited her traits. A smile that didn't quite reach his eyes got me wondering about him blowing hot and cold. 'So tell me about your little shop, Nancy. Nice little earner for you, is it? I always wonder how businesses survive in Driftwood Bay. I don't get down here very often these days but there never seems to be loads of people around.'

Sure that my eyebrows were reflecting my quizzical thoughts, I thought about what a bizarre question it was and how out of the blue. One minute we were talking books and the next, this insult about my beliefs followed quickly by a personal intrusion asking about money. It was almost as if he knew finances was my weak spot, something that I hadn't admitted to anyone.

He could see that I was a little flummoxed by his questioning and I was a little lost for words. I never was very good at hiding my thoughts, my inner feelings written all over my face, and right then I wasn't sure if he was being passive-aggressive or just downright nosy.

'Gosh, that's quite a personal question when we've only just met.'

What I really wanted to say was that it was none of his business, but my parents had always brought me up to not be rude.

'I'm a business analyst and I can't help myself. Always worrying about the money side of things of a business.'

This was clearly an explanation and not an apology, and it was getting my hackles right up. Particularly because I had no explanation on the paper front.

'Regarding the income I earn from the shop, I'm a huge believer in what will be will be, so try not to worry about such things.'

This time *his* expression showed me what was going on in his head.

'Good luck with that,' he mumbled as he took the mug of coffee I'd offered him. There was a little bit of me that was wondering whether I'd done the right thing by showing kindness to him. 'Honestly, I visit so many people who have set up a business and have absolutely no idea about how they need to run it. They get these airy-fairy ideas and romanticise that running a business is easy. Did you know that most start-ups fail? It's mainly because the owners live with their heads in the clouds.'

'Thanks for the motivational words. I'll bear them in mind. Have you ever considered doing a TED Talk? You'd be a knockout. Think of all the business owners dreams you could kill in a whole fifteen-minute speech.'

I glared at him, now absolutely wishing I hadn't bothered to invite him in.

Dennis bit the inside of his lip and had the good grace to look a little sheepish.

'Sorry, Nancy, I'm tired and grumpy and have a lot on my mind right now, but it's no excuse. I shouldn't have voiced my opinions out loud.' His brow furrowed. 'All you've done is show me kindness and I've not repaid that.' He took a big swig from his mug, put it down on the counter, and turned towards the door. 'Thank you for the coffee. See you around. And I promise to keep my views to myself if I do.' He walked out, mumbling away to himself incoherently.

As I put my mug up to my lips, to sip at my drink, I wondered what on earth had just happened. Who was this opinionated man who had waltzed into my life on this Wednesday morning, making the wonderful effects of that gorgeous sunrise, which normally put me in a great mood for the day ahead, a distant memory? He knew nothing about me and he had no right to cast aspersions on me or my bookshop. However good looking he was.

2

Preparations for my launch party had been taking place for a week or two. Dennis was true to his word. I'd seen him in the bay a couple of times wandering around the harbour with Gladys, Vi's dog. His gait lacked energy; not what I would have expected from a high-flying business consultant which is what Vi had described him as when she talked about her grandson. His constant staring out at the horizon made him look like he had the weight of the world on his shoulders. Not that I'd been observing him much of course. I just happened to have seen him a couple of times as I looked out of the window, and when I had passed him in the bay, he had just smiled and said hello, but it was one of those smiles that didn't quite reach the eyes. He was, however, the talk of the village, particularly among the womenfolk, who all seemed to bat their eyelashes at him, even though he was oblivious to the attention.

There was a little bit of me that felt sorry for him as he just didn't seem happy, but then when I remembered his previously cutting words, I tried not to dwell on them. I had enough worries of my own. What had started off as a small gathering of friends and family, to celebrate the opening of my dream come true – a bookshop of my very own – was now costing me an arm and a leg on top of what I'd already spent on stock.

My original plan was to just open the doors on a Saturday morning but Mum and Dad had insisted we should mark the occasion in a more celebratory way and host a proper gathering. The day soon came around and I'd ended up ordering cupcakes decorated with books, Buck's Fizz made with good quality champagne and freshly squeezed orange juice, and little gift bags with a free bookmark. Mum also suggested that I wrap a book up in brown paper and slip that in the gift bag too as a 'blind date with a book' gimmick, a great idea, but the amount of money I'd spent on the launch came to a small fortune.

As I was swept away with everyone else's ideas of what the day should look like, it wasn't the day I had wanted.

'Congratulations, my darling. Look at how busy your shop is. I told you they'd love the gift bags.'

'Thanks, Mum, and for all your help too. I really appreciate it.'

'I wish your Aunty Theresa could see you now. Bless her.'

Mum kissed my cheek and wandered away from the counter where I thought I might be busier, but it seems that giving away a book meant that people didn't think they had to buy one. Hopefully they'd be back another day to browse when they had more time. It was a genius idea of Mum's to open up on Bank Holiday weekend, so that people who were visiting the bay on holiday might come back on the coming Monday, and I'd included a flyer in the gift bag with the opening hours. Fingers crossed for a bit more till action on Monday.

Despite the lower-than-expected sales, it was a wonderful day and the love I felt from the locals was truly heart-warming. Floating around in my very own bookshop really was a dream come true.

A nervous throat-clearing cough from behind me brought me back to the present, trying not to think about how much money I'd spent and how long it would take me to claw it back. It would all be worth it in the end. I had to believe that.

'Nancy, do you have a minute?' I turned at the sound of a man's voice as I pottered around behind the counter. My heart sank when I realised who it was, but I pulled my shoulders back and pasted a smile on my face.

'Dennis. What can I do for you?'

'I just wanted to wish you luck for your new venture.'

'Do you though?'

'Yes. I really do and if I could take back the words I said before, I would. I should never had been so negative. I was wrong. I'm admitting I was wrong and I *am* truly sorry.'

The surprise, and that I was taken aback by his words, must have been written all over my face.

'Why the change of heart? You seemed pretty adamant about sharing failing business facts with me.'

Vi appeared at this point.

'Because I gave him a bollocking. That's why! Shitting idiot.' She gave him a short, sharp rap on the arm and he dodged out of her way.

Dennis and I both laughed. 'Please excuse my nan's potty mouth. She can't help herself.' Vi was well known for speaking her mind and we all loved her dearly despite the fact she never held back. Mum ran a cleaning company and Vi was her favourite client.

He held out his hand to me to shake.

'Truce? Friends?'

Looking into his big brown eyes, which seemed to bore right into the very core of me, my tummy did a little flip. I'd forgotten my breakfast that day in all of the excitement. Hadn't even had chance to have one of my own book cupcakes. I must be hungry.

I wasn't sure if Dennis and I would ever be friends exactly, but maybe if he was around in the bay, it wouldn't be the worst thing in the world to be pleasant with him, as long as he didn't try to impart his voice of doom on me. I had no wish for negative Nellies in my life.

'Positive vibes only?' I reached out my hand to meet his and he grinned back at me. God! His film star looks really were quite dazzling, although he appeared to be unaware of the effect he had on the ladies of Driftwood Bay. Except on me, of course. I had a business to run and a planet to save with no time or energy to have a crush on anyone right now.

3

'How many times do I have to tell you, Nancy? Don't feed the pesky seagulls.'

Mum slammed the door behind her as she walked into Books In The Bay. Looks like that was the end of my peaceful reading hour.

'They're vermin and you'll never get rid of them. Blooming scavengers.'

'It's only a bit of bread, Mum. They'll go and find someone else to feed them tomorrow.'

'That's what you said yesterday. And the day before. And...' Mum rolled her eyes but smiled at the same time.

'It's a shame for them if they're hungry. No one else feeds them.'

'There's a reason for that, as well you know, daughter dear.'

Mum had always tolerated my love of nature with good humour. Whether it's squirrels on our fence, sparrows in the garden, or seagulls in the bay, we all need to eat to survive and sometimes a kind human leaving a little food out for them gave them a little helping hand along the way.

She reached down and gave me a peck on the cheek.

'What are you reading?'

'*The Great Gatsby.*'

'Again?'

'Yeah, but it's a new embossed hardback with shiny sprayed edges.'

'Nice. Does that mean it's a different story?' She ruffled my hair and I shrugged away from her. She'd be licking her hanky and wiping my face in a minute. Sometimes I thought she forgot that I was twenty-seven years old.

'I don't know why you don't stop in bed an hour longer and read rather than come in here. Especially at this time of year now the days are drawing in.'

This was the first autumn in my little bookshop and I was so looking forward to it along with the winter ahead. Gone were the sky blue, pastel pink and mint-coloured cushions on the brown leather wingback armchairs in the window, along with similar tones of bunting around the windows. They had been replaced with rust, olive and plum-coloured accessories, with ivory sheepskin rugs and fairy lights galore giving a cosy, magical air about the place. My brother Dan called me a saddo the other day when he came in and I was arranging the books in colour order, said I clearly had way too much time on my hands. I'd laughed at the time, but it was important for me to get the ambience right. To have somewhere that people wanted to come to, to hang out, while browsing for their latest read.

Mum stood next to me in the low fronted bow window which overlooked Driftwood Bay, the gorgeous little seaside village that I was lucky enough to live in. The beach was empty apart from one lone person, strolling along the water's edge.

'I do know why you come here, darling. It's stunning. Both outside and in.'

I glanced around like I did every morning, my heart swelling with pride and joy. This was all mine and I still had to pinch myself when I walked through the door each day. This was the first September in a few years when I wasn't returning to school after the holidays, wondering what the term ahead had in store for this art teacher. In May this year, my dream of owning a bookshop had come to fruition, thanks to my dear Aunty Theresa leaving me a wad of inheritance that came out of the blue. I would rather her be here now, and would swap my dream for that in a heartbeat, but sadly her illness had other ideas. Mum had been, and still was, devastated at the loss of her best friend and missed her desperately. At first, I didn't want to spend Theresa's money but Mum insisted it would have been what she'd wanted and if she could have been here today, she'd be taking pride of place in one of those window seats and very probably bossing us all around.

'Is that Dennis out there, Nancy?'

I lifted my hand to shade my eyes from the sun and peered out.

'Mmm, yes I think so.'

'Oh, Vi never shuts up about her grandson. She totally dotes on him. A right bobby-dazzler, she calls him. I *do* like him though. He's proper handsome and a real charmer with it too.'

'Yeah, I thought that too, Mum, until he came in here telling me what I should and shouldn't do with the shop. He came to help me a couple of times to shift some boxes in the summer, but he's a bit of a know-all. Not the type of person I like to spend time with.'

Mum pulled a strange face and rolled her eyes at me.

'You are a funny one, Nancy. Nice dress, darling. Is it new?'

'Oh, come on, Mum. When was the last time you saw me buy something that was new?'

'Good point. New to you then, I mean.'

'Yep, I bought it from a new app that sells vintage clothes.'

'You do know that you can buy new clothes, don't you? You don't have to buy second-hand all the time.'

'Pre-loved I like to call them. And it's better for the environment than buying new all the time. You know that, even if it's not something that bothers you.'

'It does bother me; I just prefer to buy something that I know someone hasn't died in. Or worse, come to think of it.'

'What could be worse than dying in something?'

'I don't know. Had an accident in maybe?' She screwed up her face. 'Just imagine.'

'I'd rather not but they've all been laundered.'

'Still.' She shuddered. 'Not for me.'

'But you know that the environment would be—'

'Coffee, darling?'

I sighed knowing that she was interrupting me to shut me up. She had a tendency to do this when I wittered on about how we could all do our little bit to help the world be a more environmentally friendly place.

'Yes, please, Mum.'

It wasn't that she wasn't interested in yet another lecture from me about recycling and sustainability, it was more that she'd heard it all before. Many times. I placed the bookmark I'd been holding inside my book to keep my page and closed it, before moving over to the other side of the room and tucking it under the counter. Clem, a handyman from the village, had designed the shop so that everything that could, faced the window, so we were making the most of the spectacular view. Both the counter and the bookshelves had been made from reclaimed timber because he knew how important recycling was to me and I'd been delighted when he showed me his plans and even more enamoured when they were put into place. His partner Meredith had a real eye for interior design and gave me some fabulous advice about decor and upholstery and I don't mind admitting I had a little cry when I saw it all come together. We'd made sure we'd chosen environmentally friendly paints for the walls and the chairs had been re-covered in material made from recyclable plastic. It really was quite amazing what you could get hold of these days, if you shopped around.

I stood behind the counter now and just had a little moment where I thanked my lucky stars, and my Aunty Theresa, proud as punch of my little empire.

On the shelving unit to the left of the counter there was a display of candles and I took a moment or two to choose one which I felt was suitable for the day ahead.

Mum brought two steaming mugs through and smiled at me.

'You could just choose the first one you look at, you know.'

'I could, but where's the fun in that?'

'You do make me smile. I was watching you from the kitchen. Turning them over to read the names, then having a sniff. Some go back on the shelf and some make it to the next round before you go through it all over again. You're such a creature of habit, my little cherub.'

'If I must put up with the smell all day, it needs to be something I like. Couldn't bear it if it was something awful that stinks out the whole shop.'

'What's today's stink of choice then?'

'Pumpkin spice. Here you go.' She sniffed the one I passed her and wrinkled her nose.

'Nice. Shall I go and turn the sign round then?'

'No, you're OK, Mum, thanks. I'll do it.'

Turning the sign round on my very own bookshop, from closed to open, and putting the door on the latch, was one of my favourite times of the day.

4

Five minutes later the bell above the door chimed and Karl the postman appeared. Lovely man, like me born and bred in Driftwood Cove and always cheerful with a beaming smile when he was out and about.

'Just a few for you today, Nancy.' He handed over four letters, a couple of them in brown envelopes and both looked quite official. I thanked him but I wasn't in the mood to open them. Yesterday my latest bank statement had arrived and it was quite depressing to see all the withdrawals and hardly any credits. I knew that you had to speculate to accumulate but I was getting worried at the way business had slowed now the summer trade had died down. I'd cut back on everything I could and made sure that my minimum payments were as minimal as they could be. Luckily, living with Mum helped a great deal. It was lovely that she didn't mind me being back home.

When I left school, armed with my excellent exam results, I'd been lucky enough to be accepted by Exeter University where I studied art history, and I lived in a shared flat, but the costs of living away from home had way exceeded what we ever thought they would, so when I finished my education there, I moved back closer to home and found a brilliant teacher training college in Truro. Mum and Dad had been amazing but it had nearly crippled them. The guilt I felt at hating my job ate away at me and I became quite depressed having to get up and go to a job that I didn't want to go to. The money that had been gifted to both Mum and Dad and me, in Aunty Theresa's will, had more than replaced the money that I'd been paying them back, and meant I could take a step back and evaluate what was important to me. And now I was standing here in my very own bookshop.

I shoved the brown envelopes under the counter and tried to forget about them as I removed my paints and a bag full of scallop shells, which were still a bit whiffy but they'd be fine once they'd been painted and varnished.

As I looked out of the window to the bay beyond, I saw that Dennis was meandering round the harbour, heading in the direction of the shop, and my heart fell a little.

I thought back to Dennis's words about wanting to be friends at my open day. It had been a lovely event, people popping in and out all day long. Sadly, that only lasted that weekend; a week later most of the holidaymakers had gone home and it was back to normal here in Driftwood Bay, and I was left wondering whether opening a bookshop in a small seaside town had been a good idea after all.

When I originally bumped into Dennis in the harbour for the very first time, there had been a little frisson between us. The fact that he was a bit of a dish hadn't passed me by, and if truth be told, there was a little bit of me that thought there may be something more than friendship between us, but instead of that spark igniting, the more I got to know him the more I grew less fond of him. Being a business consultant, big in London apparently, he was very matter of fact and to the point. He certainly didn't fawn over my shop. He couldn't help himself passing on opinion after opinion, even when it wasn't asked for or required. And everything about him was about money: his car, his clothes, his demeanour. He just exuded wealth.

Couldn't be more opposite to me in fact. Yes, I knew that Aunty Theresa's money was the catalyst for me opening the shop, but as long as I could get by that would be enough for me. I didn't want to be rich. What I wanted to be was happy.

The next time I looked up, the harbour was as quiet as could be. Not a soul around. The turquoise sea before me twinkled in the early morning sunlight and I sighed, hoping that I would never forget to be grateful for where I lived and where my business had been born. I laid out my acrylic paints before me and removed a seashell from my handbag, and for the next hour or so, lost myself in creating a gorgeous beach scene with a little red and white lighthouse in the distance inside the shell.

I'd been so immersed in what I was doing that the bell above the door made me jump.

'Hey, Nancy.'

'Dennis.' I nodded, and then moved my head from side to side to stretch. Stooping over the counter painting really did make my shoulders ache.

After he'd told me that I lived with my head in the clouds and that this fluffy little world that I lived in wasn't reality, I still wasn't completely over it. I'm not sure he was even aware of how his frankness came across as offensive but my sensitive little soul had been really hurt. I couldn't really bring myself to be overly nice to him right now, but he smiled as if he'd forgotten the way he'd treated me last time. He probably had.

'Nan asked me to pop in and see whether the book she'd ordered had come in yet?'

'It has yes. It's just under the counter. I'm just going to go and wash my hands if you don't mind hanging on a minute or two. I've got paint everywhere.'

I nipped to the small bathroom at the back of the shop and had a quick wee before washing my hands, wiping them down my apron as I walked back into the main shop. Dennis stood with the book his nan had ordered in one hand and I was horrified to see that he had a pile of brown envelopes in the other. We both yelled at the same time.

'What the hell are you doing, Dennis...?'

'What the hell is going on, Nancy...'

5

I could feel the blood rush through my body, the rage building inside me as I snatched the envelopes from his hand.

'What the hell do you think you are doing snooping around in my private papers?'

'You told me to get Nan's book from under the counter.'

'I most certainly did not. I said it was under the counter. That was not an invitation. This is a bloody shop.'

'I assumed that you meant for me to get it.'

'You must have heard the old proverb, Dennis. The word assume makes an ass out of you and me.'

He dipped his head to one side and frowned. Clearly, he hadn't got a clue what I was talking about.

'The word assume *obviously*,' I explained. 'It has the letters a, s and s and then a u an m and an e. Ass. U. Me. Get it?'

His blank expression told me that he still had no idea.

'Oh, forget it. Clearly you are not as clever as you think you are.'

'More's the question, Nancy, why are all these letters sat unopened under your counter?'

'You wouldn't understand. Someone like you wouldn't understand at all.'

A great big sigh escaped from him at the same time as a tear rolled down my face.

'Try me.'

I took a big breath and just blurted it out.

'I think I'm in a spot of trouble.'

6

I walked from the small kitchen area carrying two mugs of coffee, and placed them down on the coffee table next to the two wing-backed armchairs in the bay window. Dennis didn't even look up from the pile of papers he'd been looking through.

A little fake cough seemed to break into his thoughts and he placed the papers on the table, and looked at me over the top of his glasses.

'So, what's the verdict?'
'Oh, Nancy. You just have no idea, do you?'
'Idea of what?'
'Of what it takes to run a business.'
'How dare you?'
'Nancy, I'm not saying this to be nasty.'
'Well, you could have fooled me!'
'I'm not,' he said, his voice reduced to a whisper, then returning to its normal volume, he added, 'You need to take your head out the clouds. You can't play at having a bookstore. You've only been open a few months and you're in a state already. I could help you if you let me.'

'I don't need your help.' I stuck out my chin, pulled my shoulders back and stomped across the room. Footsteps behind me indicated that I was not the only one who had crossed the room.

'You need someone's help and it may as well be me. I'm here. You know me and I know that if you'd just listen to me and accept some cold hard truths, we could get you through a tough winter. The summer holidays have been and gone. You've got one school half term left this year, so one lot of holidaymakers, apart from Christmas of course, but with some diversification, I reckon it'll be OK.'

'I'm a bookshop, Dennis. I'm not diversifying from books.'

'Look, it's no good you standing there with your hands on your hips. I've seen the bills you've got coming in. I can have a very good guess at how much the shop earns. It doesn't take a genius to work out that you can't carry on like this.'

'A business doesn't have to make money in its first year,' I said proudly.

'Who told you that? Can I take a look at your business plan?'

'My what?'

Dennis shook his head at me. 'Tell me you have a business plan.'

I chewed the inside of my cheek.

'Who else knows about this?'

I slumped against the counter and whispered, 'No one.' Another stray tear ran down my cheek but I would not give him the satisfaction of seeing me wipe it away.

His voice softened. 'Nancy, do you want this shop to work? It's no skin off my nose. Do you want my help or not?'

'Not!'

I don't care how much experience he had; he wasn't going to quash my dream. I had wanted to own a bookshop all my life. When I was a little girl, I used to pretend that I had one and lived above it and it was all I'd ever wanted. At a careers interview at school when I was asked what I wanted to do with my life and I told them, I was told that it wasn't a viable option. So, I did the next best thing and became a teacher instead. When I knew that it could happen, with the help of Aunt Theresa's money, it was literally a dream come true. I would make it work if it killed me.

'Fine,' he said. 'Let me settle up for Nan's book and I'll get out of your hair. Here.'

He thrust the bunch of bank statements he'd been analysing at me.

'How much do I owe you?'

'She's already paid.'

Dennis took the book from the counter and stamped across to the door, slamming it behind him. I watched him go before running over to the door and tugging at the handle.

'Dennis?' I shouted. He kept on walking. 'Dennis!' I yelled. He stopped still, his back still facing me. 'Dennis, please?'

He turned. God, he was infuriating. I'd like to say that the smug smirk on his face took away from his good looks, but sadly it didn't and he was as handsome as I thought he had been on the very first day we'd met. Before I realised what a total know-it-all he was.

'How much will I have to pay you?'

He looked me up and down, making me feel incredibly uncomfortable.

'Oh, I'm sure we can come to some sort of agreement.' He winked.

'Twat!' I muttered under my breath.

'I'll be round in the morning at eight o'clock. Sharp. Don't be late.'

He turned and started to walk away and childishly I bobbed my tongue at him behind his back.

'I saw that!' he shouted over his shoulder.

I can't imagine how I ever thought we might be more than friends. Despite me originally thinking that he was helpful, kind and considerate, he was the most irritating, annoying, condescending man I had ever had the misfortune to meet. However, he was also, apparently, about to be promoted, according to Vi, onto the board of directors of the company he worked at, so was clearly very good at his job. In Vi's eyes he could do no wrong. I found this particularly strange as she was normally an excellent judge of character. Maybe, sometimes in life, you just don't gel with someone. And I needed him more than I would ever let on. If I didn't take the help offered to me, the only thing Santa would be bringing me this Christmas would be a bankruptcy notice.

7

I'd left the house that morning before anyone else was up and arrived at the shop at seven thirty. I knew I wouldn't get much chance to read before Dennis arrived, so thought I'd come and switch on the fairy lights, basking in the lovely warm, cosy feeling that it gave me, before Mr Perfect came along and spoilt the vibe. I propped the door open, lit a sage stick, and wafted it around, determined to reduce any negative energy from his visit yesterday. I probably should have done it before I left last night, but after he'd gone, I felt completely shattered and closed early as I just wasn't feeling the love. This morning, as I glanced out to sea, and could see the sun starting to rise, I breathed in deeply, closed my eyes and began to repeat my affirmations out loud.

'I am a successful business owner.' I repeated these words five times before moving on to the next one. I'd been told that you needed to do it at least this many times as positive thinking can affect your brain and change the way you feel inside.

'I am resilient and can handle any challenges that come my way.' Five repeats later and I was ready for another.

'The universe is conspiring to bring me all that I want.' Again repeated five times before moving on to the final one.

'I am enough.' Apparently this was the most powerful of them all, which tackled feelings of self-doubt and inadequacy. It promoted worthiness and self-confidence and I could definitely do with some of that. Halfway through the third time, I was rudely interrupted.

'What's all this malarkey then?'

I jumped at his voice.

'I'm doing my daily affirmations.'

'Your whatimations?'

'Affirmations. They're positively loaded phrases, which challenge unhelpful or negative thoughts. They're used to encourage positive changes, boost self-esteem and belief. Oh, and they're motivational too.' I had learned this description off by heart when I was first told about them.

I saw him roll his eyes and jumped in before he could speak.

'I'm a huge believer in manifesting, asking the universe for what you want and need and trusting that it will all work out.' I smiled sweetly at him.

'And how's that working out for you so far?'

That smirk was beginning to form again. Much as I could have slapped him right then, I breathed deeply, and offered him a herbal tea. I did need some help and getting my knickers in a twist with him wasn't going to help me at all.

'I'd rather have a coffee if you have some. Stronger the better please.'

While the kettle was boiling, I had a little word with myself. I needed help. He could help me. Maybe I had to swallow my pride and see what he had to say. If he was all that Vi said he was, it would probably be worth listening to what he had to say, even if I didn't agree. He might have had one little nugget of an idea that could help.

'Look, Nancy, I feel like we've got off on the wrong foot. Shall we start over again?'

I looked into his big brown eyes. God, much as I didn't want to, I could get lost in them. It occurred to me then that he looked like Ryan Gosling in *Crazy Stupid Love*. His mannerisms were quite like him too. Much as I fought them, and in my head told them to pipe down, little fireworks went off inside my tummy.

'I'm stopping with Nan for a couple of weeks,' he said. 'Taking some time out of work. I'm going to be around anyway. I won't know what to do with myself if I'm not working. It'll give me something to do to while away my time.'

'My bookshop is not a joke, Dennis.'

'I didn't mean it like that.'

'How much do you charge? I'm not even sure I can afford you.'

'Ah, don't worry about that.'

'I'd rather know upfront before I get stung with a big bill.'

'Nancy, you've been lovely to my nan. The whole of Driftwood Bay has been amazing to her and I'll never be able to thank everyone. Your mum isn't just Nan's cleaner she's way much more than that.'

'I don't want Mum to know anything. She can't find out.' Panic was rising. 'Please tell me that you haven't told your nan about this.'

'No, I haven't. But she does know that I'm coming here to see if I can do anything to help. I told her I was coming to help you unload some boxes. Don't worry.'

'Thank you.'

'I wasn't going to charge you anything, Nancy,' he continued. 'This is a gift from me to you to say thank you for being so kind to Nan.'

Maybe he wasn't such a baddie after all. Not everyone has to be friends. If he could offer help, out of the goodness of his heart, surely I would be a fool to turn it down.

I thought about my future. Teaching was behind me now and it was something I would never want to go back to. A bookshop was all I'd ever dreamed of. I wanted to run this one until I was a little old lady. I could be stubborn and defiant, and refuse his help, or I could accept that with some expert advice, this business could give me the future I so craved. I'd be a fool to turn him down.

'Then yes please, Dennis. I would like your help.'

He smiled back at me and then that smirk reappeared.

'There you go. That wasn't so hard after all, was it?'

8

Much as I had wanted to slap him the day before, when we sat down and Dennis started to explain certain aspects of the business to me, he made an awful lot of sense. He asked what took up most of my time and got me to describe my typical bookshop day. There were so many ideas I'd had that I'd not yet put into practice because I didn't feel like I had the time. I explained that I felt like I was doing two jobs; one being the manager and the other just being a worker and I struggled to do both at the same time.

But when he questioned how I was spending my spare time, I felt like he was personally criticising me.

'Did you know the percentage of start-up businesses that fail within their first year?'

I thought back to the day we met and him telling me this information and what a surprise it had been to me.

'I did not. But I bet they didn't believe in the power of the universe taking care of everything for them, did they?' I smiled.

'Is the universe going to pay the rental on the shop when you can't afford it though? Starting a business takes extensive planning, research and implementation. What's your plan for staffing? What happens when you go on holiday?'

God, he really was a laugh a minute. How on earth did I think he was hot when I first met him? Just because he was well dressed and good looking wasn't enough to endear him to me.

'Nancy, are you listening to me? I'm trying to help you here, you know.'

'Sorry, I was just wondering what you do for fun.'

'Not really relevant, is it?'

'It's not, but it's called conversation. I say something, then you say something back and so on and so on.'

'Hilarious. Shall we get back to the business plan?'

'Yes, would love to.' I smiled sweetly again.

He sighed.

'Sorry, it's just so serious.'

'Yeah, that's exactly what it is. That's my job and that's what I'm trying to make sure you realise. Trying to get those bills paid for you. You can't keep ignoring those brown envelopes, you know? You have a business to make profitable.'

'I do know that of course, but Aunty Theresa's money is in the bank too.'

'Yeah, but that's running out. Look, last night I set up this spreadsheet. I wanted to show you the outgoings and incomings. They just don't balance at all.'

'But you have to speculate to accumulate, isn't that what they say?' You see, I did know what I was talking about. I'd show him.

'Nancy, this business is haemorrhaging money left, right and centre and you've only been open a few months. At the rate you are spending and not earning, you'll be shut down by Christmas. Is that what you want?'

'Oh, you're just being dramatic now. It's not that bad surely?'

He turned his laptop round and started talking through the figures.

'So now do you see the problem?'

'Erm, yes I think I do.'

'Praise the Lord. She gets it.'

'Has anyone ever told you how annoying you are?'

'Plenty. It's water off a duck's back. I'm here to do a job and that's what I'm trying to do.'

'I know you said you weren't charging me for this consultancy work you're doing, but if you were, how much would you charge?'

'Way more than you can afford.'

'Rude! Seriously though, how much do you charge for this type of work? And do you insult all the business owners the way you seem to be insulting me?'

'Only the stupid ones.'

'I wish I was paying you.'

'Why's that?'

'Because I could sack you! That's why.'

'You need me, Nancy.'

My hands instinctively flew to my hips and I could feel my nostrils flaring.

'There's a difference between needing someone and wanting someone, you know.'

His eyes locked onto mine and he raised an eyebrow.

The bell over the door rang then and Mum appeared, saving us from a confrontation. I quickly gathered the papers together and slammed the lid shut on the laptop and looked at Dennis, willing him not to say anything in front of her. The last thing I wanted her to know was that I was making a hash of her best friend's legacy. I didn't think she'd ever forgive me if she knew.

'Oh, it's so lovely to see you two together. I was chatting to Vi earlier when I was doing the cleaning and she was saying that Dennis was spending a lot of time here with you, Nance.'

Dennis blushed and excused himself to go to the bathroom.

'He's quite a dish, isn't he?' Mum said after he'd gone into the bathroom.

'Well, I suppose if you like that type of thing then I can see why people might look at him that way.'

'Oh yes, if I was ten years younger I'd give him a run for his money.'

'Twenty years, more like, and you meant if you weren't happily married to my lovely dad?'

'Of course, that's what I meant.'

Mum's tinkling laugh was a joy to hear. Mum and Dad had a wonderful marriage and they'd not long celebrated their thirtieth wedding anniversary. I couldn't imagine being married to someone that long. That was longer than I'd even been alive. At twenty-seven, I hadn't had many serious relationships in my life, prioritising my career ahead of everything, but also being a teacher wasn't just working nine to three every day and having all the school holidays off. There was all the other stuff that went alongside it – the marking, the talking to parents, the counselling and social work side of being a teacher and that didn't leave me an awful lot of time for a social life. Also, I idolised my father, and so far, I hadn't managed to find anyone who lived up to my high expectations of the perfect man.

'What's he like?' Mum asked, tilting her head towards the back of the shop where Dennis had just been.

'Serious. Annoying. Dull. Money mad. Did I mention annoying? Shall I go on?'

'Oh, he must have some endearing qualities, surely?'

'Nope! I don't think so.'

'He told Vi he thought you were really pretty.'

'Dennis did?' I couldn't have been more surprised.

'Yep. She thought he… What were her words now? Oh yes, that's right. Has the hots for you.'

'I don't think that could be further from the truth. And he's certainly not my type at all.'

'So why are you spending so much time with him then? It looked like you were as thick as thieves when I came in, poring over that laptop.'

Neither of us had realised that Dennis had returned until he was right behind me and when he spoke it made me jump.

'I just had a few ideas that I thought might help Nancy, and she was telling me about some ideas she'd had too. She just wants me for my business consultancy skills. Isn't that right, Nancy?'

'Err yes, that's right.' I chewed the inside of my cheek and Mum raised an eyebrow.

After a few seconds' hesitation she started talking again.

'Oh, how lovely. That's so kind of you to offer your advice, Dennis. I know that Nancy is living her dream here in her little bookshop and that her aunty Theresa would be so proud of what a fabulous job she's doing. She saved up for years, you know, and when she knew she was ill, sold everything she had just so she could help Nancy fulfil her ambitions. I'm so glad it's all working out for her and she's doing so well.' She squeezed my cheeks in the same way she did when I was the sheep in my primary school nativity play. 'My little entrepreneur.'

Nothing like a little bit of pressure of that type to give you a kick up the backside. Maybe I did need Dennis a lot more than I'd originally thought.

I couldn't bring myself to look at him. He must have thought I was a complete numpty. Only open for a few months and making a right blooming mess of everything. Someone like me must have seemed so ridiculous to someone of his standing.

'Right, I was only popping in to bring your lunch. I'll go and put it in the fridge. It'll probably feed both of you if you are stopping around, Dennis.'

'That's very kind, but I have things to do. Thank you though.'

We both watched her as she left, both silent in our thoughts.

'Look, Nancy. I feel like we've really got off on the wrong foot. We don't have to like each other for us to work together. I've worked with plenty of people that I don't like.'

'You really do have a way with words, don't you?'

'You know what I mean. I'm trying to help you here, you know. Why don't we just start again? Deal?'

He held his hand out to me.

I sighed. Sadly, I didn't think I had much of an alternative.

I put my hand in his and immediately we both jumped back as an electric shock jolted us both.

He shook his hand and pulled a face.

'Right, what are you doing after the shop has shut later?'

'It's Tuesday. I close early as it's my afternoon to be a beach angel.'

'A what?'

'Beach angel. There's a group of us that take it in turns to collect and remove rubbish from the beaches.'

'That's all very commendable, but does it pay?'

'Not everything in life is paid, Dennis. There are people who don't treat our beaches the way they should. There are fragments of plastic being dumped all over the place. If someone doesn't clean them away then they'll be here for generations to come. Maybe you should come with me. See for yourself. You could even help.'

'Thanks for the offer but no thanks. I've got better things to do.'
'Such as?' My hands had rested themselves on my hips again.
'I'm sure I'll think of something.'
'It's easy to sit back and do nothing.'
'If it's such a big issue then a small group of people in the corner of Cornwall aren't going to have much of an impact.'

It was opinions like this that really riled me. If everyone made more of an effort to help then the world would be a better place. Sitting back and doing nothing was not an option for me. Ever since I was a little girl and heard of the beach angel scheme, I'd been at the beach every free chance I had, collecting rubbish after the holidaymakers abused our little seaside sanctuary. Yes, they spent money in our shops and yes, they ate and drank in our establishments, but then they littered our beaches and it broke my heart to see what they'd left behind. To think of all the marine life that was in danger because people just don't think. I might not be able to do everything but I could certainly do something and I would. Awareness and action were top of my agenda.

'OK, well that's clearly more important to you than your bookshop so I'll pop by again tomorrow lunchtime if that's OK and we can run through some more ideas. We'll put a firm plan into place and start taking some quick action. Then you can go off and do your beach cleaning later. That OK?'

'Yep.'

He slung his Gucci leather man bag over his shoulder and winked at me before he slowly slid on his aviator sunglasses.

Blimey.

OK, so maybe Mum did have a point and every so often I was reminded of what I'd thought of him when we first met. When he smiled, his eyes crinkled and his whole face softened. If I was the type of person who succumbed to the powerful smile of a handsome man with perfectly manicured designer stubble, then now would be the time I would melt into a little puddle.

'See you tomorrow.'

As he walked towards the door and into the street, I got a funny little fluttering in my tummy. It must be dinner time.

9

The following day was quite productive and much better than I thought it was going to be. I'd had a chat with Mum the night before and she told me that she'd found Dad quite annoying when she met him and then decided to ignore that side of his personality and they'd become friends.

Being friends with Dennis didn't sound totally horrendous. Maybe we could work together after all if we put our differences aside. Also, I had an idea up my sleeve that might change how he felt about beach cleaning and hoped to put my plan into action over the next few days.

* * *

'Morning, Nancy.' He breezed in, leaving a cloud of Hugo Boss aftershave behind him. I would like to say it wasn't my favourite but the fact I knew exactly what that fragrance was probably explained how much I loved it. 'Shall I pop myself over in the window seat?'

There were only two seats there and he didn't wait for my answer before heading over. How did he manage to sit in the one that was my favourite? The one where I had the best view of the bay one way and the harbour the other. I breathed deeply. There were two chairs after all. I could sit in the other one. It was not a big deal. Was it?

'Coffee, Dennis?' I held up the pot, which I'd been keeping warm on the counter. Most people I knew had these new-fangled machines that were overcomplicated and I preferred my very basic filter coffee machine. 'Fairtrade of course.'

'I wouldn't have expected anything less from you. Yes please, milk and half a sugar please. It smells amazing I have to say.'

What *did* smell amazing was the very masculine musky spicy aftershave that wafted my way as I plonked his coffee on the table next to where he'd set up his computer. I noticed that he had certainly made himself quite at home. Dennis clearly had style and liked expensive clothes. Today he was wearing a pair of dark navy jeans and a white Ralph Lauren polo-shirt. As I looked at his feet, which looked huge, by the way, I noticed he was wearing a pair of Prada trainers.

Telling myself to say something sensible before I started thinking about what people said about a man with big feet, I blurted out the next thing that came into my head.

'They do say that if you are selling a house, you should always have a pot of coffee on the go. I was rather hoping that the same extended to a bookshop and that people would want to stay if it smelt nice in here. That's why I always have a scented candle on the go too.'

'It's a good idea. Though I was going to ask if you knew how much you'd spent on candles since you've opened.'

I could feel my eyes about to roll as I looked over his shoulder and he pointed to a figure on the screen.

'That's never right.'

'I'm afraid it is.'

My voice became very high pitched.

'Twelve hundred pounds on candles? Really? In six months. That's impossible.'

He shook his head. 'Sadly not.'

'Bloody hell, Dennis!'

'Money literally going up in smoke. I'm sure the ones you light and sell are lovely but... I think we can definitely make a difference here.'

'I've always wanted to make candles but never got round to it. The ones I buy are very expensive but they are eco-friendly with no synthetic fragrances and they use soy wax. That's why they cost so much I suppose. I wonder how long they would take me to make.'

'At the moment, you are using three a week which at twenty pounds is costing you £60 a week. Times that by the twenty weeks you've been open and that's your twelve hundred pounds. How about one of the first things you do is source some cheaper ones? That would cut costs initially and then you could research making your own. What do you think?'

I smiled. Maybe this wasn't going to be so hard after all.

'You'd obviously have to look at where you would make them, what the legalities are, the costs of the ingredients, bottles, etc.'

Oh, maybe this idea didn't sound so appealing after all. I was sure he could see my interest waning and he quickly continued before I could speak.

'How about if you did make your own, you asked people to bring back the glass candle jars and you would give them an amount off their next purchase? That way, you are encouraging them to spend more with you, but you are giving them a discount at the same time and it fits in with your ethos of recycling.'

That sounded like a great idea but I didn't want to let him know he'd won me over that easily.

I shrugged.

'It could work I suppose,' I said as nonchalantly as I could, secretly thinking what a fabulous idea it was and why I'd never thought of it myself. It resonated with me on every score. Maybe he was the bloody genius that Vi kept telling me about after all.

He looked away but not before I saw his lips twitch, not quite a full-on smirk, but a smidgeon of one.

'Maybe I need a nice new notebook to write these things down in. I've got some gorgeous ones over there.'

'Those really expensive ones that you sell, you mean?'

'Yes, that shelf over there.' I pointed to the side of the counter.

'Great idea. *Or* you could just use this A4 lined pad that I've brought you and let the customers spend their money buying the posh stuff?'

He tilted his head, not waiting for an answer as he passed over the very dull-looking hardback book. While I was thinking that I couldn't possibly write in such a plain notebook and would have to source some pretty stickers to add all over the cover, he mumbled, 'I did take the liberty of buying you one of these though.'

He handed me a pack in which there was a four-coloured ballpoint pen. At first, I thought this was one of those we used to have at school, but while this one was similar, the ink was in pastel colours: pink, green, blue and purple. I raised an eyebrow at him.

'Well, I saw that you were writing in different colours yesterday so thought I'd get you one of those. You might have a crappy old book, but at least you can jazz it up a bit with funky-coloured writing.'

I couldn't have been more surprised.

'Right, let's get on. Are you going to write about the candles?

Don't forget to list all the jobs you need to do so you don't forget anything.'

'You're enjoying this, aren't you?'

'God, yes!' He licked his lips, while locking his eyes onto mine and that funny fluttering feeling came back in my belly.

Maybe I was too.

* * *

As I locked the door at the end of the day, shattered, I reflected on what I'd learned about Dennis so far. He talked about colleagues but not about friends, so I wondered whether he had many. When I asked him what he loved doing in his spare time, he looked at me like I'd got two heads. He told me he didn't get much spare time but when he did, he liked to analyse the stock market and read self-development and business books. When I offered to give him a discount, in exchange for all the help he was giving me, he shook his head and told me that every time I offered a discount to a customer, it meant less money in my till. When I tried to explain that customer loyalty and repeat business could come from it, he tried to tell me that my first loyalty was to myself and keeping my shop trading.

He had opened my eyes up to how much I had my head in the clouds, loving the feeling of running my own bookshop and trusting that everything would work out OK when I could take more control over my destiny and make this a viable long-term business.

'I think I'm finally learning. What an idiot I was to open a shop without knowing all this stuff.'

'Not at all. You only know what you know. We've only just touched the surface,' he stated as he packed up his belongings, 'but it's great to see that there's loads we can do to turn this around into a profitable proposition. This is what I'm brilliant at. This is why I'm paid an absolute fortune to teach people like you. See you tomorrow.'

Just as I was starting to warm to him again, he came up with this cocky sentence.

An idea popped into my brain and I only faltered slightly, before speaking up.

'What are you doing tonight, Dennis?'

He looked at me for longer than I thought totally necessary, and raised a querying eyebrow before saying that he was just planning a night in with his nan. Crikey, I hope he didn't think I was asking him out on a date.

'Fancy meeting me back here for an hour later? I have something I'd like to show you.'

Another raised eyebrow and a moment's hesitation made me backtrack.

'Don't worry. It was just a thought.'

'Are you going to give me any more information? I like to know all the facts before making an informed decision.'

A loud sigh escaped me.

'Have you ever considered that you need more spontaneity in your life?'

'Have you ever considered you might need less?'

We stared each other down, before we both gave in and laughed at the same time.

'Oh, what the hell. Why not? How's that for spontaneity?'

'Impressive.'

He grinned and I thought the similarity and mannerisms between Ryan and real-life Dennis was uncanny.

'What time do you want me?'

Gosh it was getting hot.

'Six o'clock OK?' I squeaked.

'Yep. It's not like I've got offers left, right and centre. See you then.'

We were moving two steps forward and one step back.

It would be interesting to see how tonight went.

10

'Hey!'

I looked up from my book as Dennis towered over me.

Musky, spicy tones hit my nostrils.

'Ooh, you smell nice!'

Oh God, did I say that out loud? What was wrong with me?

'Thank you.' The surprise that I'd complimented him was written all over his face. 'Just got out of the shower.'

'Oh!'

Trying very hard not to think about Dennis in the shower and hiding my blushes as I put my book into my cross-body bag, I guided Dennis out of the shop, and into the street, locking the door behind me.

'Where are we going then?'

'You'll see.'

It was clear by the way he clenched his jaw that he was hating someone else being in control.

'Trust me. You might even enjoy yourself.'

He huffed.

Leading him over to the beach, I unlocked the door of a little wooden hut and removed two litter picker-uppers, two large clear plastic bags, two fluorescent tabards and two pairs of gloves. Picking up some jelly beach shoes for us both too, I slipped off my trainers and left them at the side, indicating that he should do the same.

'You're not serious. These are Prada, Nancy. I don't want anyone stealing them. They cost a fortune.'

'Are they? They look more like Primark to me, but you can lock them in the hut if they're so precious.'

He grumbled his thanks as I locked the hut back up and handed him one of each of my wares.

'You want me to pick up litter and wear those?' He turned his nose up.

'Yeah. I'm making you an honorary beach angel.'

'Gee, thanks. Just what I've always wanted.'

'Oh, get over yourself, Dennis. You're not in your posh London office now. You're at the seaside and we all need to do our bit in conserving the planet for future generations.'

'Yippee do!'

He held up his hands in protest as he could see from the way I'd crossed my arms and huffed that I was annoyed by him.

'You're quite cute when you're angry, you know, Nancy. Right, come on then. What am I doing?'

He really was infuriating and I never knew where I stood with him, constantly blowing both hot and cold. I stomped away from him.

'OK, OK! Wait for me.' He caught up and grabbed at my arm, spinning me round. 'I'm sorry! I'm here and I'm happy to help.'

'Well, tell your face that then.'

He grinned widely and the corners of his brown eyes crinkled.

'You should smile more often, you know. You're not so ugly when you're not being petulant.'

'Gosh, is that another compliment? Wonders will never cease.'

'Dennis, can we stop all this? I haven't got the energy.'

'Deal. And, to be honest, neither have I today. Come on, let's get this over with.' I looked up and he held his hands up again. 'Last joke, I promise. I'm done now. So, what are we looking for?'

Surprisingly, he did listen quite attentively as I explained that we needed to collect any plastic matter from the beach and he was staggered at the amount we found in just the first half an hour. When I enlightened him on how the plastic gets washed up from the ocean on the tides, he asked many intelligent questions and I felt like he was really taking an interest in what we were doing. I explained that I'd recently found a sweet wrapper from the seventies, which had clearly been floating around for years, and talked about how crisp packets can lurk around for decades. This, I think, made him realise the extent of the issues and he really started to take it all on board. I could see his brain was working overtime and wondered what he was thinking.

'Do you know, Nancy, it would be great if we could think of some ideas to incorporate your love of the environment with your love of books and the shop. Maybe a recycling project.'

'That's not going to make money though, is it, which is really what you need me to be focusing on.'

'I get that, but it would get people into the shop and maybe while they're there, they'd buy something. If they don't come in, they're never going to buy anything, are they?'

I imitated his deep voice. 'It's all about the numbers, Dennis, and fishing where the fish are.'

He rolled his eyes.

'I do not sound like that.' His hands rested on his hips. 'Do I?'

I chewed the inside of my cheek, then turned away, hoping I hadn't offended him too deeply.

'So all the books you buy are new? You buy a lot of hardbacks, which are expensive, aren't they?' he asked, and I nodded in response.

An idea popped into my head and stopped me in my tracks. I spoke it out loud before I had to think it through.

'I wonder if I should consider selling second-hand books?'

It wasn't something I'd ever considered really. I always thought charity shops were the place for second-hand books, but with our nearest charity shop being three villages away, people seemed to hang on to them.

'I wonder if people would buy them though. I suppose they might, depending on the condition. Or would it put people off buying new books if they could buy second-hand books cheaper? That's my worry.' I was wittering now, randomly blurting my thoughts.

'Look at you thinking like a businessperson.'

I narrowed my eyes at him.

'You could do a bit of market research,' he suggested. 'I'm not sure I'd want to buy a book when you don't know what someone else had been doing while they were reading it. Specially some of those saucy ones you ladies read. Maybe you could find out, whether people would still buy new. And whether they'd buy something that was second-hand.'

'Market research? I could probably ask my friends what they thought.'

'Well that wasn't really what I had in mind. Business decisions have to be made on more than gut feelings. It's all about the data.'

'It's definitely something to think about, Dennis. I could maybe have a second-hand section at the back or something.'

'Pre-loved.'

'Sorry.'

'Pre-loved sounds much more romantic than second-hand.'

I laughed. 'Blimey, Dennis being all romantic.'

'Not likely. No time for romance in my life.'

'So you don't have a special someone in your life then?' Gosh, I really should engage my brain more before I let my mouth open. I blushed. He must think I'm being way too direct.

'Nah. No time for all that malarkey. Too busy at work. I work long hours and I can't imagine anyone would want to put up with that.'

'Maybe the right person would.'

'I don't have the time to find the right person. I'm busy. I fly around the world. I don't need anyone, despite what Nan says.'

'What does Vi say then?'

'Oh, you know, the normal. I haven't met my soulmate yet. That I shouldn't work so hard. That money isn't everything. Blah, blah, blah.'

'Maybe she's right.'

'Nah. I'm fine as I am. Quite happy on my own. Pleasing myself. Doing what I want, when I want.'

He looked out towards the sea and I could see his Adam's apple bob when he swallowed.

'Wouldn't you like someone to do things with though? Go on holidays and stuff like that?'

I felt like I was projecting my own feelings into this question. There were times that I would love someone to do things with.

'I've got mates I can do that with. Couple of guys from work are my holiday pals. We head off to Dubai or Las Vegas a couple of times a year and have fun, playing golf, hanging out in the casinos and bars.'

'Sounds exhausting.'

'Not having to consider anyone else. Just myself to worry about and not having anyone worrying about me. Suits me just fine.'

It seemed that we were both pondering what he'd said when he cut into my thoughts.

'What about you, Nancy?'

'What about me?'

'No one special in your life? Who are your holiday companions?'

'Definitely not a special someone. I've spent a long time focusing on my work. Being a teacher, despite what everyone thinks, is not a nine-to-three job with tons of holiday time. It's a vocation. You are everything to some of the kids. Their parent, their mentor, their social worker, their doctor. It's exhausting and then when you do get home, you have marking to do and lessons to plan. And targets to meet and grades to achieve so the school looks good. It's an awful lot of pressure and it was starting to affect my mental health. Yes, I did get summer holidays off, but that was when I'd throw myself into this passion project. I spend my spare time doing this.' I swept my arm around me.

'So, no Caribbean holidays for you then?'

'God no! You won't find me contributing to the air pollution of the world. If more people stopped flying we wouldn't be having the global warming issues the world is experiencing.'

'And we'd all be a little more miserable too.'

'Not necessarily. There's nowhere nicer than Cornwall in the summer. It's as hot as the Caribbean at times and probably just as beautiful too. I mean, why would you ever want to be anywhere else?'

I spotted a bottle lid poking out of the sand.

'Interesting...'

'Not really, just life. I don't feel like I'm missing out on anything. And, when the opportunity came along for me to start the bookshop, when Aunty Theresa left me some money, I jumped at the chance. It had always been a dream of mine, and she'd left me a note saying life was short and that you should spend it doing something you love.' I reached down and picked up the bit of blue plastic. 'Did you know that bottles and bottle tops in particular take longer to break down than many other plastics?'

'I did not know that. Thank you for enlightening me.'

I swung round towards him, ready to reprimand him for making fun of me, but he was standing still, staring at me.

'What?'

'I was waiting for your next jibe, that's all.'

He held up his hands in surrender.

'None coming. I *am* grateful to you for explaining all of this to me. I suppose despite visiting here when I come to see Nan, it was stuff I never considered.'

'Well, raising awareness is important to me. I don't really have time for proper holidays any more because I'm busy doing this. Mum and I sometimes go and hire a lodge in the countryside from time to time, but when you live here in Driftwood Bay...' I took a deep breath and stood and appreciated my surroundings: the golden sand beneath my feet, the gentle waves lapping at the shore, the autumn sun brightly shining low in the sky, the boats in the harbour in the other direction and the pretty pastel houses around the harbour '...why would you want to go anywhere else?'

Dennis looked around him and sighed loudly.

'I don't think I ever really appreciated it before.'

Dennis was a little bit of an enigma to me. Despite spending time with him talking about business, I didn't really know an awful lot about him.

'Why are you here, Dennis?'

'Because Nan lives here?'

'No, I don't mean that. You said you were here for a month.

Why are you here? Why not in Las Vegas, or Dubai or somewhere else exotic? And why are you helping me?'

Dennis dropped to the sand and patted the space next to him, placing all the paraphernalia he'd been carrying on the other side of him.

'I fucked up.'

11

I turned to face him and he hung his head in shame.

'What do you mean?'

'Ah, it's nothing. Don't worry.'

'It clearly is something. I'm a good listener, Dennis, and sometimes a problem shared is a problem halved.'

A quick lift of his eyebrows showed me that he was dubious about that statement.

'Up to you. No skin off my nose if you don't want to tell me. I know we don't always see eye to eye on stuff, but maybe you just need a friend right now. Someone who can listen to you, not judge you, and let you talk.'

His shoulders were rising and falling with the deep breaths he was taking. It clearly wasn't easy for him to confide in someone.

'Years of working all the hours God sends, at full pelt, took its toll on me. I made a bad decision and it cost someone a lot of money.'

I rubbed his back, not really knowing if it was the right thing to do but he looked like he needed comforting.

'Shit happens, Dennis. It's not the end of the world.'

'It was the end of someone's world.' He turned to me with a tear in his eye.

'Money isn't everything.'

'It is to some people. You can't just go through life without making it safe and secure for yourself. You need money to do that. I know that more than anyone.'

Wondering how this random statement was related, I tipped my head to one side, and waited until he felt he could continue.

'I gave someone some bad advice and they lost everything they had. I told them they should take a risk on something, with some of their investments.'

'Well, surely that's not so bad?'

'No, but I hadn't done my due diligence and what I didn't know was that they were in a lot of trouble financially and they risked not just *some* of what they had, but *everything*.'

'Ah.'

'Ah, indeed. He lost his business. His wife walked out on him. His children won't speak to him and he has literally nothing. He's now had to move back in with his parents while he tries to sort his life out. He's fifty-seven years old and, thanks to me, hasn't got a penny to his name.'

'That wasn't your fault though. Surely you can't blame yourself.'

'But I do. If I'd known the extent of his difficulties, I would have advised against risking anything let alone everything. That's kind of my job. I should have known.'

'But if he didn't tell you, how could it have been your fault?'

'Well, they said that at work too, but it hurts, Nance.' His voice caught and I put my hand on top of his, which was resting on his knees. It hadn't gone unnoticed that he'd abbreviated my name to something I'd never liked as a child but when he said it, it sounded... well, it kind of sounded good.

He smiled at me, but it didn't reach his eyes and then he looked away out to the horizon. He looked like a crestfallen little boy and my heart reached out to him. Gone was the brash, self-assured man who was normally brimming with confidence, telling me what I should do to turn my business around. And there before me was a man who was vulnerable and full of self-loathing. A very unfamiliar Dennis.

I looked to see what he was fixated on and saw a boat bobbing on the horizon.

'I should have asked more questions. I should have shown more interest and not just seen the pound signs flashing. I stood to make a big commission from him and for the company I work for. I was about to be made a partner. That was important to me.'

'And can that not still happen? Surely if you're good at your job then this won't stop you.'

'Not sure to be honest. They gave me some time out for us both to do some thinking. About whether they want to still make me a partner after all of this. And I'm wondering whether I want them to. I don't know what I want any more. And that's why I'm here, Nance. Bet you wished you'd never asked now.'

He glanced across at me, looked deep into my eyes and bit his lip. I knew this was not the time or place to even think this, but when he did that, it did something very strange to my nether regions and all I could think about was how his lips would feel on mine. Or how they'd taste. I blushed at how inappropriate I was being.

We both looked out to sea and at the little dot in the distance.

Eventually he broke the silence.

'I wonder who is on that. Whenever I see a boat, I wonder where they've been and where they are heading to. It's like a metaphor for my life right now.'

It's good to talk when you have something on your mind. I

knew from working with children that keeping stuff inside didn't help anyone. It was an honour that he'd confided in me, but I felt quite responsible that whatever I said next should be significant and meaningful, yet I couldn't think of anything intelligent to say.

'Everything happens for a reason, we just don't always know what it is. Maybe it'll all work out well in the end for him.'

This was a very different Dennis to the one I normally saw. This was a sweet, caring man who, I felt, I could really get to like. Someone I wanted to know more about. He was clearly feeling guilty for something that was not his fault, but I don't think it would matter what anyone said to him in that moment, he had to work it all out for himself.

He sat upright, sniffed, and wiped his nose on the back of his hand before standing abruptly, reaching out for my hand. I looked up and took his, until I was standing too.

'Is it helping to be here?' I asked. 'Giving you some perspective? Helping you to decide what you want?'

He looked deep into my eyes, as if he could see into my very soul. His gaze flickered to my lips and back, and he stepped closer, narrowing the gap between us. I held my breath, knowing that I wanted him to kiss me more than I had wanted anything before.

Suddenly, he took a step back.

'You have no idea, Nance.'

He grinned that cheeky grin and it was like a switch had flicked inside him. At the same time, my tummy did that funny little skip thing again.

'Come on. Let's go and find some more beach to rescue. At least I can do something practical here that will help. And you never know, we might find a tree or two to hug. It won't earn you any money, eh? But hey ho! We get to save the planet. Yay!' He winked at me as he walked past, bent down, and grabbed a plastic water bottle from behind a rock, cockily throwing it up into the air and, to my annoyance, catching it in his rubbish bag.

Just like that, the other Dennis was back. The one that wound me up, irritated the hell out of me and the one that for some unknown reason was getting me all hot under the collar.

The sound of a text arriving on Dennis's phone interrupted our companionable silence as we picked up bits of plastic from the beach. Blood drained from his face.

'I'm sorry, Nancy, but I have to go.' He hurried back over to where he had locked his stuff, retrieved it and swapped his shoes over.

'Is everything OK, Dennis?' His behaviour was bizarre.

'Tickety-fucking-boo, Nancy.' Without even saying goodbye, he practically ran away from the beach.

What an odd man he was.

12

There was no word from Dennis the next day. We hadn't made plans but I suppose I must have been expecting him. I'd felt like we'd really connected the day before. His barriers definitely seemed to be lowering and it felt like where he normally tolerated me, that he'd trusted in me; opened up to me and shared his personal problems, like I was sharing my business issues with him.

It had been a quiet day in the shop and I felt a little discombobulated all day and couldn't get him off my mind and how he'd gone as white as a sheet when he received the text. I was just cashing up when the bell went to signify I had company and I turned to the door.

'Dennis.' I was surprised to see him. His eyes were red and he looked like he'd been up all night. 'Is everything OK?'

'The text I had last night was to say that the man I was telling you about, Steve, was in hospital after he'd attempted to take his own life.'

My heart leapt into my stomach.

'Oh, Dennis. I'm so sorry.' I flew across the room and put my arm around his shoulders and pulled him towards me.

'He's not in danger any more but to think that something I did caused the ripple effect for this to happen is really getting to me.'

'Come and sit down.' I led him over to the bay window where we sat. After a while of him staring out to sea, I felt like it was OK to interrupt his thoughts.

'It wasn't your fault.'

He looked up. 'It wasn't? It sure feels like it.'

'He's a grown man, Dennis. You gave him information and he took that and did what he chose to do with it. *You* are not responsible for any of his actions.'

'Others have said the same but it all just feels quite raw at the moment. What a shocker it was. Honestly, Nancy, if he'd died, I don't know what I'd have done.'

'He didn't though, did he, Dennis? He was clearly desperate and that's really sad, but now hopefully he'll get the help he needs. Look at me.' I reached across and put my fingers under his chin guiding his face upwards until his eyes met mine. 'It's. Not. Your. Fault. OK?'

His eyes filled with tears and he put his hand on my arm.

'Thank you, Nancy. You don't know what this means to me.'

We held each other's gaze, sharing a moment that felt really quite special.

I dithered over my next question but decided to go ahead with it anyway. I really needed to eat.

'Don't know about you, Dennis, but I'm starving. Fancy grabbing some food?'

'I'd love to. I've not eaten all day. I just couldn't until I'd heard that Steve was in the clear. Also, Nan was cooking liver and lime, and while she said it would be good for me, the god-awful smell was making me heave and I was pleased to get out of the house.'

I laughed and the mood lightened, which felt good. Vi was well known in the village for her random concoctions, sometimes bringing along things like carrot and coriander cake, or banana and Bovril, and while people wanted to avoid these like the plague, because she was such a lovely little old lady, no one had the heart to reject her offerings. It was, however, lovely to hear that she was cooking again after a recent spell Mum had been telling me about. Apparently, her house had been in such a state, she couldn't even think about cooking and that if she'd put something in her cooker, she would have died from salmonella.

It was nice to know that now the house had been sorted, and Mum was Vi's regular cleaner, Dennis was staying close by. I liked the feeling that he wasn't far away.

I jumped up. 'It's Wednesday!'

'Well done, Nance. Yes, it is. Do you want a medal?'

Aha. And just like that, he was back.

'Don't be a smartass, Dennie. It doesn't become you.'

'Dennie?'

He stopped still in his tracks and then repeated the name that for some reason had, without thinking, popped out of my mouth.

'Sorry, I don't know why I said that.'

'Don't be sorry. I like it. I've always thought Dennis makes me sound like a right old fart.'

I giggled, remembering that when someone first told me that Vi's grandson called Dennis was visiting, I thought he was going to be quite old and past it. I got a very pleasant surprise when I first met him and realised he was very much far from it. You know what they say, never make assumptions.

'Anyway,' he continued, 'what's with it being Wednesday?'

'Gemma from the bistro sells fish and chips from the catering van. We could sit outside if you fancy it and have some tea.'

Dennis's stomach rumbled loudly. We laughed.

'I take it that's a yes then?'

'It's a big yes from me. I could eat a whale.'

'Well, it's normally cod or haddock but we can always see if they have a really big one.'

* * *

Fifteen minutes later, we were sat on a bench in the harbour, scoffing the most divine fish and chips and drinking beer. Gemma's idea of extending the bistro's offering and starting up a fish and chip shop in her catering van was genius. She'd drive around the village, honking her horn when she arrived and then when she'd done the rounds, she'd park up at the harbour and sell from there. She didn't know if it would be as successful in the winter, when the holidaymakers were no longer around, but it was thriving so far and not many people in Driftwood Bay cooked on a Monday night. Her licence at the bistro meant that she could serve alcohol too, so a bottle of Becks was going down particularly well with the food.

We'd argued over who was going to pay. I insisted on it as a little way of saying thank you to Dennis for all his help at the shop. I felt it was the least I could do when he wouldn't take any money from me. Though he said he was still being paid, very handsomely, from his job, so he wouldn't think of accepting my money and that I needed every penny I had.

Dennis took the empty wrappers from me and took them over to the bin where about twenty seagulls swooped down and started to peck at the paper. I had to pull my eyes away from him to stop myself staring. Seeing him being more vulnerable over the last few days had made me feel differently about him and I couldn't get that moment when I thought he was going to kiss me out of my head.

I knew I was being ridiculous, as he clearly hadn't intended that at all, so I was trying hard to ignore the vision that I'd had in my head.

'Thanks, Nance.' He reached out and gave my hand a gentle squeeze.

'Yeah, it was delish, wasn't it? Told you Gemma's chip supper was a winner.'

'I don't mean for the food. I mean for listening earlier.'

'You're welcome.'

As I searched his face, his eyes softened before closing. He tipped his head back and looked up at the sky and gave a deep sigh. I hoped that chatting had helped to lighten his burden a little. Talking is really good therapy when you are stuck in your head.

'I don't have many close friends. Yes, I have the lads at work that I sometimes go away with, but not anyone who I can pour my troubles out to. I appreciate you very much.'

I nudged him with my shoulder.

'Are you saying that we are friends, Dennie?'

'I think I am. Oh wait.' He put his bottle down on the bench and lifted his hand to my face. I held my breath as he brushed my cheek with his thumb.

Oh blimey. Was he going to kiss me *this* time?

'Bit of mayonnaise there, Nance. S'OK, I got it for you.'

I let out a huge intake of breath. All these moments were playing havoc with my emotions. One minute I didn't know if he liked me, or me him for that matter, and the next minute, I was willing him to kiss me, throw me down and roger me senseless. I needed to get out more. There was clearly of a lack of male company in my life, so when a newbie did arrive in Driftwood Bay, particularly when he was a dead ringer for the Gozzer, I lost my senses. We were just friends and I had to remind myself of that.

He held his bottle up to mine.

'To friendship, Nancy.'

'To friendship, Dennie.'

13

Dennis burst through the door the following morning.

'Nance, I've had the most amazing idea.'

The moment I saw him, I blushed. I'd dreamt last night that we were married and had a family and that we were lying in bed together, with him lying behind me, holding me. Where the hell that dream had come from, I didn't know, especially as we'd only just agreed that we were mates. I'd woken up totally out of sorts. It had been years since someone had properly held me like that, and while it felt nice, it was just a reminder it had been that long, and got me thinking about whether I should put myself out there into the dating pool again. Maybe it was time I let someone else into my life and opened up to them. It might be nice to wake up to a warm body next to mine.

I quickly closed the book I'd been scribbling in. Morning journaling was a big part of my day. Writing down my innermost thoughts and desires was a great way of getting things out of my mind, and stopped my brain working overtime. I certainly didn't want Dennis to see what I was doing. The things I'd written down that morning weren't anything that anyone should ever read – they were X-rated and for me only – and I told myself I must remember to rip them out and burn them in the fire later.

I tucked the notebook into my apron pocket as I stood and walked towards the counter, trying to not to think about how Dennis's body had felt pressed up against mine in my dream, while he was spooning me.

'A relaunch party, are you sure?'

'I think it would be really good. Obviously, we wouldn't call it a relaunch party, but we would know that's what it is. We could have it in say a month's time when we've had time to source new stock and get the pre-loved section underway. What are you thinking?'

What I was thinking was why he kept saying 'we'. Like it was our shop. I suppose he was just helping. It was his project after all. As normal, I was probably just overthinking everything.

'Well, I suppose so, but is a month enough to do all of that?'

'I think so. I've called in to work this morning and requested another month off. I've got to go up to London tomorrow for a couple of days, to sign some stuff, but once I'm back I'm back for a while, and am all yours. So, you can get me doing anything you'd like me to in that time.'

Now there was a thought!

I blushed again and turned away. The more time I was spending with Dennis, the more confused I was becoming. At times, it felt like he was properly flirting with me, then at others, it was like I was the most annoying person in the world to him. I was trying my hardest to learn what he was teaching me, but all that academia stuff was just not doing it for me, like it clearly did for him. We were total opposites.

He turned me to face him.

'Don't be scared, Nance. I'm here for you. We've got this.'

I'd been doing stuff on my own for so long, it felt nice to know that someone had my back. Mum was busy running her own cleaning business and Dad was an engineer, and they didn't have time for my 'airy-fairy' bookshop ideas. I'd launched the bookshop entirely on my own with no knowledge of how to run a business and had been muddling my way through. However, that's why I was in the mess I was in right now and why I needed Dennis's help to turn the shop around.

'So, why don't I go and make us a cuppa and we can discuss our plans?'

I smiled.

'Sounds good.'

I'd forgotten what I'd left out in the kitchen on the draining board, and when Dennis came back through, he was holding a large scallop shell in his hand.

'Dare I ask?'

'Well, you kind of did. They're shells.'

'No shit, Sherlock. I could work that bit out for myself. I just wondered why there were about twenty of them sat on your draining board?'

'They're drying.'

'Again, I'm not a thicko and could work that out. But for what purpose? Maybe that's a more straightforward question for you?'

This was something that was hard for me to admit to. I was a little bit embarrassed about this hobby. It was something I thought was quite amateur and probably looked awful.

'I paint them.'

'Uh?' He screwed up his face. 'You paint them. What do you mean?'

'I'm a shell painter. It's one of my many skills.'

'What, so you paint them a colour and then what?'

'No, I paint pictures on them. Pass me my phone and I'll show you some of the recent ones I've done.'

As he handed me my phone, his hand brushed against mine

and our eyes met. We both looked away at exactly the same time and I distracted myself by pulling up a picture on my phone. I took a deep breath before I handed it over to him sheepishly.

He looked at the image and then back at me. Studying the image again, and enlarging it on the screen, he focused in on the intricate painting I had done on the inside of the scallop shell. It was of a pastel-coloured beach hut on golden sands, with a turquoise ocean in the background, a shining yellow sun and seagulls gliding through the sky.

'Jeez, Nance.'

'I know they're crap but they're not meant to be professional or anything. It's just something I like doing to de-stress. When I'm painting, it lets me shut off from the world outside. That's all I think about. It's good for mindfulness. It was something I started doing with my art class at school and I've just kept it up since I've not been teaching.'

'They're *not* crap.'

'Well...' I looked at the floor. I never did like showing people my artwork. Not since Denise Wilson had ridiculed me in primary school and my ten-year-old self didn't know how to handle the whole class laughing at me. It was one of the reasons I went into teaching. I never wanted a child to ever feel like that when they were expressing themselves.

'Nancy, they are exquisite.'

I looked up and he was flicking through other pics on my phone, enlarging each one and studying the images.

'Really?'

'I can't believe you are doubting me. Honestly, Nancy, they are stunning. Look at the way you've captured the total essence of Driftwood Bay.'

At that point, my mum walked in and we jumped apart.

Surprise showed on her face for a split second before she smiled again.

'Morning, you two. What are you up to?'

The word 'nothing' in unison was not particularly convincing and she raised an eyebrow until she saw the phone in Dennis's right hand and an empty shell in the other.

'Talented, isn't she?'

'Amazingly so. You really should be selling these, you know.'

'Ah, Dennis, you are a man after my own heart. I've been telling her that since she's been doing them. We've got bloody hundreds of them at home, and to be honest, much as I love them, I don't know what to do with them. They're definitely good enough to sell, but I just can't convince her of it.'

'I couldn't charge anything for them,' I said sheepishly. 'They're nothing special at all.'

'I beg to differ with you there, daughter dear.'

'Me too!'

All I needed was Mum *and* Dennis ganging up on me.

'You should bring them in here, Wendy. Nancy could clear off a shelf and make a lovely display. What a gorgeous memento of Driftwood Bay for people to buy. A hand-painted scene on a shell.'

I tried to grab the phone from him but he held it behind his back.

'They'd never sell. You're being ridiculous.'

'*You're* being ridiculous. You'd sell them for good money. I know it.'

Mum smiled at me over Dennis's head, mouthing, 'I told you so.'

I could feel myself chewing the inside of my cheek, a nervous habit I knew I had when I was a little unsure of something while I was pondering. I suppose I didn't really have a lot to lose by trying it. Apart from my dignity if people thought they were a load of old crap.

'Maybe I could put a couple up for a couple of quid each and see if there's any interest.'

'A couple of quid. More like twenty I was thinking.' Mum looked at me smugly, clearly on Dennis's side.

'Twenty quid!' I exclaimed. 'That's way too much.'

The bell above the door tinkled and Lucy from the B&B reversed in, pulling a pushchair in with her.

'Let's see, shall we?' Dennis winked at me and that little tummy flip happened again. I did wish he'd stop doing that. If he only knew what it was doing to my insides. 'Let me help you there,' he said to Lucy. 'Do you mind me asking you for a little bit of market research?'

'Of course not, Dennis. Anything for you.' She fluttered her eyelashes. Shame on her. Her, a married woman. Was I the only female in Driftwood Bay that hadn't fallen under his charm?

'How much would you pay for something like this?' He passed her the phone.

'Wow. That is stunning. Probably about £50. Oh, look. It's Driftwood Bay. Look at the little houses in the harbour. I'd love to know who the supplier is. I'd sell these in the B&B to our customers. They'd love them.'

Dennis turned round with an 'I-told-you-so' expression on his smug face.

'Thanks, Lucy, that's really helpful. Are you looking for anything in particular?'

'I've got a birthday present to buy for someone, but, as always, I've left it till the last minute and I could really do with getting something in the post. I wondered if you'd got anything suitable. I was thinking about maybe a notebook or pen or something but now I've seen that, I want that. I wonder if the company sell them online.'

'What company?' I asked, not quite following her train of thought.

'The company that sells them.'

'Tell you what, Lucy,' Dennis said with a grin. 'As it's you and I know the owner, I'll drop one round to the B&B later in a gift box if you like. It'll be twenty pounds. How does that sound?'

'Oh, Dennis, you could sell me anything. You're such a charmer. That would be amazing. Do you really know the owner?'

'I do. Not only is she kind, incredibly pretty and generally lovely, she's also super talented too.'

'Oh, you should date her. She sounds perfect.'

'Now there's an idea.' His raised eyebrow and mischievous grin made me shake my head as, totally embarrassed, I excused myself and sloped off to the back of the shop. Because Lucy and James were all loved up and playing happy families, she took every opportunity she could to pair up everyone in the village. If she'd have known it was me that Dennis was talking about, she'd have been doing it even more. Thank goodness she didn't.

I could hear Lucy shout, 'See you later, Nancy,' but I couldn't bring myself to show my face just yet. I wondered if Dennis meant what he'd said or whether he was just teasing. Either way, I had decided that I was going to stay in here as long as I possibly could, but it seemed like others had different ideas.

14

There was a knock on the kitchen door.

'Nance.'

I ignored it and the little tap came again.

'Nance.'

This time the door burst open and Dennis filled the doorway. Rather nicely I must admit. Gosh, I had to stop thinking about him in this way, but he'd said those lovely things about me. I was confused. Did he really like me? I thought I was just the annoying bookshop owner that he felt he had to help because I lived in the same village as his nan.

'You OK?'

'Erm, yes thanks. I was just...' I couldn't think of a thing to say.

'I think you should go to your mum's now and collect all the painted shells.'

'I can just bring a few in each day. They'll all need packing up and wrapping carefully.'

'No, let's go now. I'll come with you. Two hands are better than one.'

I held my hands up to him.

'I already have two of my own, thanks.'

'Don't be contrary. You know what I mean. Come on, your mum says she'll hold the fort while we nip back to yours.'

It was quite clear that he was taking no hostages. Dennis on a mission was not someone to challenge, so I grabbed my denim jacket from the hook behind the door, and when I failed to even find the armhole and made myself look like a total muppet, Dennis rescued me again, holding it behind me for me to slip my arms into.

Mumbling thank you, I stomped past Mum, like a sulky teenager, and headed back to my cottage. Mum and I didn't live far from the bookshop so there didn't seem much point in me ever really looking for anywhere else to stay, although there was quite a large flat above the shop which Dennis had been asking about. I said I'd show him later that day. The old owner used it as a storeroom and it was full of cobwebs and dust and needed a bloody good clean out. But when Dennis suggested it could either be used as more rooms for the shop, or even converted into a flat which brought in rent every month, it had got me thinking. I'd been in Gemma's flat above the bistro and it was stunning. Maybe I could eventually do something like that here and move in – if I could afford to, that is. If not, I'd have to rent it out, but that would be a real shame. Imagine walking down the stairs to your very own bookshop. It was the stuff of dreams.

I turned the key in the front door of our house and told Dennis to wait in the lounge. Most of the shells were already packed away, in a couple of boxes which were kept on the top shelf of my wardrobe. My bedroom was a complete tip and Mum was always nagging me to tidy it up, but there was always something more interesting to do. A shell to paint, a book to read, a book to buy even.

Balancing on top of a footstool, I reached to grab the boxes and righted myself once I started to wobble. However, a couple of seconds later, I completely lost my balance and fell, though I made sure that I was the one that landed on the floor first rather than the box of shells.

'Fuck! That hurt!' I muttered as I righted myself.

As I was rubbing my leg, I heard footsteps thunder up the stairs and the door burst open. Dear God, did this man never walk through a door properly? Why was his default setting to burst into a room and fill it completely?

He strode across the room and took the boxes off me.

'Why didn't you just ask me to help you, Nance?' He tutted. One of my pet hates was tutting. It was something the kids in my class used to do and it drove me insane.

'I don't need your help, Dennis. I can do things on my own, you know. I'm not the weak, pathetic person you think I am. I don't need you to rescue me all the time. How do you think I managed before you came to Driftwood Bay?'

He raised an eyebrow. I knew my words were harsh and that I'd raised my voice but I couldn't seem to help myself. Dennis standing in my bedroom was freaking me out. And when he sat down on my bed, it was even more bizarre, especially after the dream I'd had last night. It was like he didn't belong here, while at the same time it was like it was perfectly normal for him to be lowering himself onto my bed now. His face reflected how uncomfortable he was and when he ferreted about beneath him and realised that the culprit that was digging into him was a scarlet lacy bra, his face matched its colour.

'I'll be waiting downstairs,' he said.

He picked up the boxes of shells, excused himself and went downstairs quicker than I'd ever seen him move.

After gathering my things together, I held my head high as I walked downstairs. I decided that, while it was nice he was thinking about me and my business and my future, it might be better all round if he stopped working on my shop as his little side hustle and found himself something else to occupy his time. And yes, OK, while it might have been nice to know how it felt to kiss him and even to go out with him, he'd made it perfectly clear he was only in town for a short while, while he was taking a rest from his real world. The one in which he earned lots of money, wore designer suits, went on lavish holidays, and lived a completely different life to mine. Our worlds had collided but they were never aligning so it was time for me to realise this and move on, and stop thinking about how, in my dream, his body fitted perfectly into mine.

When I lifted the heavy boxes, which were actually really awkward to carry, that smirk appeared on his face again. Typical. Now would have been a really good time for him to help, but after my little outburst earlier, I couldn't blame him for not coming forward. He stood to the side as I put the boxes down and pulled the door shut behind us. It had now turned into a battle of wills. He clearly wasn't going to offer and I clearly wasn't going to ask, even though I could hardly see over the top of the boxes.

'Ready, Nance?'

'Yep!' I mumbled from behind the boxes.

When I tripped up over one of the cobbles, he took the top box from me without a word and I grumbled my thanks. It was so much easier when I could see where I was walking and also take in my surroundings. Being here in Driftwood Bay always lifted my heart and I tried to never take this amazing place for granted.

The harbour was bustling today, the late-autumn sunshine bringing out many of the locals. Boats were being scrubbed down, some owners packing things away for the winter months, doing the last few jobs that needed to be done before the boats were retired until the spring. Others were preparing to clear off to take in the winter sun in other parts of the world, preferring the Mediterranean temperatures rather than the harsh Cornish winters that can sometimes be bestowed upon us. The drone of lawnmowers in the distance signified that people were also taking the opportunity to do an autumn mow, never quite knowing when the last one of the year would be.

When we arrived back at the shop, Mum was just checking the stock system for a man who had come in asking for a copy of *A Christmas Carol* for his wife. As I heard what he was after, I jumped in to save her some time as I placed my box down on the counter.

'I'm so sorry, I know that I sold the last one yesterday.'

'Oh OK, no worries. Thanks very much.' He turned to walk away.

Dennis quickly flung his box down too and approached him.

'Was there anything else we can help you with instead?'

'Ah thanks so much but no, it was that one in particular I was interested in.'

'Such a shame because those particular editions are beautiful. We do have some other ones in if it's the classics that interest your wife. We can show you where they are if you'd like us to.'

We all watched as the customer's brain seemed to tick away. We waited. I cringed inwardly but tried not to let it show on my face. I hated being sold to in a shop and never wanted to be pushy with anyone who came to visit. If we didn't have what they wanted, I was happy for them to leave.

'Yeah, go on please. That would be great.'

'Fabulous. Nancy, could you show... sorry what's your name?'

'Phil.'

'Hi, Phil, I'm Dennis. Nancy, could you show Phil where the classics are please?'

Smiling sweetly, knowing that as soon as Phil left, I'd be giving Dennis a bollocking, I showed him over to the section of the shop that held all the classic books that we had in stock. I was reminded of how beautiful they were, when Phil stroked the covers, and remarked on the gorgeous shiny fronts and how pretty the sprayed edges were, and how much both his wife and daughter would love them.

'Do you know what?' Phil began. 'I know she said there are loads of classics that she's not read and it's our daughter's birthday, so why don't I take a selection. Something both a woman and little girl would like? Five, I think. But you'll have to choose. Is that too cheeky?'

'Not at all, I'd love to.'

'And we could order you a copy of *A Christmas Carol* too if you'd like us to?' Dennis shouted up from behind the counter. He'd made himself quite at home behind there and was definitely acting not only like he worked there, but more like he was the boss. I'd swing for him when Phil left the shop.

'Oh, yes please. That would be perfect.'

I carried the selection of books over to the counter and put the order through the system, letting him know that the other book should be in the next afternoon.

'I don't suppose I could pay now, leave them here and pick them up all together, could I?'

'You can indeed.'

Dennis cut in again. 'As they're a present, would you like us to wrap them for you, to save you a job?'

'You, mate, are a lifesaver. You don't do cards too, do you?' He laughed nervously.

'We can do that,' Dennis replied before I even had chance to speak. My hands shot to my hips and I was just about to spout off when Phil's next words stopped me in my tracks.

'I've only just popped out while the carer has gone into ours to relieve my wife and me. It's our daughter, you see. She's not well and is on dialysis. We don't get much time these days and my wife has sent me out on this book errand while she's gone out to get ingredients so she can bake a birthday cake. It could be her last one.'

I didn't know whether or not to ask more. Would he think I was prying?

'How old is she?'

'Ten.'

Mum, Dennis and I were all silent. How could any words at all be right in this situation? It was so sad to think it might be her last one.

After a few moments of all looking at each other, I had to break in.

'What sort of card would you like?'

'If you could just get any tenth birthday card for a girl, that would be amazing. Honestly, I can't thank you enough. I have a list as long as your arm that I'm working through.'

At that moment I knew I had to make sure that it was the most beautiful card she'd ever had. In fact I was going to make it myself. A perfect, hand-painted, unique card for a very special little girl.

'We're happy to help. If there's anything else you need just let us know.'

'You've done so much already. I can't tell you what a weight this is off my mind. Thank you so much.'

Sometimes you just don't realise how lucky in life you are. And at that moment, Dennis didn't realise how much he had to thank Phil for. Because Phil had just saved him from getting a massive bollocking.

15

As the door slammed shut, Dennis turned to me.

'Before you say anything—'

'How do you know I was going to say anything?'

'Well, your face was like thunder earlier and the fact that you've gone from your hands on your hips to the crossed arms and puckered mouth with slightly less thunderous glares, I thought it was quite a good indication really.' He looked over at Mum. 'It's a good job Phil softened the way for me a little, don't you think, Wendy?'

'I'm off,' she said in response. 'You can leave me out of...' she turned her index finger around in a circle in the air '...whatever is going on here.'

Mum scooted off after giving me a very quick kiss on the cheek and Dennis a shy little wave.

'So, would you please just hear me out?' he said. 'Shall we have a drink and a sit down?'

'I suppose you want me to make that too, don't you?'

'I'm happy to make it, but I don't want you to feel like I'm getting in the way.'

His eyebrows raised at the extremely loud huff that escaped me but he walked towards the coffee machine anyway and poured us two mugs full of coffee, putting just the right amount of milk in mine. As I sipped the drink, I realised it was exactly how I liked it.

I narrowed my eyes at him.

'Nothing to be suspicious about. I noticed how you had it yesterday. Now, I hadn't obviously had a chance to mention anything before Phil came in, but it was the perfect opportunity to show just how much you can upsell things.'

'Upsell?'

'Well, firstly, and I hope you don't mind me mentioning it, but I'm going to because I am here to help and it wouldn't be right for me to not say anything. When you told Phil that you hadn't got the book he wanted, he would have left, without buying anything.'

'Yes, because we hadn't got what he wanted.'

'But he'd have gone somewhere else to buy it if we hadn't shown him the other books and offered to order it for him. You don't really want customers to leave without buying anything, so you have to upsell. Upselling is kind of telling the customer what they want. Or highlighting it to them, should I say? Offering them something they didn't even know they wanted. Like the other classics, and then the gift wrapping. And that's something you could be offering anyone, not just at Christmas. You could just keep some nice paper under the counter and learn how to make pretty bows and charge them an extra fifty pence or a pound to have their purchases wrapped. Who, in this day and age, can be arsed to wrap presents? Who has the time?'

'I love wrapping presents. It's one of my favourite parts of Christmas.'

Dennis raised a brow.

'Well, there you go. Wrapping doesn't just have to be for Christmas. Who wouldn't want to receive a book that's been beautifully wrapped up in gorgeous tissue paper? That's why the brand Jo Malone does so well. The way they gift wrap their products is second to none. Tissue paper, a spray of their fragrance and then in a lovely gift bag. It makes the buyer feel valued and they always leave the shops with a smile, swinging their gift bag.'

I tilted my head to one side. It would be nice to get a present wrapped up beautifully like that, I had to admit. Even if it was something I was buying for myself. Dennis really did seem to know his stuff and these could be little ways we could help others, and help my business at the same time.

There were still questions I had though.

'You don't think it's being too pushy? That's what I always worry about.'

'I honestly think these days we have so many choices thrown at us on a daily basis, we don't know whether we're coming or going. Anything that takes choices out of the equation, and makes the consumer journey as short as possible, I reckon is worth all the money in the world.'

'What do you mean?'

'So, when I'm talking about the consumer journey, I mean give them what they want but not only that, give them what they didn't realise they wanted. For instance, cards. If you sell something you know is a present, and you'll know that because you can ask whether they want it wrapping, you can offer them a card. You're offering them something they already need and they can always say no, but if you have some here, then there's no need for them to go elsewhere.'

My brain clicked into place. So pretty hand-painted cards might be a nice addition to the shop stock too. Something else I could be doing in my spare time, which was reducing quite dramatically. Another thought occurred to me.

'Ah, so I suppose you mean like offering table service in a pub or restaurant?'

Dennis looked delighted with my comparison. He looked like a proud parent when something had finally clicked in a child's brain.

'Yes! Exactly that! So, you probably spend another tenner or so on drinks, which you wouldn't have spent otherwise if someone offers to get them for you.'

'But isn't that wrong? Too pushy?'

'Not when it's something they need or want. You just have to make it easy for them. It's like everything you do on your website or Facebook page. You need to make sure it's easy for people to see the thing they want, click a link, and buy it. They don't want to be searching around for other stuff and getting distracted on the way.'

'Well, we don't have to worry about those because I don't have either.'

'Yes, I know. And that's something else we'll be talking about soon too, don't you worry! Social media and websites will probably take up a whole other day!'

This time it was my eyes that had gone wide. It sounded like I was in for another lecture. Life was a dream with Dennis. It was a blooming good job he was easy on the eye, even if I did wonder where that thought had sprung from.

'Let's go back to choices. Think about when you go to a large supermarket, you know you want milk, but there are so many varieties of milk that it's like a brain overload. There's fresh, skimmed, there's semi-skimmed, full fat, sterilised, UHT, and now you also have soy milk, almond milk, oat milk. Your brain is just being fried constantly with loads of information and choices. That's before you've even got out of the milk aisle and you've probably got a whole week's worth of other food shopping to do too. I'm a firm believer that we have to do all we can to calm our brains. Does that make sense?'

Much as I didn't want to give him the benefit of the doubt and let him think he'd won, he was right and I had no alternative but to admit it, even though the words stuck in my throat a little.

'Yes, it does. I suppose.'

'So, if you can limit the choices in as many situations as you can, people will normally say yes. He's gone to the trouble of visiting your store, and you want him to buy from you, and come back, and not only that but tell all his friends about you too. So they come and visit and spend their money here instead of online or elsewhere. There's so much competition out there these days. And the most appealing one, most of the time, is the one we take when we can just click a button or use an app on our phones. So, you have to make the in-person shopping experience an incredibly good one and be super helpful, therefore making it a no-brainer for them not to use you again. It's not being pushy, it really isn't.'

My brain was working overtime taking all of this in. Dennis talked a whole lot of sense and I did trust him to be giving me good advice. Sometimes, though, there's a huge gap between giving advice and receiving that advice, taking it on board, but I knew I wanted this business to work. I needed it to work more than anything else in the world. And so Dennis was a little gift sent to me from heaven. Maybe via Aunty Theresa. Who knew? What I did know was that he charged a fortune for this type of advice and he wasn't charging me a penny. I'd be very stupid not to look this gift horse in the mouth.

'OK, smarty-pants. I presume you might have lots of other little gems like that up your sleeve and I'm ready to hear them. Only I have a favour to ask first.'

'Knock yourself out.'

'Next time you have a bright idea, can you maybe let me know first, so that I can get my head round it before announcing it to my customers, please?'

'Yes, ma'am.'

He clicked his heels together, saluted me and gave me a wink that turned my insides to jelly. I needed to change the subject before I got lost in those eyes again.

'What are you up to tonight, Dennis? Anything exciting going on at Chez Vi's?' I asked as I started to cash up.

'I've got some papers to read through and a great book I'm reading.'

At that, my eyes widened. Nothing excited me more than discussing what people were reading. The poor people who stood next to me at the huge supermarket in Truro when I was browsing the books section didn't know what they were in for when they asked me if I had any recommendations. They'd be there for hours desperately trying to get away.

My guess for Dennis would be a gritty crime thriller. Couldn't put my finger on why, but I could imagine him cosying up in an armchair, putting his glasses on and settling down to read one of those, maybe with a whisky over ice in a cut-glass tumbler by his side.

'What are you reading?' I asked, not quite believing that we'd never had this conversation before.

I was dying to know if I was right.

'Oh, it's an autobiography of a businessman who lives out in America. He turned things around from a struggling start-up to being a multimillion-dollar enterprise and selling out to a big conglomerate. Things like that fascinate me.'

'Do you ever read fiction?'

'Nah.' He dismissed it immediately. 'I find fiction a total waste of time and energy. If I'm not learning from it, I don't want to be reading it.'

'But there's so much to learn from novels and stories. Lots of books have realistic characters and storylines and the way that they overcome obstacles in their life is totally inspiring and makes you want to up and change the world.'

'Nance, don't you think you try to change the world enough as it is? It's a big world out there and you can't change it all.'

'No, but I remember reading a quote once that said, "helping one person might not change the world, but it might change the world of one person", so for me every small change makes a difference. Imagine if everyone did the same.'

Dennis stared out of the window to the bay beyond.

'Maybe you're right, Nance, but I'd need a lot more convincing than it's worth it.'

I loved nothing more than a challenge.

'You're on!'

He turned and winked at me again and my brain went to mush. I sighed. I knew that I was in trouble because I was finally ready to admit to myself that I liked him. Really liked him.

16

That night, when I got back home, Mum asked me how my day had ended up and I practically threw myself into the armchair like a petulant teenager.

'I'm knackered!'

Mum laughed and I saw her share a look with Dad who grinned back at her.

'Good, that means you must have had a busy day then. Are you ready for your dinner yet?'

'I'm ready for a drink. A strong one. Spending a day with Dennis isn't the most riveting of experiences, you know.'

'Oh, really? I always thought he's an incredibly interesting character. Lots of layers to him, I reckon, and you just need to peel them away. And with those spectacularly good looks of his, he could be a character in one of those romance novels you love reading so much.'

Why on earth did Mum have to mention peeling away his layers? Now all I could think of was his layers being clothes and peeling them all off him. I needed to change the conversation, quickly.

'He's not all that good looking, you know. I've seen far better.'

'Really? How many Hollywood film star lookalikes do you get in your little bookshop in Driftwood Bay then, darling?'

I sighed.

'Maybe not enough. And if I did, the chances of them being a reader and buying loads of my stock are pretty slim. Anyhow, enough about him. I've had enough of Dennis for one day. Him and his spreadsheets and his budget planners. What's for tea? I'm starving.'

I saw Mum's mouth twitch as she raised her eyebrows and looked over at Dad, who winked at her.

'You are very lucky to have him in your life.'

'You think?'

'I know. Vi talks about him a lot. He's a proper bigwig in his world, you know.'

'Well, he's not in his world now though, is he? He's in ours and we don't like show-offs around here.'

'I don't think he's showing off, love. He's just trying to help you. Vi tells me that he really likes spending time with you.'

This couldn't have come as more of a surprise to me. Dennis seemed to be exasperated by me most of the time. By the way that I thought I could run a business without really having the knowledge or commercial acumen that went with it. How I thought I could just open my shop and it naturally would just all fall into place and it be a booming business, without having a business plan or any real plans of any kind. How I felt that the universe had my back, so it didn't really matter what I did and didn't know. I felt like I was just the annoying customer that he was working with. So, for Vi to say that he enjoyed our time together, it was a real revelation.

'He's had a tough life,' Mum continued. 'Vi told me some bits and pieces and I'll fill you in on what I know another time when

I've learned a bit more. But don't be so hard on him, love. Maybe if you stopped fighting him, you'd realise that you could learn to like him too. She said he came back, almost lighter, the other night after being on the beach helping you on your cleaning shift. She worries about him so much. Always seems to have the weight of the world on his shoulders. Always trying to prove something to the world. But he just seems to want to help you. He was telling her about all the plastic on the beach and how he couldn't believe how long it would stay around if people like you didn't clean up after everyone. He seemed to be really interested in what he'd learned. She was surprised because he didn't normally care about anything much apart from how much money he could make for himself and for his company. She said she felt like there'd been a bit of a shift in him. She also said it was about time he learned from others. He's always been so fiercely independent, not accepting help from anyone. Reminds me of someone I know.'

She walked past me and kissed my head.

I sat up straight in my seat. I didn't think Dennis had learned anything from me. Although I suppose he had opened up to me when we'd been on the beach. Had I been too quick to judge him when I really didn't know him at all? I'd learned so much from him already, even if it was hard to admit to myself, let alone anyone else. And yes, Mum was probably right. I did strive to be as independent as I could be. In today's day and age, it was hard to get on the property market, and especially hard in a place like Cornwall where the prices were massively inflated by people from outside the area buying second houses or moving to the coast for a better way of life. Even a small starter house or flat here was way out of my price range, and that's why at the age of twenty-seven years old, I was still living at home with my parents. It would be nice to start earning a good salary from the shop and to be able to invest in a future of my own rather than just live day to day not knowing what the next week would hold. I think holding on to my independence at the shop was the only bit of control I did have.

'Sometimes it's nice to have new friends in your life, Nancy. I didn't like Theresa, you know, when I first met her. When she arrived at school, she got loads of attention. She was the new pretty girl and there was a boy I fancied – and who fancied me back – who took a liking to her and went off me. You can imagine it, can't you? I was fuming. I was fourteen and full of raging hormones and then the new girl came along and took away the love of my life. But then I fell over in PE and she was the one the PE teacher made take me to the school nurse and she was really kind to me. Over the next few weeks, I got to really know her and like her. And the boy was an arse anyway. If I'd have gone out with him, I'd never have met your dad, and you wouldn't exist. It's just a lesson to us all that you have to give people a chance. Give Dennis a chance, love. You could be the best of friends for years to come. And friends help each other, in many different ways. He could be your life-changer. And who knows? You could be his.'

Maybe, while Dennis was starting to have an impact on me, in his world, I was starting to have an impact on him. If he could teach me something about forecasts and investments, and profit and loss accounts, then maybe I could teach him something about conservation and sustainability, and recycling and regeneration.

Struggling to think about anything else but this all the way through dinner, I pottered off upstairs after I'd loaded the dishwasher citing that I was going to have an early night and read in my room, but really, I wanted to consider how I could educate Dennis about the things that mattered to me. Maybe he could pass this on to the people within his company, so that instead of just thinking about the money side of the business, they also looked at the environmental issues too and how they could incorporate them. I also thought about how I should use the opportunity of having someone in my life with the life skills that I was so clearly lacking, and how I could use those to start to shape my future more.

My last thoughts, as I put down the romance novel that I was reading, before turning off my bedside light, was whether Dennis was sitting up in bed reading the autobiography and whether I could persuade him to branch out into something a little different – he might think novels were about the lighter things in life, but they could be equally as inspiring and life-changing as the highly successful profiled autobiographies he chose.

17

Dennis was a bit later turning up at the shop the next day. As I handed him a mug of coffee, I noticed that he also looked a little less formal, this time dressed in a pair of denim blue jeans, and a sky-blue polo shirt. Still impeccable and clearly very good quality, and most probably all designer gear, but just a little less stiff. More casual. It suited him.

I looked down at my own clothes. Today, I'd chosen a vintage wrap dress in red and brown tones, which were perfect for autumn, along with a pair of knee-high brown suede boots which Mum had picked up at a charity shop in Truro.

Dennis smiled as he took the coffee from me and our hands touched briefly. Our eyes locked and I was the first to look away.

We both started speaking at the same time.

'You look nice...'

'I've been thinking...'

'That sounds dangerous.'

'Not really,' I said, 'but I have been thinking that I should have been, and should be, more grateful for the advice you're offering me. I'd like to apologise. I suppose criticism is hard for me to take.

I've always been the teacher and it's hard for me to be the student, but I have had a word with myself and I am prepared to learn.'

'Great. That's great, Nance. I just want to help you, you know.'

'I know and thank you.'

'And you have so much to teach me too.'

'You really think so?'

'I do. I've never even thought about our environment before. It's just all money, money, money with me. It's been the one constant in my life and the one thing I can control. That might sound daft but...'

'It doesn't at all. I kind of know where you're coming from.'

'You are so talented, Nance, look at those amazing shell paintings you do. They're incredible. And I've been thinking about how you can do more book-related things like that too.'

'Now that would be fun.'

Dennis hesitated before taking a deep breath and blurting out his next words most unexpectedly.

'You inspire me, you know, Nancy.'

'Me? How so?'

'You are doing something you're totally passionate about. Running a bookshop. Living your dream. All I do is make money. And taking this time out from work is making me realise that maybe it's not everything.'

A little light bulb went off in my head. I knew just the thing to make Dennis realise that there was more to life than work.

'What are you doing on Sunday?' I asked.

'No plans. My life consists of no real plans at the moment.'

'Does that bother you?'

'It did at first. I didn't know what to do with myself when I got up in the morning. I'm a get-up-at-six kind of guy and rarely lie in. But somehow, the Driftwood Bay air is getting to me and I'm having early nights and lie-ins. I've not done that since I was a teenager. Nan has got me walking Gladys most days. Said it's not right for Meredith to be doing it when she's got a perfectly able-bodied person in the house and, to be honest, it's been lovely. On the mornings that I've still got up reasonably early, Gladys and I have snuck out and strolled along the beach. I have to say, it's a much nicer way to start the day than looking out over the rooftops of loads of other buildings and seeing the cloud of smog that sits across the city.'

'I don't think there's a better place on earth than Driftwood Bay first thing in the morning. When the rest of the world is still in bed asleep. At this time of the year, I sometimes wrap up and come down here while it's still dark. It's lovely, and life-affirming to see Mother Nature do her thing, and watching the sun come up. I always think it's really kind of special. You have to check on the weather forecast to see if it'll be clear but it's a sight for sore eyes. It really is. I know when we first met it was over a sunrise, but to see it from dark to light is incredible. Meredith's mum is normally round the corner in her little bay doing her early morning yoga. And if you're lucky you'll see the Driftwood Babes paddleboarding out on the water.'

'They even do it at this time of the year?'

'You bet! They make a special event of it on Christmas Day. It's quite spectacle, you know. Everyone gathers on the beach and we have hot chocolate and bacon sandwiches to start the day when those who choose to go in come out of the water.'

'They must be mad.'

'It's supposed to be exhilarating.'

'I'll take their word for it!'

'I go in, in the summer, but you wouldn't catch me going in much after the middle of September.'

I laughed out loud remembering something that had just popped into my head.

'Care to share?'

'I was just thinking that when I was at school there was a young boy called Paul Shepherd who said he loved me. My best friend told him that if he loved me, he'd go in the sea on Christmas Day and prove it, and after that, he said he didn't love me *that* much.'

Dennis laughed too, his eyes crinkling up at the corners.

'I can't say I blame him!' He laughed.

'Me neither.'

'Right, lady,' he said, slapping his thighs and going to stand up. 'You ready for some learning? And then we can talk about my latest brainwaves.'

'As long as you weren't trying to avoid my earlier question about what you're doing on Sunday.'

'Ah, you noticed. Sorry. On Sunday you can have me for the whole day if you can think of something to entertain me.'

He grinned, there was a flicker of an eyebrow raise and he tilted his head to one side. God! I was sure he was properly flirting with me.

Trying to ignore the little thoughts that might be running through my head right then, about what we could get up to with a whole day, I brought myself back to the task in hand.

'OK, meet me here on Sunday morning at ten and I'll promise you a few hours of fun.'

His mouth twitched.

'Best offer I've had for a while, I have to say.'

I could feel the heat rise up my neck and into my face.

'I'm sorry,' he said, 'I don't mean to tease you but you look so cute when you blush. I'd be delighted to spend a few hours with you on Sunday. Shall we get to work now then? I thought we could talk about business expenses today and then maybe you can have a treat.'

Withholding the desire to groan, I forced a smile. I knew it was important stuff that could help my future so I would grin and bear it. I would listen to his words of wisdom and I would learn from him. But he seemed to also be adjusting to my way of learning and in the same way that I probably would have done with the children I used to teach, I would reward them with something nice, after they had to do something they didn't like as much.

True to my word, I listened intently. He was actually a very good teacher, excellent at explaining things in detail, without making me feel stupid and giving me analogies to relate to. By the time lunchtime came around, and he offered to go and grab us some soup from the bistro, I was actually looking forward to him coming back.

My afternoon treat was not only a huge slab of Victoria sponge, but that he suggested doing some workshops in the bookshop. These would probably be on a Sunday, which would mean I'd be working extra hours, but when I learned his thoughts, I realised it wouldn't be like work at all. He suggested doing a creative writing session, a making-a-bookmark workshop and we brainstormed some ideas for others, my favourite being the Christmas bauble making. He thought that by getting people who loved book-related things involved, they'd be happy to spread the word about the shop. I absolutely loved these ideas and was super happy that we could put some dates in the diary.

The only negative part of the day was when he asked me where I felt we could advertise these things.

As a teacher, social media was something I was always quite wary of. I didn't want the children or their parents being able to get in touch with me so my profiles were very small and protected where possible. My homework for that evening was to think about what sort of posts I could be putting up and we would discuss it tomorrow. I knew that I could get a few people locally to come to these workshops but Dennis was so right when he said we could attract a much bigger audience if we were able to spread the word online, possibly even getting a website when I had a bit more experience and had got the technical side of things sorted. All of this planning was happening around customers coming in and I was still getting used to his upselling suggestion. That afternoon, I'd noticed that while a couple of people said no to things I suggested, the majority said yes and what was normally a quiet day turned into being quite a busy and productive one.

'Great work today, Nance. I've enjoyed it.'

'Me too, Dennie. Sorry – Dennis.'

'No, let's go with Dennie. I like it. I think it suits the new Driftwood Bay me.'

'Not sure it'll suit the London Financial Dennis though, eh?'

'I'm not sure I know who that guy is any more.' He looked down at his feet. He was like a lost little boy. I felt a little sorry for him. He'd been having a tough time and he'd also been helping me out of the goodness of his heart. An idea popped into my mind.

'Why don't you come to the pub quiz with me tonight?'

His head shot up at the same time that I wondered why those words had come out of my mouth. I wasn't usually one to invite people to my inner circle, which was rather small and only really consisted of me and my family.

'It might be fun. When was the last time you had fun, Dennis?'

'You've already promised me fun on Sunday, Nance. I don't want to be overdosing on it.'

I laughed. 'Maybe Dennie likes fun.'

'Maybe he does. Go on then, yes. Dennie accepts. Quiz night it is.'

'Great, we'll be leaving at about ten to eight. Starts at eight.'

'Can I bring Vi too?'

'Absolutely. She'll definitely liven things up.'

'That she will. Shall we knock on the door as we pass yours?'

He was full of smiles when I nodded. And his eyes sparkled. His lovely brown eyes. I liked Dennie. I just had to keep reminding myself that he was just my friend, and somehow find a way to stop those flipping summersaults in my tummy every time he smiled that Ryan Gosling smile.

18

As I heard the knock at the door, my heart did another little skip and I took a deep breath. I let Mum open the door, while I put the finishing touches to my make-up, telling myself that I was an idiot and not to get carried away with feeling anything more than friendship for Dennis. He wouldn't be sticking around long term, so even if I was interested in him in that way, which I wasn't of course, there was no point.

He winked at me when I went down to the hall, where he and Vi, Mum and Dad were waiting. We all fell into step, Vi between Mum and Dad, with an arm hooked through each of theirs. Dennis and I walked next to each other.

'You look nice, Nance.'

'Thanks,' I mumbled and could feel my cheeks warming up in the cool night air. 'You any good at quizzes?'

'I can hold my own. How about you? As an ex-teacher, you must have expectations that your team has a good chance of winning.'

'I can get by. Don't forget that I was an art teacher though, not maths, so if there are any number questions, it'll be all down to you.'

'No pressure there then, thanks, Nance!'

Dennis was the first at the bar and offered to get a round in. We were lucky enough that someone got up and left the window seating area as we arrived, so we took over that area, which was my favourite space in the whole pub with a huge picture window that overlooked the harbour.

After a lot of laughs and a great deal of good-natured shouting at each other, in the spirit of winning, we were delighted to have come second, only pipped to the post by Clem and Meredith, Lucy and James and Gemma and Jude, all locals, and our protests that they had six in their group and we only had five, fell on deaf ears. Mum, Dad and Vi all said that they wanted to go home after the quiz had finished, but I was having a really nice time. Dennis said he'd stick around and make sure I got back safely if I wanted to stay, if Mum and Dad would make sure his Nan got back OK. I did notice that Mum and Vi pulled strange faces at each other and grinned, and I pretended I hadn't noticed.

'Right, you 'orrible lot,' the landlord, Geoff, shouted at the customers across the bar an hour or so later. 'Time you all buggered off home and let me lock up. I need my beauty sleep.'

I felt quite light-headed as I stood, and Dennis steadied me. I wasn't a big drinker and I'd had a couple of glasses of wine which I really wasn't used to. I'd noticed that Dennis had had a couple of pints though he was looking quite relaxed.

'I've really enjoyed myself tonight,' he said. 'Thanks for asking me.'

'You're welcome. It's been a really nice night. Fun too.'

He grinned back. That grin. Wow.

We didn't have far to walk but spending time with Dennis had been lovely. And if I could get over this silly little crush, which I appeared to have, it seemed like we could become good friends. I didn't really want the night to end, though, not just yet.

'It's a lovely clear night,' he said. 'Fancy a walk along the beach?'

'Yeah, go on then.'

Because there was hardly any light pollution, Driftwood Bay on a clear night was amazing. The myriad of silver sparkling stars above us looked like someone had cast a net of fairy lights across the sky. Even the sand looked like it was scattered with glitter and the moonlight made the sea look like it was shimmering away. We approached a flat rock at the back of the beach.

'Shall we sit?' he suggested.

I nodded and he shouted out loud before my backside hit the rock.

'Wait, sit on this.' He took his jacket off and let me sit on it. 'Nan always says you'll get piles if you sit on something cold.'

'How thoughtful of you to bring piles into the conversation, Dennie, but thank you.'

We smiled at each other before staring out at the sea; its spellbinding beauty still at times took my breath away, never ceasing to amaze me even after all the years of living here. Being in Driftwood Bay made my heart happy and filled me with joy.

'What's it like living in London?' I asked, fascinated at why anyone would want to.

A loud sigh escaped him.

'I used to love it. The city that never sleeps. There's always something going on. No one in your business. People leave you alone. It's fast paced. Everyone rushing around.'

'I feel like there's a but.'

He turned and looked at me intently before whispering, 'But being back here this time feels like I've come home.'

I smiled. It appeared that Driftwood Bay had weaved its magical spell on him, like it had on many others.

'How so?'

He held my gaze before looking back out to sea.

'I used to like the fact that London was quite anonymous. Now I love that here people really care about each other. Look at what you all did for Nan. It's a real sense of community spirit. All the things I loved about London in the past seem to be the things I can't bear about it now.'

The silence between us wasn't in the least bit awkward. It was needed for us both to process what he'd said.

'I like being part of a community,' he continued. 'I feel like it gives me a sense of purpose, which is something that I didn't realise I was missing. Now when I head back, it feels dirty and the air doesn't feel clean. I get off the train at Paddington and everyone is so focused on where they're going, they cut across you or bump into you. No one has manners, it's almost every man or woman for themself. Nobody makes eye contact with you. You're constantly checking that you've still got your wallet in your back pocket in case someone's swiped it, and hold on to your laptop bag like it holds the crown jewels for the same reason. I suppose I'd lived in that for so long that I never really noticed.'

I shuddered at the thought.

'I've hardly left this part of the world apart from uni in Exeter which isn't that far away, although I suppose it is a different county,' I said. 'I feel like I've hardly seen the world, but I've never felt like I needed to. Everything I want is here.' I scanned the beach, looked across to the harbour and leaned back to take in the hills. 'I love it.'

Dennie's eyes locked onto mine. 'Yeah, I'm beginning to love it too.'

We both sat quietly, together, but alone in our thoughts.

'We should get off,' Dennis said eventually. 'We've got a busy day ahead of us tomorrow. I've got some brilliant ideas that I want to run by you.'

'OK.' I heaved myself off the bench, reluctantly tearing myself away. 'I've got some of my own to share with you too.'

Dennis nudged my shoulder gently. 'We'll make a businesswoman of you yet!'

'You are quite annoying you know, Dennie!'

'Rubbish. You're growing quite fond of me, I reckon.'

I shook my head and laughed his words off. 'Whatever.'

If only he knew.

19

'You have got to be kidding me.'

'Nope, you said I could do with you what I wanted.'

'Yeah, but that didn't include this.'

'Ah, you promised, Dennie. Remember, Dennie is a fun-loving guy! You're not going to let me down after all this, are you? You're not going to back down?'

'I most certainly am not. I'm no quitter!'

'Glad to hear it. Right, come and take this from me then and let's go.'

I laughed as Dennis tried to mount my brother's bike. It was a similar size to mine, so I knew he'd be fine on it. I could feel his fresh minty breath on my face as I helped him fasten the helmet under his chin. Embarrassed by our closeness, I moved as fast as I could to get away from him and how warm he was making me feel.

'Right, come on then. You ready?'

'Yep, let's go!'

When I glanced back at him, wobbling from side to side, he looked like a little boy learning to ride for the very first time.

'Christ, I haven't ridden a bike for literally years.'

'You'll be fine,' I shouted over my shoulder. 'It's, literally, like riding a bike.'

'Oh, you're so funny. Whoa!' He wobbled and leaned the bike on one side, balancing it with his foot which was closest to the floor. 'Right, I'm ready, just go and I'll follow you.'

I started to pedal and we just did a little gentle ride round the harbour wall to get him used to it. I kept turning to look back, and he looked more confident every time. Trust me to pick someone who's naturally good at everything he does. Now there's a thought.

Back to earth, Nancy.

I could, however, immediately tell that Dennis was definitely not one to give up. He was someone who would persevere until he mastered something and it wasn't long before he was riding beside me and chatting comfortably about the things he was seeing around the bay. Before long, I had stopped at the top of the cliff waiting for him to catch me up. He wasn't that far behind me but it gave me time to catch my own breath. I was trying to prove a point that I was happy to do this all the time.

'Wow. This is kind of amazing,' Dennis said when he'd caught me up. 'Thanks, Nancy.'

'Told you it'd be something you'd enjoy. It's fun, isn't it?'

'It is, although if you'd asked me to come on a bike ride with you, I probably wouldn't have agreed.'

'That's why I didn't tell you.'

'You know me so well already.'

I smiled at him, thinking about how my mum said he'd be full of layers. I hardly knew Dennis but it was kind of fun learning about what made him tick. We were such different characters that I knew we wouldn't always see eye to eye on everything but we could definitely teach each other things that we might need to learn, even if those were things like having fun.

'The bay looks stunning from up here. And I'm blooming roasting.' He took his helmet off and hung it over the handlebars and pulled at the bottom of his Tommy Hilfiger hoody to drag it over his head. Unfortunately for him – but fortunately for me – he also pulled at the bottom of his T-shirt and gave me a glimpse of a rather defined stomach. I had to tear my eyes away but not until he'd noticed my raised eyebrows.

He patted himself.

'Been working on getting my six-pack back after Nan told me I was looking a bit porky. Been back in the gym before work, and if I get time at night, I try to get a run in too.'

'Do you like exercise?'

'Not really. It's just a necessity, isn't it?'

'I'm not one for the gym to be honest. It's all a bit boring and repetitive.'

'It is but that's kind of the point.'

'I'd rather be on my bike,' I said. 'I love taking in the countryside, noticing things about the place I've lived in all my life that most people don't see when they're driving.'

'Funnily enough that's what I was just thinking. I've always driven down to Nan's and parked up at the harbour side outside her house. So it's only been when I've been out walking with Gladys that I've seen more than ever before – and I've been coming here for years to visit Nan.'

'It's strange that we've never really bumped into each other before really.'

'Well, to be truthful, I don't normally get that involved in the village life. Since I've been working, I've not been to stay with Nan for much longer than a weekend at a time. I've always been too busy to stay for longer. But it's actually really rather lovely. I'm loving it more by the day.'

I turned to him and found he was staring at me. I didn't want to presume anything here, but it felt like we really had a connection again. I had felt it when I first met him, on that day when we collided and it wasn't until he started dishing out the advice to me that I started to feel differently. Maybe it was because I felt like he was criticising me when all he was trying to do was help. There was a bit of me now thinking that it was just a communication issue. Like in most cases in life.

We locked eyes.

'Maybe you'll come and stay again.'

'Maybe I will.'

We both grinned at each other like lunatics.

'Come on, slowcoach. Race you to the next stop.'

As we cycled around the wide coastal path side by side, we settled into a more relaxed pace and I pointed out some landmarks to him as we travelled. Finally, we reached a bench and we stopped. My bike, with its basket on the front, might look like the bike of a little old lady, but it was actually incredibly practical and Dennis was impressed when I handed him a bottle of water and started to unpack a picnic blanket and some food packages.

'Wouldn't it have been easier to pack them in plastic bags?' he asked, looking at the wraps I'd used.

'Easier, yes maybe. But environmentally friendly, no. I try where possible to limit the amount of plastic I use. These are made of beeswax. You can swill them and use them time and time again. Much better for the world.'

'Oh yes, I suppose it is. I'm so much better informed now, Nancy. I did some reading last night about how we can all do our bit. There are lots of things that I think I could do and I wondered if you'd mind me running the ideas by you.'

He was now talking my kind of language and once on this topic, I could go on for hours.

'Just stop me when I'm boring you,' I said as I passed him a packet of sandwiches.

He unwrapped them and grinned. 'Have you made me chicken and stuffing sandwiches? These are my favourite.'

'I know they are. Mum said that your nan is always talking about you and your favourite.'

'Oh my God! Chicken crisps too! You are spoiling me.'

'Yep, that made me laugh because I thought that I was the only person in the world that loved chicken crisps. But now there's two of us.'

'We're clearly made for each other.'

I turned my head but he was looking down at his sandwiches and I wondered if I'd imagined what he'd.

He started to tell me about his ideas to be more sustainable.

'Maybe I'll buy myself a bike and stop using my car so much.'

'That seems like a waste of money if you're not stopping long.'

'Well, maybe there might be a reason to come back a bit more often.'

This time, it was my turn to look down at my sandwich. Did he mean me? Was I reading this the right way?

I looked up and our eyes locked again. This kept happening. It was almost like he had a magnet that was pulling my eyes towards him. Much as I liked him, the emotions that he had stirred up within me were ones that I was feeling uncomfortable with. I was quite happy on my own, in my own little world. Love brings complications with it. I saw that every day when I looked at my brother and his relationship with his girlfriend. She was demanding and high maintenance and he spent his life doing things he didn't want to do, just to make her happy. That wasn't the sort of relationship I wanted. I wanted the dream that my parents had. Years of being with someone who loved you for being you. I knew deep down that my brother wasn't the best role model, but it was the only one I had apart from Mum and Dad. Dan's was the one that I knew wasn't right. But when I questioned him about it, he always said that that was just the way love was and that it was better to be with someone who loved you, like she loved him, than being on your own. He was happy to make all the compromises.

Their relationship had put me off and was one of the main reasons why I wasn't looking for anyone in my life. I was busy enough – with my beach angel work, my bookshop, and the other stuff that I did in the community. I didn't really have the time or energy for anyone in my life. And certainly didn't have the time or energy for anyone who didn't even live here. A holiday romance was not my thing at all. Even if he was a Gozzer lookalike.

* * *

My mood was pensive when I packed the food back into the pannier. We were just about to ride off when I peeked over at Dennis. He was gazing out to sea and the gentle wind was blowing his normally gelled-back hair, and it almost looked fluffy after he'd been wearing a helmet for the last two hours. Some women were lucky that their hair fell into gorgeous natural waves when they shook their head out of a hat. Sadly, I was not one of them. I was more the type whose hair was stuck to their head, and looked hot and sweaty, so it was a good job I wasn't trying to impress anyone.

I got my phone out of my cross-body bag and took an inconspicuous shot of Dennis. His eyes were closed and he was letting the wind wrap itself around him. I'd never seen him look so relaxed and happy. The next time he told me he didn't know how to have fun, I would remind him of this moment.

As he came back to reality, I turned away, pretending that I hadn't been staring at him for the last minute or so.

When we arrived back at our house, where he insisted he should return the bike, he offered to take the helmet home to clean it. 'I'm sure your brother doesn't want my sweat inside the next time he wants to wear this.'

'It's fine, honestly. He won't mind at all. We're used to having sweaty helmets in our house!'

The smirk on his face was enough to make me blush and I looked away, removing my own helmet and trying to fluff up my hair which I'm sure was plastered to my head and sticking up in all the wrong places.

'Well, you still look gorgeous to me, Nancy.'

I giggled in response, thinking he was taking the mickey out of me, but when I looked over at him, he looked deadly serious. I couldn't work him out at all.

'I really have had fun today,' he continued. 'Thank you for showing me what I could be doing with my life instead of working all the time. You've really opened my eyes, you know. There's a whole new world outside.'

'You're welcome, Dennis.'

'Dennie. I think I'll definitely be Dennie from now on in Driftwood Bay. He feels more at home here than he's ever felt in his life before. And he has you to thank for that.'

'Well, that's what friends do for each other, right?'

'Yeah, that's what friends do.'

To my sheer surprise, he handed me back my brother's helmet then leaned across and kissed me on the cheek.

As he walked away and I touched the place where his gentle lips had brushed against my skin, I shivered. That did not feel like something a friend would do.

Before I went to bed that night, I flicked through the photos I'd snapped along the way today. The autumn heathers that gave purple colour to the lush green landscape. The birds that were circling around us. The views across the bay. My finger stopped at the picture I'd taken of Dennie and I lingered, drinking in all of his features – the way his eyebrows were in perfect symmetry with each other, the way his nose ever so slightly turned up at the end, at the little dimple in his chin that was so tiny it was hardly noticeable and the freckle on the brow of his nose. The thoughts that were going through my mind right then were not thoughts of things that friends should be doing with each other. I had a feeling that I might be in a little bit of trouble.

20

We'd settled into an easy routine. Every day I would arrive at the shop and have an hour of cosy reading in the window, and I'd get a pot of coffee ready for when Dennie arrived around nine. The mornings were normally quiet and we could chat around the customers who came in and I'd also try to spend some time painting, although the shells were going down really well and I was nearly running out of my stock. The nights were drawing in and it was getting darker earlier so there wasn't as much time in the day to go and do the things that I wanted to do, and my weekends were full of beach angel work and finding shells to paint. I wasn't sure what Dennie got up to normally on a weekend. He said that he'd been enjoying spending real quality time with his nan and he told me that she loved reminiscing and sharing stories about his parents when they were younger and less selfish. He didn't speak about his parents much and didn't seem to give anything away about them. He had shared that he loved listening to those stories even though they seemed to be about people he didn't know and said that he could understand a little more about why she liked reading fiction, because it was as if she was telling him fictional stories.

'So, today, my friend, we're going to be learning all about manifesting.'

Dennie put his head in his hands but I immediately reached out to him and removed his hands, holding on to them for a split second too long before I realised what I was doing. I had, however, in that short time, realised how soft his hands were, and felt like I could probably count every single one of the light brown hairs on the back of them. I dropped them back onto his lap and smiled sweetly.

After I'd explained what manifesting was, he paraphrased it back to me.

'So, I tell the universe what I want, and it listens and through its vibrations, it sends me back the thing that I want. Is that it?'

'Yep, that's about it,' I said. 'I told the universe that I wanted a bookshop, and then a few weeks later, I got a letter telling me that Aunty Theresa had left me some money in her will and wished that I would be able to follow my dream.'

'And you don't just think that was a bloody great big coincidence?'

'No, I don't.'

'But why?'

'Because the universe doesn't work like that. That's why.'

He scorned, huffing out loud.

'OK, let's try this. Close your eyes. Now think of something you'd really like right now.'

His left eyebrow lifted ever so slightly. So slightly that I wondered if I'd imagined it. He opened one eye and smirked at me.

'Be serious. It won't work if you don't.'

'Yes, miss!'

I giggled. I was not a giggler but somehow in his presence I became one. He was dry and full of one-liners that were hilarious. I don't think he even realised how funny he was. I rolled my eyes at myself and told him to relax.

'I've told you before, I find it hard to relax.'

'Oh, Dennie, you're a nightmare. Chill out!'

'Nancy, I'm finding it quite unrelaxing to have you bellowing at me. Not really conducive, you know? Can we not have some twinky-twonky music playing and some smelly candles to help the atmosphere a little?'

'We're trying to talk to the universe here, not have a romantic night in.'

'Well, perhaps we need to woo the universe a little more. Make it a little more ambient.'

'Dennie!' I warned.

He held his hands up to me.

'OK, OK. I'm relaxing. Honest.'

'Now think of the thing you really want.'

'Mmmm! I am.' His deep guttural elongated pronunciation of such a small phrase hit me with a power I didn't know existed. Blimey, just imagine if... No! I couldn't allow myself to imagine anything more than us being friends. Since our bike ride, I had taken stock of our situation and we'd been getting on like a house on fire. As friends. He would be heading back to London soon, I would be here alone, and with a thriving business that I didn't have to worry about any longer. My plan for the next year was coming along swimmingly and I was going to be so busy I wouldn't have time to even think about him when he was gone.

'Now, you ask the universe in your head to make it happen. Then think about it in the present. Imagine how it would feel if you had the thing that you wanted. Can you see it?'

'God! Yes!' The tone that he said those two little words in was sexier than I could ever imagine. Was he doing it on purpose to wind me up?

'OK, so you can open your eyes now.'

'Thank you.'

'How did that feel?'

Again, those gorgeous brown eyes locked onto mine and I felt like he could see right into the very soul of me. I sincerely hoped that at that very moment he could not read my mind. I was thinking things that one should never be thinking about a friend. But then most people didn't have friends who looked the spitting image of Ryan Gosling.

'OK. So, let's see if it happens now then. See whether this bullshit you spout comes true.'

'Harsh.'

'The proof will be in the pudding.'

'It really is.'

'Anyhow, what are you doing at the weekend?'

'Beach angeling on Saturday and then on Sunday I really need to see if I can get some more large shells. I've used all but the last one. If not, I'm going to have to buy some, but I don't really want to do that unless I have to. Keep the costs down and all that.'

He put his hands together in prayer. 'Thank you, Lord! She listens.'

I swatted him with the pad I'd been using to do some journaling in. Another manifestation tool was to write down what you wanted. I was a big believer in vision boards too but thought that might definitely be a bit too woo-woo for him.

At that point Mum walked in. She'd brought us both some sweet potato and cinnamon soup. Dennis was still struggling with Vi's food. She'd offered him banana and spinach cake the day before and he'd refused, saying that he didn't want to start putting on weight again, rather than hurting her feelings. Mum had laughed when he told her this – apparently Vi had told her that Dennis was turning his nose up a lot at all the things she suggested and said that he could do his own cooking.

'This smells gorgeous, Wendy,' he said, taking the package. 'Thanks so much.'

'My pleasure, treasure. If I'm doing some for Nancy, then another mouth being fed makes me happy.'

'Mum's a feeder. You may have noticed.' I laughed and Mum narrowed her eyes at me.

'I suppose I am really. I think it comes from when your brother was bullied at school. I used to feed him things I knew he loved when he got home so it would cheer him up. I think that's why he has all these issues these days with his girlfriends. I don't think he feels like he's ever worthy of anything else after all that trouble he had back then.'

'That's so sad,' Dennis said. 'I wish my mum would have been more like you.'

It was the first real time he'd mentioned his mum and I was glad that he was speaking about her, even if it was to my mum and not me. By this time, I'd moved over to behind the counter but I could still hear him talking.

'She was just not maternal. She was never around much. I used to have to come home from school and get myself something to eat. I couldn't cook so it was normally a bowl of cereal or some toast, which I could just about manage to make. It's why I used to love coming to Nan's in the school holidays.'

'So, did you never learn to cook then, Dennis? Can you cook?'

Typical that Mum picked up on that more than the emotional side of things and wondering why his mum was never there.

'I'm a wizard with a microwave, Wendy. I have a very good cleaning lady who has been more of a mother to me than my own ever was. She makes me home-cooked meals while she's doing them for her own family, and she loads up my freezer, so I just have to get them out in the morning before work and then I heat them up when I get home. I wish I could cook, to be honest. It's something I've always said I'd learn but never seemed to find the time.'

'You have more time on your hands now than ever, don't you?' she asked. 'When do you go back to London?'

I nearly broke my neck at this point, craning to hear as best as I could.

'I'm heading back at the weekend actually. Got some things I need to sort out.'

'Will you be away for long?'

'I don't think I can stay away. Even if I wanted to.' We both looked up at the same time and our eyes locked. 'Driftwood Bay seems to have got right under my skin.'

He didn't take his eyes off mine, and when I broke eye contact, Mum looked from one of us to the other, a sly smile appearing on her face.

'Well, you let me know when you are back and have some time, young man. I think I have a wonderful idea that could help both you and Vi, and maybe some other people too.'

Intrigued as to what she was plotting, I stepped back over to where they were standing, but she didn't elaborate any further, though she did wink at me as she gave me a little kiss on the cheek before she left.

'He's a good one, you know, kid,' she whispered in my ear. 'Not many of them around. You should snap him up before someone else does. Or before he goes back to London for good.'

This thought wouldn't leave my mind that evening. I locked the shop door and Dennie and I agreed to meet later at the pub for quiz night. We were getting into a proper little routine and I think I'd been kidding myself into thinking that being friends was just fine, and that we'd just continue to plod along in the way that we were. But now all I could think about was the fact he might not be here for much longer and that thought gave a little twang on my heart. The thought of him not being in my life every day was not filling me with joy. It wasn't that long ago that we barely knew each other, but now, I couldn't imagine my life without him in it.

21

Life just seemed a little less bright without Dennie. I sent him a text on the Saturday morning to say have a nice weekend and just got a thumbs up in return. It was all I could do to stop my thoughts running away with me. Wondering what he was doing and who he was doing it with. Worrying about whether he'd hook up with anyone while he was back in London or realise that life there was better than life here. I was scared that now he was back where he originally belonged, he wouldn't want to return.

I tried to keep myself occupied. Saturday in the shop was a very busy day. It was nice that people came from further afield. In the downtime that I did have, I set up social media profiles and started taking what Dad called 'arty-farty' photos of the books along with the other items that I was now branching out into. And my pièce de résistance of course were my painted shells. Inspired by Dennis's idea of making the shells book related, I started to copy the covers of the books. So far, I had done *Wuthering Heights* and *Little Women*. They just needed to be varnished and photographed before I could put them on sale.

To stop thoughts of Dennis filling my head all the time, I made sure that every minute of every day was accounted for. I had to distract myself to stop me from thinking. Thinking about Dennie and how much I missed him.

More than what seemed like at least a hundred times, I resisted the urge to message him, to tell him the most ridiculous of things which I knew would either make him laugh or make him think, make him smack his head at my commercial ignorance or shake his head at me. It felt like a part of me was missing. Like something I'd always worn, a piece of jewellery for instance, was lost from my life and I kept reaching out for it. A ring that I might spin on my finger, or a necklace that I constantly touched, which had been there once upon a time and now wasn't any more.

My day off was the worst. It was simple – I missed him. We'd got into a little routine on my days off and Dennie and I had spent them going on bike rides around the surrounding areas and we'd had such fun. Me pointing out places of interest along the way, telling him a little of my history and my youth, and him very nearly a few times opening up to me. On a couple of occasions, I even thought we were on the brink of a breakthrough. Vi had told Mum he wasn't a person who shared things easily but I felt that he did open up to me. This made me feel like I was special to him. He made me feel like we were the best of friends. He made me feel like we could be a whole lot more if we had more time together.

And when Mum came into my bedroom that night to check that I was OK, I pretended that I had the start of a cold and was feeling a bit rotten, when, to be honest, I think a little bit of my heart had gone back to London with Dennie. When she told me that she'd popped in to see Vi that day, to check that she was OK, and that Vi said Dennie was having to stay in London for the next couple of weeks, I felt physically sick. This was the exact reason why I didn't want to be in love with someone. People said that it was better to have loved and lost but I didn't think it was. I'd seen the state that my brother had been in when his girlfriend dumped him. He was literally a broken man. Then how grateful he was to her when she deigned to take him back after he begged her to. I'd never been fond of her, and after that performance, I was even less so, even though I had to be nice to her for his sake. That's what love does to a person. And it wasn't something that I wanted to be part of. Not a feeling that I wanted to have.

Not that I was in love with Dennie of course. Absolutely not. Of course.

22

It was two weeks later when life changed again for me. On a quiet Monday morning, while the rain pattered against my window and I was having a lie-in, there was a knock at the front door. Mum and Dad were both out at work already and I'd been reading in bed.

I muttered all the way downstairs, while pulling on my fleecy dressing gown and tying the belt around me. I flung open the door ready to give Karl the postman a mouthful for spoiling my peace and quiet. He was the only person I'd seen wandering around the harbour when I'd looked out of the bedroom window, taking in the moody grey sky which was full of rain.

'Dennie. What the—'

'Hello, stranger!' He was leaning up against the wall outside of the front porch and I honestly couldn't have been more surprised, delighted yet horrified all at the same time.

My hands immediately flew to my head where I tried to smooth down my wayward hair. I knew there were coffee stains all over my dressing gown and I hadn't brushed my teeth since yesterday morning, because I just couldn't be bothered to do them before I went to bed last night and I was pretty sure that, in a competition, my ogre breath would have won against Shrek.

'What on earth are you doing here?' My voice seemed to increase in both volume and pitch.

'Well, that's a nice welcome. You got any of that lovely coffee of yours on the go?'

'No, but I can go and put a pot on. Come in, come in.'

He followed me through into the kitchen, while I was trying to rub my teeth a little, and even though I was all fingers and thumbs, I managed to get the coffee percolating.

'I'd better go and put some clothes on. Can you give me a minute?'

'You don't need to do that on my account.'

'Oh, I think I do. I must look a fright.'

'You look lovely, Nancy, like you always do.'

My heart was beating ten to the dozen, and I had to shuffle past him because he was standing in my way and there was no other way to get out of the room.

'Make yourself at home. I won't be long.'

For some unknown reason, for the first time ever, I felt nervous in his company. What was he doing here? Was he just visiting? Maybe I'd find out if I stopped fannying about and got myself washed and changed.

I flung open my wardrobe door. What did you wear when the person who you think you might have fallen a little bit in love with turns up unexpectedly and you have two minutes rather than two hours to make yourself look presentable? I grabbed the first thing that caught my eye, which was a pretty vintage Joules dress. I quickly went into the bathroom and splashed my face with water and brushed my teeth. My hair, well, that was a different matter. I hadn't dried it before I went to bed last night, so it was literally all over the place. I scraped it back into a reasonably neat chignon and quickly covered my face in tinted moisturiser and put a lick of mascara over my lashes. That would have to do.

'You look even lovelier now, Nancy.'

'Oh, Dennie, you're such a smoothie,' I retorted as I fumbled getting cups down from the top cupboard. Sadly, not as well as I'd hoped as my favourite of all, a spotty Emma Bridgewater mug that I'd had for years, fell through my clumsy fingers and smashed onto the tiled floor.

I bent to pick up the pieces at the same time as Dennie did and our faces ended up inches apart. He reached out and tucked a stray piece of hair behind my ear. I couldn't look at him. He was literally millimetres from me and I held my breath, waiting for the moment to pass.

'I've missed you,' he whispered.

'Have you?' I whispered back, lifting my eyes to meet his.

'More than you can know. I... Well... I...'

His eyes flickered from mine, to my lips and back again.

'I couldn't stop thinking about you, Nance. I tried to throw myself back into London life, but I couldn't get you off my mind.'

Time stood still. I couldn't believe what he was saying. I'd only just got used to him not being around.

'Oh.'

I was shell-shocked, I couldn't speak.

'Tell me I haven't got this all wrong. That you feel the same.'

I grinned.

'I do feel the same, Dennie.'

'Thank God.' He shuffled onto his other knee and somehow was now even closer to me.

Was he going to kiss me? Shit! Dennis *was* going to kiss me.

I closed my eyes and closed the gap between us.

Suddenly, the front door flung open and we sprang apart. A voice from the hallway stopped us in our tracks.

'Mum, Dad, Nancy? Anyone home?'

'Dan, what are you doing here?'

My brother came bumbling into the kitchen with a holdall slung over his shoulder. That wasn't a good sign.

'Hey, sis, how are you doing?' he asked. He then noticed Dennie. 'Oh, hello. Interrupting something, was I?' He grinned.

'Hey, I'm Dennis.' He offered Dan his hand. 'You must be Dan. I've heard a lot about you.'

'Oh, so *you're* Dennis. Been hearing about you from Mum.'

'All good I hope.'

'Well, that's a matter of opinion really.'

I looked away, totally embarrassed, not wanting Dennie to think that we'd been talking about him. We actually hadn't. No one had really mentioned his name out loud since he'd gone. His loss just wasn't acknowledged by any of us, even though I had felt it so deeply.

I grabbed the dustpan and brush from the cupboard under the sink and started to sweep away the mess from the broken crockery.

'Coffee smells good, Nancy. Got one for your bro?'

I grabbed more cups from the cupboard and with shaky hands still, poured us all a drink, then added milk and handed them out.

'So, what brings you home, Dan?'

'Guess!'

'Sabrina kicked you out again? What have you done to piss her off this time?'

'Nothing – again. Well, apart from living and breathing of course.'

'Dan, you can't let her keep doing this. You're worth more than this.'

'Oh, it'll be fine again after a couple of days on her own. She just needs her space.'

'But that's not how relationships work. She can't just kick you out every time she feels like it. You need to stand up to her more.'

'Can't. She scares the shit out of me.'

Dennie laughed.

'Don't laugh. It's not funny, Dennis. She's been doing this to him for years, then we're expected to pick up the pieces every time. She'll take him back and it'll be all hunky-dory for the next few months until the next time she wakes up in a bad mood.'

'She can't help it.' My big brother looked so dejected and sad that it broke another little piece of my heart. Like it did every time this behaviour repeated itself.

'You deserve better, Daniel.'

'I love her,' he whispered.

'You're a fool and that's not love.'

'Well, you're a fine one to talk. Look at you. You've never been in love in your life so how do you think you're so qualified to tell me what to do? I'd rather be with someone than on my own and too scared to love. Like you are.'

'And why do you think that is, Dan? Do you think you're a good example to follow? Do you think I want to be caught up in a relationship like yours? I'd like to think I'm worth more than that.'

'Yeah, and that's why you're on your own, like a sad sap.'

I hadn't known Dennie for long and I didn't like that Dan was taking the mickey out of me in front of him. It felt particularly awkward. I felt like Dennie liked me for the me that I was around him and not for the me that I really was. The sad sap that my brother knew I was.

'Hey,' Dennie said, stepping in and raising his voice. 'That's no way to talk to Nancy, sister or not. You're out of order, mate!'

My head snapped around. While there was a part of me that loved that Dennis was sticking up for me, I was my own person and could stand up for myself. I didn't need anyone else to fight my battles. I was perfectly capable of fighting my own.

Also, anyone with siblings would surely confirm, *I* could slag off my brother, but no one else could.

'Thank you, Dennis, but I can handle my own arguments thank you very much. I've managed perfectly well fighting my own battles for the last twenty-seven years, without anyone else interfering. I don't need you! I don't need anyone. You don't know anything about us as a family. If you did, you'd know that he follows the same pattern every time. She upsets him. He takes it out on me. It's just the way it is. Welcome to our family!'

'And she'll then tell me why she's on her own,' Dan added. 'That she doesn't want to end up like me. And that's why she'll never take a chance on love. Never gives anyone the chance to get close to her. She's too scared that her heart will break. But sometimes you have to take the risk. To love is to live. How can you have a life without love?'

'Well, I'd rather be alone, thank you very much. At least that way you don't get hurt. Life is just full of people letting you down and at least my heart will always be protected if I don't give it away to anyone. No thank you. Not for me. I'd rather live without love than go through this shit.'

Dan's lip quivered. One minute he was talking about me and then he realised that he was actually talking about himself. His eyes welled up. I knew him well enough to know when he was about to break down and he flew across the room and into my arms. His body was heaving with sobs and we clung onto each other for dear life. My poor battered brother. I hated the way Sabrina treated him. I wished he'd wake up and realise what she was like. I wished he'd find someone else to show an interest. I stroked his back, trying to calm him down. Just like I always did.

Then I turned to Dennis, but he wasn't there. All that was left on the table next to where he'd been standing was a full cup of coffee, hardly touched. He'd clearly left us to it.

I sighed. Dan looked up at me.

'Sorry, sis, have I interrupted something?'

'No, it's fine. Don't worry. It was nothing important.'

The click of the front door *after* that sentence, indicating that he had probably heard every single word, was a sound that I could never forget.

23

Once Dan had calmed down, I left him curled up under a blanket on the sofa watching *This Morning*. I really did wish he'd sort things out with Sabrina once and for all. He couldn't go on like this, for all our sakes as well as his own. His mental health was so fragile and I worried about him so much. But I also knew that he needed to be in the right place to deal with it. Sabrina was controlling him and she loved it. Classic narcissist behaviour. If you looked at the list of characteristics, she literally showed every single one. And it was so unfair.

My brother, my gorgeous, kind, lovely brother, was being totally and utterly manipulated. And I hated her for it. One day I would have my say with her, but not yet. Not until he was ready for me to do that. I just hoped that as a family we could pull together and get him into that place.

Dan's words about my own love life had really hit home this time. Normally, they were like water off a duck's back. They never really bothered me. But that was before Dennis had come into my life. This time it felt like he'd cut to the very core of me. And yes, I was scared. Scared of ending up in a relationship like this, where I was a puppet, and my strings were being pulled by my puppet master. But maybe he was also right and that if I never gave myself a chance, I'd end up alone for ever.

Dennis deserved an apology after my little outburst. He was important to me and I needed to show him that. After he'd opened up to me about the neglect from his own family, I could see now that my words may have seemed cruel towards him, and I owed it to him to say sorry. I genuinely was. I wouldn't hurt him for anything in the world.

I practically ran and knocked on Vi's door, and she seemed to take an age to answer. She smiled when she saw me. I must have looked like a drowned rat, the rain dripping off my hair.

'He's gone to the train station.'

'He's leaving?'

'Yeah, not sure what's happened between you two, but he was mighty hacked off. Said there was nothing here for him any more. Mumbled about the fact he thought there was but he was wrong. Said no one needed him here and that he'd be better off back in London. Charming, eh? Cheeky little bugger. What about his old nan? I've loved having him here.' She looked at my face and could see how upset I was. Glancing at her watch, she said, 'His train to Truro is in ten minutes. If you go now, you might catch him. Hurry though. And sort everything out, you daft tart, or I'll have to bang your heads together!'

I leaned forward and kissed her papery soft cheek and she put her hands up to my face.

'Go, Nancy. See if you can stop him leaving. He's so shitting proud. Such a silly lad! He doesn't realise what a little treasure he really is and how loved he is. Letting someone into your heart is hard you know, but it's worth it.' I wasn't sure if she was talking about me or Dennie. 'I could swing for his parents, they've damaged him more than they'll ever know. Just when he felt like he was belonging somewhere, and fitting in, and well... you know. He loved spending time with you. And now he's run away.'

I ran home, grabbed my bike, and pedalled with all the energy I could muster. My heart filled with joy at the thought of potentially having a relationship with Dennis and declaring my feelings to him. Butterflies in my tummy kept me going, but as I approached the level crossing and the gates came down, my heart sank. I frantically kept checking my watch until they were ready to rise again and allow the traffic to continue, and I sped towards the station as fast as the pedals would allow.

As I pulled into the car park, I saw that the train was still there on the opposite platform. I looked to the sky and mouthed 'Thank you.' Maybe Aunty Theresa had my back in more ways than one. I slammed on my brakes and leapt off my bike at the same time. The sound of clattering metal echoed around the empty car park as I tried to fling it into the grassy verge, but the back wheel caught on my dress. The bike didn't go down fully, landing on my foot, and pulling me over in my haste, the bike somehow landing on top of me.

The whistle blew. And as I tried to pull the bike off me, I could only watch as the train slowly pulled out of the station.

And then the heavens opened.

* * *

Sobs wracked my body, and I wiped my snotty tears with my sleeve. I was too late. Too shitting late as Vi would say. As I sat with my head in my hands, I heard a gentle cough. I uncovered my eyes, and saw a pair of pristine white Prada trainers in front of me. I gasped as my gaze travelled further up the dark denim-clad legs, and the hem of a crisp white shirt.

Dennie removed the bike, which was balancing precariously on my leg, and propped it up against the nearest wall. Then he returned to where I was sitting, knelt before me, and I breathed him in as he took my face in his hands.

And then he kissed me.

A million fireworks went off inside my head, my heart, my tummy and my legs, as time stood still. His lips were gentle at first, his delicate kiss becoming more urgent and demanding. I didn't care if anyone was watching. I was going to savour this moment forever. The taste of his lips was a heady mixture of mint and coffee, like a box of divine chocolates.

When he eventually moved away, he plonked himself beside me on the wet damp grass and grinned.

'Hey!'

'Hey yourself!' I replied. 'Your jeans will get wet and dirty.'

'Just how I like them.' His eyebrows shifted upwards. 'Like my women.'

The joke broke the tension and we both laughed out loud, Dennis smacking his forehead with the heel of his hand.

'Sorry. That sounded so much better in my head.'

He stood and held out his hands to me, helping me up. Then he lifted one of mine to his lips and kissed it, grinning at me like a lunatic. And I mirrored him.

He lifted my bike with one hand with ease and carried it over to his car, the other hand clinging onto mine. My hand fitted into his perfectly. Like it was always meant to be there. And apart from loading my bike into his boot, he didn't let go of my hand for most of the journey back into the village.

When we arrived back at Driftwood Bay, a full rainbow arced across the bay and we looked at each other and smiled. The rain was petering out and the sun was peeping out from behind the clouds. The seagulls, which were normally so noisy when the rain came teaming down, were just starting to resurface and caw once more. It was as if the bay had returned to its rightful beautiful state. I felt like my world was once more complete.

24

We both hovered outside of the car, neither of us knowing what our next move was.

'So, what now?' he said, broaching the subject.

I had no answers for him and shrugged my shoulders, scared to speak. This was all new to me. I had no flipping idea what came next. And it scared the living daylights out of me.

'I suppose you could make me another coffee. I never did get to drink the one you made for me earlier. Then maybe we could talk. Maybe I could apologise for storming off. Maybe I could even come to my senses and realise I might have been over-reacting?'

The inflection at the end of his sentence turned it into a question rather than a sentence.

I nodded. Seemingly all my words had disappeared.

As I fumbled to put the key into the front door of Books In The Bay, Dennie took the key from me and opened the door, before closing it gently behind him. The click of the lock being put across made my spine shiver with anticipation. I headed out back to the kitchen and started to fill the kettle but could hear his footsteps behind me, and as I turned, I literally bumped into his body. His firm, hard body.

He took the kettle from my hands and placed it on the counter. Every hair on my skin stood to attention as he closed the gap between us and took my face in his hands and kissed me once more. His fingers reached to the back of my head and unleashed my hair, which fell to my shoulders, and he let his fingers slide through it as his lips pressed down on mine, more urgently and passionately than when he'd kissed me earlier.

Somehow, before I knew it, he'd moved me so I was now leaning against the door and his body was pressed against mine, every tingle I'd felt before magnified by a million per cent. My knees were trembling and my hands were shaking but I knew that this felt more right than anything in my life had ever felt before. We kissed for what seemed like hours, his lips on my neck and his hands roaming my body. He could have literally taken me there and then. I wanted him more than I ever thought possible.

My mind was running away with me and before I could take a breath, I realised he'd pulled away.

'God, I'm so sorry! I never meant to...' He ran his hands through his hair and exhaled.

'Do it again, Dennie!'

'Sorry?'

'Kiss me again. Please.'

I didn't have to ask him twice this time. He kissed me as if it were the only thing in the world that we could do, and right there and then I knew I would have let him make love to me, had there not been a knock at the door.

'Ignore it!' I whispered breathlessly. We both held our breath. I buried my head in his chest and we both giggled.

'Nance!' There was a shout and a harder, more urgent knock at the door.

'I know you're in there. The light is on out the back. Open the door.'

'Ignore it!' I urged him again. 'He might go away.'

'He's your brother and he clearly needs you right now,' Dennie said. 'Go and let him in.'

I groaned as I tore myself away. I opened the kitchen door and walked down the hallway, shouting at Dan to calm down and stop banging on the door.

'Hey, sis, how are you doing?'

'Erm, yes. I'm good thanks.'

'Are you sure? You're a bit flushed in the face.' He held the back of his hand to my head. 'You're not sickening for something, are you?'

Dennie coughed as he came out of the kitchen with two coffee mugs in his hand and walked towards the chairs in the bay window. Dan and I followed him.

'Oh, right, that explains everything. Sorry, I didn't know you had company. I woke up and you'd gone so I figured you'd be here.' He was totally oblivious to the hugely momentous scene that had just happened at the train station.

'Yeah, we were just...'

'It's fine, we were just...'

Dennie and I couldn't look at each other but I could hear from his voice that the corners of his mouth would be turning up.

I said 'stocktaking' at the same time as he said, 'ordering some books'.

'Oh, so that's what you call it.' My brother grinned at me. 'About time, Nancy. About time.' He winked at me and flung himself down one of the armchairs in the window. 'No sugar for me thanks, Nance, and while you're doing that, I'll have a little word here with yer man.'

Shaking my head and wondering what the hell my brother was

going to say to Dennie, I headed back to the kitchen. I felt like my whole life had changed in the space of an hour. What did this now mean though? I frowned as lots of thoughts flew through my mind: was he stopping here in Driftwood Bay, or was he heading back to London again? How could we conduct a long-distance love affair? How was our story going to end? All of this, just as our story was beginning, and it scared the crap out of me. I was forging ahead too fast, almost seeing it not work out before I was going to give it a chance. I needed to get back out into the shop and stop my brain working overtime.

I got back to the shop floor just in time to hear Dan say to Dennie, '...or I'll break your legs!'

'What's going on here then?'

They were both smiling so I knew it was nothing too serious.

'Your brother was just telling me that if I broke your heart, he'd break my legs.'

'Oh, right.' My hands wouldn't stop trembling as I put Dan's coffee down on the table between the chairs. They were both sat extremely comfortably, seemingly at ease in each other's company.

Dan continued. 'I just wanted to say that I'm sorry, Nancy. For letting you think that my relationship is normal. I think I've finally realised that it isn't.'

Dennie lifted himself out of the chair. 'I'll leave you two to it.'

'No, it's fine, mate,' Dan said. 'There's nothing you can't hear. It's probably good if you do to be honest. I want you both to hold me accountable. I know I've made a lot of mistakes and I know I've been the one who stopped you wanting to put yourself out there and find someone to love you, Nancy. But you are a wonderful human being, who deserves the very best of everything in your life. Everything you do, you do for others and not yourself. The beach work you do, the teaching and now this.' He swept his arms around the room and swallowed before he continued. 'You deserve love in your life, Nancy. Don't let me and Sabrina be the example of how things should be. Look to Mum and Dad instead. They got the fairy tale and there's no reason that you shouldn't too.'

'I do, Dan, but not many relationships end up like that either.'

'But it doesn't mean you shouldn't get your happy-ever-after. You deserve to have someone in your life who puts you first. To love you, to cherish you, to help you and support you to flourish.' He nodded towards Dennis, who was looking down at his feet, trying not to get involved.

'And so do you,' I said.

'I know, and I promise that I'm going to sort things out with Sabrina once and for all. Remember that lodge that we all used to go to in the woods?'

'I love that lodge,' I said, looking up with a smile.

'I know you do and I do too. We have so many happy memories there from our childhoods, don't we? I've just called the owners and it's free right now so I'm going to go and spend some time there on my own, to work out how I'm going to break the cycle and start being me again. I haven't felt like me for years. I might need your help, though, sis.'

'You've got it. Anything you need it's yours.'

'You're the best.'

'Yeah, I know.'

'No, I am.'

Snotty tears streamed down my face as we fell into a childhood competitive tradition. I was so glad that my brother had finally realised that I wasn't the only one who deserved a different life and I hoped beyond words that one day, his princess would come and she would not be called Sabrina.

As I glanced over at Dennis, I saw he was grinning at me and I mouthed the word 'sorry' over my brother's shoulder as he grabbed me in a bear hug.

'It's fine,' he whispered and winked and my heart felt a little safer than it had before.

'Sorry, mate, I interrupted you again, didn't I?'

'It's fine, Dan. I really hope you get yourself sorted out, and if there's anything I can do to help, just let me know. Nancy and me. We've got all the time in the world.'

But had we?

25

Once Dan had gone and we'd got the place to ourselves again, we talked a lot of shop. For some reason, we were a little nervous around each other now, so it was easier to focus on Dennis's ideas. He wanted to do another open-day event, so we could invite Cornish bloggers and authors. The shop was large enough to run a workshop at the same time. He'd clearly been working on lots of ideas while he'd been away. I didn't want to think about what else he'd been doing but by the time he left he seemed to be more relaxed.

'What are you doing later?' he asked.

'What, tonight you mean?'

'Well, for the rest of the day? And then tonight too?'

The way he looked at me made a shiver run down the whole of my spine. He looked like he wanted to devour me. I'd never felt so wanted. It was an unusual feeling. Sure, I'd fancied people in the past and they'd fancied me back, and I'd had my moments over the years but it had never set off fireworks in my body like in the books that I read.

'I thought we could go and do some beachcombing for shells. I know you love to do that.'

I felt a little disappointed. But then realised that it was a lovely thing to do.

'I'd love to.'

'And then, I'd like to take you to dinner. Maybe we could go to the bistro?'

'Oh, you are kidding me. If we go to dinner at the bistro, we'll be the talk of the town and they'll have us marching up the aisle before the night is out.'

'Ha, yes, I forget that Driftwood Bay is a lot smaller than where I come from. I do think we need to go somewhere to talk though. I think we've got a lot to discuss.'

'Yeah, we definitely do. I want all your ideas for this launch event.' I smiled at him, and narrowed my eyes in what I thought was a seductive way, but hey what did I know?

'You OK there? Something in your eye?'

I over-blinked a few times. 'I'm fine. I think it's gone now.'

Embarrassed, I told him about a little Italian restaurant I used to go to sometimes on a teachers' night out. It was hard being a teacher in a small community. Parents didn't respect the fact you might need a night off and would happily approach you in the local bistro and question you about little Tommy's in-growing toenail over your tagliatelle.

Dennie went out the back and booked a table and then we headed off to the beach. Walking side by side seemed a little strange after we'd kissed so passionately only hours before, but he took my hand in his and we strolled along the furthest away beach, scouring the sand and collecting several large shells between us. Holding his hand seemed the most natural thing to do even if people might see us. I just didn't want to live out the whole of our relationship in front of prying eyes. There was enough pressure itself that I was putting on the situation without everyone else throwing their oar in too. Dennie might not even be seeing it as a relationship. In fact, I had no clue what we were doing, and at that thought, I started to panic again. It was almost like I was willing things to go wrong before they'd even had a chance to go right. Even though I'd spent a lot of time with Dennis over the past few weeks, I really didn't know him at all.

After we dropped the shells back at the shop, he gently kissed my cheek and told me that he'd pick me up at 7 p.m.

* * *

I was all fingers and thumbs getting ready, trying to curl my hair when Mum came in and offered to help.

'You really like him, don't you?'

'Yeah, he's nice.'

She smiled.

'I knew it at your book event, you know.'

'Knew what?'

'That you'd get together. I can tell that you had some sizzling chemistry going on under all that disagreeing with each other. I know you had your moments when you didn't really like the way he was telling you to run your business, but I think even under all of that, you still liked him. Give him a chance, love. That's all I'll say. You should give you both a chance. Who knows what will happen? None of us can ever say what the future holds, but if you don't give love a chance, then you'll be missing out.'

'But what if it ends up like Dan and Sabrina? They were madly in love at first and everything was fabulous and then things changed.'

'That doesn't happen to everyone though, love. Look at me and your dad.'

'Yep, but love like that doesn't come along very often either, does it?'

'No, but it's not always been plain sailing for us either. You have to work at things. We're very lucky though, I know that much. Just relax tonight and get to know each other. You don't need to plan the rest of your lives tonight. You just need to spend some time together. And you don't have to jump into bed with each other either if you don't want to.'

'Muuuum!'

'Darling, you are twenty-seven years old. We don't need to have the sex conversation, do we?'

I put my hands over my ears and sang 'la la la!', blocking out what she was saying. When she finished talking, I removed them.

'But if you do want to roger him senseless then go for it, I say.'

'Muuuum! Enough! Get out!' I threw a towel that had been lying on the floor at her and she ducked and laughed.

'Just saying, it's perfect when it's with the right person.'

I slammed the door behind her and could hear her laughing all the way down the stairs.

If that wasn't enough to get me wondering about how the evening might end up, when Dennie turned up on my doorstep looking as hot as hell, my head was all over the place and I was a dithering wreck. When he winked at me as he put his arm over the back of my seat, to see better to reverse the car, and I got a whiff of his expensive aftershave, I shuddered. God, if this is how I felt when we were fully clothed, imagine how I'd feel if we were...

'Ready?' he asked as we drove out of Driftwood Bay.

I just nodded and he laughed.

'Don't know about you, Nance, but I feel a bit nervous.'

'God, me too!' Thank goodness he was honest enough to admit it.

He held my hand all the way there and it was really rather lovely. Our nervousness melted away within minutes. Dennis asked lots of questions about my dreams and ambitions in life and what my passions were even though he already knew about them. He was quite cagey when I asked him similar questions, and a lot of his answers were routed in ambition and being the best at what he did and how much money he made. Even though we were very different, I felt now that our opposing personalities complemented each other. He was clearly an excellent listener, and communicator in general, making me feel like he was really interested in everything I said.

We talked loads about the open day. It didn't seem to matter that we were mixing business with pleasure. Maybe when people were working together on things they were both passionate about, it all blended into one and it didn't matter whether it was work or passions. We decided on a date which was only two weeks away and even though we knew it would be tight, we knew that we'd work together to make it happen. I showed him the social media profiles I'd set up while he'd been away and he showed me a projection plan he'd put together for the next year ahead to keep on track. I was staggered by what an amazing team we made, once we put our differences aside and had a joint goal. We set a further date, one year from the launch party, where we'd look at things again and discuss my successful bookshop and think about the plans for another year after that. At least we were talking about a year ahead and still being in contact. That was a positive sign.

Before we knew it, the restaurant staff were dimming the lights and coughing politely, to alert us to the fact they were ready to go home.

We then spent hours in the car outside my house, kissing and talking. And kissing. Much as I didn't want to tear myself away, I didn't want to ask him in, as I didn't know if Mum and Dad would still be up and I certainly didn't want Dan to be giving us the Spanish Inquisition. So we said our goodbyes and I said that I'd see him in the morning at the shop.

It had been one of the loveliest nights – and days, for that matter – of my life, and I went to sleep that night with a smile on my face as wide as Driftwood Bay itself.

26

The eve of launch day soon came around. We'd been really busy over the last couple of weeks. The guest list was huge. There was no way that everyone who had been invited would fit in if they all turned up. I'd spent hours trawling social media, inviting influencers who might not have the biggest followings, but those who looked like they really did love books. A number of Cornish authors had also agreed to come, along with Pep the Poet, who did a lot with local schools and was totally awesome.

Mum and Dad were staying away on the night before the launch event. I think maybe on purpose. They never went anywhere, but they said that they were going up to the lodge to see Dan, making a point of saying they would be staying overnight. While Mum didn't give away any more than that when she told Dennie to look after me that night and make sure I got home safely, I was pretty sure she was insinuating there would be no one else in the house.

Dennie and I had been struggling to keep our hands off each other, necking in the car or in the back of the shop like teenagers every chance we got. Ridiculous really. I was twenty-seven and he was a good ten years older.

We'd been rushed off our feet all day so I said I'd cook for us at mine. I'd showered and curled my hair, put on some light make-up, and hoped he would notice the change from the tatty old dungarees I'd been wearing all day. I uncorked a nice bottle of red wine and was nervously cleaning the already perfectly clean wine glasses when there was a knock at the door.

Taking a deep breath, I opened the door and Dennis thrust a bouquet of flowers at me.

'These are just to say good luck for tomorrow.'

'That's so lovely, Dennie, thank you.' I reached out to kiss his cheek and inhaled the expensive woody scent. Everything about Dennie exuded style and money. He was everything I thought I hated in a man but right then it was far from hate that I was feeling for him. 'I'll go and put these in some water.'

We danced around each other in the kitchen, both a little nervous again, and I fumbled to put the flowers in a vase while making idle small talk. As I turned to him, he shook his head at me.

'Nancy, I don't think you know what you do to me.'

I looked at my feet and he strode across the room and lifted my chin with his finger. His lips were suddenly on mine. Gently at first, but then more demanding, more passionate than I'd ever known him. Mid-kiss, he lifted me from the floor so that I was above him, and I could feel him pressing into me.

'How long till dinner?' His voice was deep and low, and oh-so incredibly sexy.

'It's ready now but just keeping warm in the slow cooker. We can have it whenever we want.'

'Maybe we should put a hold on it. I can think of something much more interesting to do than eat dinner. Much as I feel like I'd quite like to throw you on that table, how would you feel about going up to your room? I don't trust your brother not to interrupt us again but I really need to be inside you right now.'

I shivered and laughed nervously but nodded. We'd struggled to keep our hands off each other over the last couple of weeks, snatching moments to grope each other like kids in the storeroom in the back of the shop. There was nothing that had ever felt more right in my life. As he suddenly grabbed me and picked me up, I gave a little high-pitched squeal and he practically ran up the stairs with me in his arms, stopping only briefly to put the lock on the front door. He grinned as he placed me down on my bed, which I was very glad I'd changed earlier that day, as well as having made a huge effort to tidy my room.

Kicking the door shut behind him while shedding his coat, which he hadn't even taken off yet before our kisses, he still hadn't taken his eyes off mine. As I reached out to him and slowly removed every single piece of his clothing, before he did the same for me, he waited for my approval before showing me just how much he wanted me.

27

'This is delicious. I've worked up quite the appetite, you know.'

'Oh really, Dennie? I hadn't noticed.'

He winked at me again and my heart gave such a skip. Everything seemed to be falling into place. Me dressed in just his shirt, and him bare-chested and just in his jeans and bare feet, we sat opposite each other at the kitchen table, my cheeks aching from the constant smiling. I didn't think I could ever have been so happy.

'Looking forward to tomorrow?'

'Can't wait. I just hope it all goes smoothly.'

'Of course it will. With you doing everything I tell you to, how could it possibly not?' He stood and put his plate on the side of the sink and came and stood behind me. The hairs on the back of my neck stood on edge, and he ran his finger down my spine. I gave a little shiver, and to my own surprise, also groaned out loud. 'Let's run through the checklist one last time.'

He removed a piece of folded paper from his back pocket and started to unfold it, before reading it out loud.

This time my groan wasn't from pleasure, but from repeating

this exercise for the fourth time today. Ever the professional, even now, Dennis had business on his mind.

I stood, moving my own plate, and took the paper from his hand. I wedged myself between him and the kitchen table, hitching myself up so that I was sitting on the edge.

'I've got this, Dennis. Don't worry. I'm sure there's something more interesting we could be doing.'

I pulled him towards me so he was up against me and my knees were either side of him, and ran my finger up his chest. He gasped as I circled his left nipple, and groaned when I reached the right. My fingers travelled further south and reached the waistband of his jeans.

'We'll get indigestion, you know,' he murmured against my neck as he started to shower me with soft fluttery kisses which were driving me wild with desire.

'It's always life on the edge with you, isn't it, Dennie?' I smiled in the most seductive manner I could. 'Let's live dangerously.'

As I loosened the button and fly on his jeans, he was soon gasping for breath again, but definitely didn't seem to mind as we devoured each other right there on the kitchen table.

* * *

'Shit, get up, Dennie. It's 7.30 and we said we'd be at the shop by now.'

I sprang out of bed and darted for the bathroom, where I threw myself under the shower. I hadn't even thought to set the alarm the night before because I never slept past 6 a.m. – I'd never overslept in my life. Although I also hadn't ever been up most of the night alternating between talking and having incredible sex with Dennie before.

I walked back into the bedroom, dragging a comb through my

freshly washed hair and Dennie was sat propped up on my pillows, his hands behind his head, watching my every move.

'You need to get up!' I yelled at him.

'That's exactly what I was just thinking.' He tried to grab the towel I'd wrapped myself in and flung the duvet back. 'Come back to bed.'

Shaking my head and laughing at the same time, I moved away and started to blast my hair with the hairdryer. I couldn't believe that we were already running late on the one day that I really needed to be on the ball.

'You need to go home and get ready and back to the shop pretty damn smartish.'

'Oh no! I can't.'

'Why on earth not?'

'Don't want anyone seeing me do the walk of shame now do I?'

I laughed.

'You're nearly forty years old. Is that not a bit past you?'

'How rude!'

'You did text Vi last night to tell her you weren't going home, right?'

'Yeah, look.'

He showed me the text and I laughed out loud when I read the message trail.

> I'm going to stop out at a mate's house tonight, Nan. Don't wait up. Be back in the morning.

> About time you got your end away with Nancy. Give her one from me. Love Nan

I groaned.

'I hope she keeps schtum when she comes to the shop today. I don't want everyone knowing our business. Mum and Dad don't even know yet.'

'Oh, I'm sure they do.' He laughed. 'You don't think it was a coincidence that they went out for the night and stayed out, do you?'

I put my head in my hands.

He reached over and kissed me tenderly.

'I had the best time with you, Nancy.'

'Me too.'

As he kissed me again, I melted into his arms before realising once more that we really had to get a shift on and get this day started. The open day was starting at 10 a.m. and we still had quite a bit to sort out before we could open the doors and I was gagging for a cup of coffee.

'Be off with you!'

'That's a fine way to treat someone you know. After you've had your wicked way with me too. Casting me aside. Charming.'

I ran my tongue across his lips. I wasn't quite sure where this new confident sex goddess version of me had come from but I felt totally liberated. 'I'm sure I could make it up to you later.'

'See you at the shop as soon as I can get past Nan and the Spanish Inquisition.'

I finished getting ready. Luckily, the previous afternoon I'd hung up the dress I was planning to wear so I didn't have to waste time sorting that out, and quickly applied some light make-up. I hoped no one would recognise the 'Hi-I'm-Nancy-and-I-spent-last-night-shagging-Dennie' glow that I would be sporting. I grinned as I grabbed the box that needed taking to the shop and slung my backpack on.

I made it somehow at one minute before eight and it wasn't long before Dennie appeared, smelling freshly showered and gorgeous as always. He bent to kiss my neck, and knowing what influence that had on me, I pushed him gently away.

'No time, Dennie. Come on, we need to sort out the furniture.'

'You drive a hard bargain, lady. I don't want any wages for working here, but I hope you know I'll be expecting you to repay me in kind later.'

It took all the strength I had not to jump him right there on the counter but there really wasn't time for more sexual shenanigans, there was still so much to do and I was starting to feel quite anxious about the day. Dennie seemed to anticipate my mood, so his first port of call was the kitchen to get the coffee pot on the go. I needed it to both give me a kick-start and to keep me awake.

'OK, tell me what you need me to do and I'll just do it.'

He really was a great help to me and we moved the furniture around so the workshops could take place in the back part of the shop. We wrapped the tables with three lots of paper, so we could just rip the top layer off and then be clean for the next one. I wanted a quick turnaround.

We really had no idea of how busy the shop would be. As well as the private invites, we'd also shared the event on social media, and the local school had put a note out to all of the parents. Mum, Dad, and Dan had all said that they'd come and help if needed. Mum knew how to work the till and I had printed some blank order forms so that if people wanted a book we didn't have in, they could fill in their details and we would order it for them.

Dennie also came up with the idea of giving a free raffle ticket away, which would serve two purposes. One was to get people to hang around until the time the raffle was drawn – we thought we'd do one at lunchtime and one later in the afternoon – and the other was so we could get people's email addresses to add to my mailing list. We'd had some of the local businesses give us vouchers, including Gemma who'd been really helpful, giving everyone a twenty per cent off voucher at the bistro so they could go and get drinks from there. That way, we didn't have to worry about refreshments and were just providing nice things like sweets and nibbles. If anyone wanted something substantial, they could go to hers.

Whilst I was titivating the shelves for the umpteenth time, ten minutes before the doors were due to open, Dennie called me into the kitchen.

'Before the excitement of the day, I just wanted to say something.'

'Oh, OK,' I said, wondering what on earth he was behaving so formally for.

'I just wanted to say how much I've enjoyed working with you over the last few weeks. I feel like we've been the perfect team, and while I've been teaching you how to make your business more profitable, you've taught me that there's so much more to life than work. For that, Nancy, I'm so very grateful to you.'

He put both of his hands on my shoulders.

'I've loved it too and thank you for all that you've done for me. I really had no idea and you've really changed the way I think. I have so many plans and ideas for the future. I'm ready to plan my future now instead of winging it and hoping that the universe deals with it all in the right way. Thank *you*, Dennie.'

When he pulled me into his chest, my heart welled with pure unadulterated love. This man before me, despite my original feelings for him, now meant the absolute world to me.

'I'm incredibly proud *of* you and proud to know you,' he said, 'and I didn't know your Aunty Theresa but I reckon, she'd be over the moon with you too. Her legacy is now in very safe hands and it should be a wonderful business for years to come.'

As I thought of how lovely it would be if Theresa were here today, a tear trickled down my cheek. Dennie reached up and wiped it away with his thumb.

I took a deep breath and couldn't help but wonder what this was. I lived in Cornwall and Dennie lived in London. Our lives were so very different. Was this just a short-term romance while he was here or something much more? My brow furrowed while the main question circled my mind: where were we going?

'This is not a day for tears,' Dennie continued. 'It's a day for you and for your dream.' It was almost as if he could read my mind when he then said, 'Let's not worry today about what comes next, I don't have the answers but I do know that I love being with you, Nancy. You've made me happier than I've ever been and we'll work it all out. All I can say is that we'll sort it. I don't know how, because your life is here. You live with your parents and I live hundreds of miles away, but somehow, we will make it work. We'll have a repeat of last night and this time it will be slower and even more fabulous than that, and then we're just going to keep on repeating it every time we get the chance. I can promise you that. But for right now, just enjoy your big day.'

He kissed me, soft and long, and I literally felt like I could swoon into his arms, lost forever. Maybe the future would work itself out. If ever there was a time that I wanted the universe to work something out for me, more than ever before, this was it.

'Go be the badass bookshop owner that you are and have your best business day ever.'

He kissed me again. I would never stop wanting to kiss those luscious lips of his. Ever. The taste of them was forever tucked away in my memory bank.

'You really think I'm a badass bookshop owner?'

'Hell yeah!' He put his hands on my backside and squeezed. 'Now get your gorgeous arse out there and open your bookshop, Nancy. And let's have a fabulous day.'

28

I took a deep breath and turned the sign on the door to 'open'. I couldn't believe my eyes when I saw a line of people snaking up the street. Only a small snake of around fifteen people, but a snake nonetheless.

'Welcome to Books In The Bay. Thank you so much for coming along today.'

The first person who introduced himself was Tim who said he was from the local paper and asked if it was OK if he took photos during the day and covered the story for not only the paper but also a local county magazine. It just so happened that Dennie was walking past the door at that time, so I grabbed him and asked him to keep an eye on Tim. I had a hunch that if we looked after him well, he might just look after us and write lots of gorgeously favourable things about the shop.

Next, were two lovely book bloggers that had seen the advert on the shop's Facebook page and couldn't wait to come down to Cornwall, saying they were making it into a long bookish weekend, going to go and visit some of the places they'd read about in a lot of books they'd read. They'd shared the event with a number of their followers who had also said that they'd be along sometime during the day.

Feeling a tap on my shoulder, I spun round to see James from the B&B.

'Hey, James, thanks for coming along. I wouldn't have thought that this was your cup of tea.'

'Ah, if only I had the time. Lucy has sent me up to tell you that we have two rooms left just in case anyone asks about somewhere local to stay. This event hasn't just been good for you, Nancy. We've had an influx of people booking in over the last few days and we've been rushed off our feet. Thank God for Meredith and Lydia who've been wonderful helping with Taran, so we could get ourselves sorted. We thought we'd be having a quiet lead-up to Christmas but that's not been the case! And there's a queue at the bistro too. Gemma is running around like a woman possessed, barking orders at the staff. The whole village is a hive of activity, Nancy. Well done you.' He reached forward and gave me an awkward hug. 'Right! Best get back before she thinks I'm skiving off.'

My heart was bursting with joy. To think that I'd created this, with Dennis's help of course, was quite amazing. I knew the bookshop would be a lovely idea and my dream come true, but to know that everyone was enjoying it as much as me was remarkable.

Looking around, I saw a number of familiar faces. It was purely delightful that many of the locals had also come along to support me. I had a feeling, and rather hoped in fact, that they'd be staggering their visits throughout the day as the room was filling up quite quickly, but it warmed my heart to hear the oohs and ahs of all these book lovers who were finding my shop as wonderful as I did.

We were hosting an author panel at midday and I wanted to prepare myself for that too. As a former teacher, I wasn't particularly nervous about hosting it, but I did want to find some time to go over the questions so I wasn't reading from a script.

Mum walked past at one point and whispered in my ear, 'Look at your shop, lady. I hope you are happy because I'm beside myself with pride. You are amazing.'

'Thanks, Mum, but so are you. I feel like you, Dennie, Dad and Dan are doing all the hard work while I'm just floating around being nice to everyone.'

'That's because you are a slave driver!'

Dennie grabbed me by the waist and squeezed past, giving me a wink as he went by. I did everything I could not to melt into a little puddle. He had such a heady effect on me.

I needn't have panicked about the day at all, because the panel event went incredibly well, with conversation flowing, and in fact, I had to try really hard to wind it up because, goodness me, those authors could go on for ages. I had to wrap it up as we needed to start the first of three workshops, the paper-folding, even though it broke my heart a little bit to see books being used in that way. After that was a wizard workshop for children, which went down really well. My favourite was the final one of the day, where we made Christmas tree book baubles. I'd been practising for days and been having the time of my life experimenting with lots of different styles and designs, utilising materials from both the beach and my craft box. I couldn't wait to get started on that one.

'Excuse me, Nancy, but the lady behind the counter said that you're the owner. Firstly, I'm so sorry that I approached her first. I thought it was her shop.'

I turned towards the voice and was met by a handsome, tall man with grey hair and a beard to match. He had one of those faces that just looked happy and made other people smile in return.

'Oh, it's an easy mistake to make. It happens all the time. I know I look quite young and people don't expect me to be the owner at my age.'

'Well, doesn't that just go to show that you should never judge a book by its cover?'

We both laughed.

'I don't suppose you might be interested in hosting some murder mystery parties at all, would you? My name is Roger and I'm the owner of a company that runs these types of events.'

Bizarrely, this was something that I'd already been pondering but hadn't mentioned it to Dennie because I didn't want him to think that it was a daft idea. I was going to try to work it all out in my head first before I presented a fully formed plan to him. It was really important to me that he knew I'd been listening and learning from him and thought everything through rationally.

'Roger, this is amazing. I think I've been looking for someone like you but didn't realise that companies like yours existed. I was trying to work out how to go about organising one.'

Maybe manifesting wasn't the rubbish that Dennie thought it was after all, I thought. *I must remember to tell him later.*

'Well, let's hope that this is a wonderful partnership in the making. Your shop would be absolutely perfect. I can just see it all decorated up and looking glorious. And you don't have to do anything but enjoy it. We'll do all the hard work for you. Oh, hello there.'

Vi had sidled up to Roger and started flicking her hair with her hand, a bit like Miss Piggy.

'I know you're busy so I'll catch you soon, Nancy. Perhaps you could give me a call and we can chat.' He handed me a business card, which I put into my cleavage.

When he raised an eyebrow, I replied, 'Just so I don't lose it.'

He laughed as he walked away.

'What a saucepot he is,' came a voice nearby. I turned to see Vi fanning herself with her hand. 'I'd roger Roger if I was twenty years younger.'

'Nan, you can't say that.' Dennie was floating past again with a couple of books in his hands. 'Also, make that thirty years, if you don't mind me saying.'

She clipped him on the arm playfully.

'Sorry, darling, but I'm only human.' Vi cackled. 'And to be frank, it's been a while since I—'

'Naaaan. Not for your grandson's ears.'

'Be off with you. After what you and this one probably got up to last night, I can't believe you've turned into a prude now. Coming in at eight o'clock in the morning...'

Dennie tried to quieten his grandmother at the same time as I said, 'Viiiii!'

She laughed and tapped the side of her nose.

'Your secret is safe with me. I'm off to chat to Rog! I'm having such a lovely day. I might even buy a book.' She winked and scampered off to follow Roger to the other side of the room. Poor man.

A phone was practically thrown in my face.

'Smile, you're on a TikTok live!'

The Booktokker, as I learned they're apparently called, went off filming all around the shop and I could hear her shouting 'Oh! Em! Gee! Look at all this fabulous merch! You can buy this all right here in the shop or order online. I'll drop the link in the comments, book lovers! Come and get it before it all sells out.'

I'm not sure if poor old TikTok was ready for this very bewildered bookshop owner but I was so incredibly grateful to everyone that had come from near and far to be with me today. I knew that book bloggers and book influencers were book mad, but I had no idea how much they would love my little bookshop.

The event finished with a reading from a bestselling thriller author, who happened to also be local, and who, somehow, a friend of a friend knew. They'd very kindly offered to come and read from their latest blockbuster and do a meet and greet and signing. I'd bought a lot of copies of her books on a bit of a whim and luckily had got them on a sale or return basis, but I needn't have worried because the shop was swamped with her fans and the books sold out entirely.

'Your shop is stunning, Nancy. A proper little treasure trove. Thank you so much for having me. I hope you don't mind but I've shared some pictures on my Instagram page. I couldn't resist.'

'I'm so grateful to you for coming,' I said after she'd finished. 'Your fans have not just bought your books, but others too. It's been amazing to have you here.'

'Yeah, they can be a bit overzealous where books are concerned. But it's good for business. We have to support local bookshops like you, my dear. I'd love to chat to you about maybe a launch event next year if you fancy it. We could get my publisher involved and they could give you some promotional material and all sorts. Have a think and perhaps we can have a chat when it's not quite so mad. I know lots of other authors too that might be interested. We're always looking for somewhere we can show off our latest books. Some of us have huge egos that need pandering to, you know.'

She couldn't have been further from a diva if she tried. I always put authors on a pedestal but the ones I'd met today were wonderful and down to earth and so complimentary about Books In The Bay. I honestly couldn't believe that they had loved my shop as much as I did.

The day had absolutely flown by, and by the time I closed up, I'd made so many friends new and old, the till was fit to bursting with cash and Dan said that the card machine had been 'battered'. There were so many promises from people that they'd be back, book onto future workshops and I'd given away a whole bunch of fliers with our details on and the dates for the next book club. My book shells had also gone down a treat, with the authors asking if I could do some for all of their titles as a little memento that they could keep to recognise their achievements.

I would have to do a huge restock tomorrow. A lot of the shelves were showing big gaps and the shelving unit with the stationery and book-related jewellery was completely out of stock. It was a good job I had a couple of days before the shop opened up again to place some orders and get the shelves replenished.

I couldn't have been happier with the results of our relaunch and I literally could not stop grinning. Dennie was right. It was a bloody good idea! A huge success.

29

After locking the shop door, I flung myself into the wing-back armchair in the bay window, closed my eyes and gave the biggest sigh of my life.

A loud pop snapped me back to the here and now and the glug, glug, glug of glasses being filled was music to my ears. Dennie had somehow managed to produce a bottle of chilled Dom Perignon and six glasses.

'Here you go, my darling. I think you've deserved this.'

Mum handed me a glass of champagne and passed them around to everyone that was left in the shop.

'Darling, you are wonderful and brave and bold and fabulous and Theresa would be absolutely thrilled that you've had this day. What a brilliant day. To Nancy.'

We all raised our glasses and when Vi got hers, she necked the lot in one.

'Nan, that's really expensive, you know.'

'I know, bloody gorgeous too! Got any more? My throat's as dry as an eighty-one-year-old's fanny. And trust me. I know.'

'Oh my God. I'd like to apologise for my dear old grandmother, folks. She's incorrigible.'

'No need to apologise for me, lad. At my age, I don't give a shit what people think of me. Shame I didn't feel like this years ago. Might not have wasted a lot of my life trying to change to please others.'

She did make an excellent point.

'Well, I'd also like to thank Dennie for all his help with the shop,' I said, raising my glass. 'It's his ideas and business acumen that's put me on the right track and I'm really grateful.'

'I bet you are.' Vi guffawed.

'To Dennie.' I raised my glass and we locked eyes and grinned at each other. He nodded back at me, his eyes not leaving mine as he brought his champagne flute to his lips.

'Oh, get a room, you two, for God's sake!' Dan grinned at us.

We'd been sharing 'looks' all day and didn't realise that anyone had cottoned on. I hadn't even said anything to Mum yet.

Vi was having none of it.

'Oh, Christ. Just kiss the girl, will you, Dennis. We all know you spent the night with her last night. Rogering her senseless no doubt. Coming home this morning with a dirty great grin on your face, looking absolutely shattered. Lucky bugger!'

The shame I felt was reflected in the heat that was rising in my body, and I could feel the flush going up my neck into my face.

Everyone burst out laughing. This wasn't really the way that I wanted my family to find out, but when I looked across at Mum, she just smiled back at me. Dad looked at his feet and Dan winked at me and shout-whispered, 'Get in!' It would seem that this was no surprise to any of them.

Dennie walked across to me, kissed me gently on the lips and slung his arm around my shoulder.

'Better, Nan?'

'Perfect, my boy. Perfect.' She smiled at him and the love that shone between them was quite overwhelming. They really did have a lovely relationship and it had bloomed over the last few weeks. 'You're so good for him, Nancy. I've noticed such a change. Not so uptight as he normally is.' We all laughed. 'It's been lovely to watch him finally start to relax and not be so focused on work and bloody money all the time. To have the love of a good woman is doing him the world of good.'

'A good shag always helps too,' my brother mumbled.

'Language, Daniel!' my mother said, using her warning voice like she did when we were youngsters.

As I put my arm around Dennie's waist and he looked down into my eyes, smiling that gorgeous smile of his, I felt the happiest I'd ever been in my life.

* * *

The hammering on the door startled us all, and when we looked up, there was a man that I didn't recognise peering through the glass. I heard a little gasp from Dennis as he seemed to register who it was.

I headed for the door. Whoever he was, he wasn't giving up the banging until he came in. As I opened it, immediately the stench of alcohol hit me and I took a step back.

The man stumbled into the shop and made his way over to Dennie. He went to high-five him but was left hanging while Dennie looked at him in horror.

'So, this is your little project, Dennis. This is what's been keeping you away. Nice, mate. Nice.'

'Craig. What are you doing here?'

'Come to see what it's all about. I was hoping to get down earlier for the open day but got caught up at a business lunch instead. Bit too much to drink and ended up falling asleep on the train and not long arrived in this little seaside town of yours. Where the fuck even is this? The arse end of nowhere?'

Craig was clearly a bit of an arsehole and I took an immediate dislike to him. He had a permanent sneer on his face and an attitude that made it seem like he thought he was better than everyone else. Little man syndrome, in my opinion. Five foot nothing with spindly little legs. Not that I was generalising about short people, of course. But I'd come across his type many times before. Think they're the dogs' doodahs but don't realise what a total tosser they look!

I looked across at my brother and giggled as he wiggled his little finger and mouthed 'tiny dick' at me. It was something he'd done for years when he encountered someone who thought they were something special.

The irony of years of dealing with people like this, who despite being huge dickheads most probably had tiny todgers, was something that Dan and I laughed about all the time. He wasn't a lover of David Beckham but I was, and while Dan insisted he'd only have a very small appendage, my love for Becks had assured him many times that it would be absolutely fricking huge!

Dennie's arm had immediately dropped from my shoulder and I was puzzled by the horrified expression on his face.

'He's off his head,' he whispered in my ear. 'Let me get him out of here.'

Sadly, Craig clearly had an acute sense of hearing because he shouted back at him, 'Dennis my mate! No need to get me out of here. I'm not planning to stop in this dead-end shithole. I only came to give you your hundred quid.'

My puzzlement was growing. Why on earth would he have travelled all this way to give Dennie a hundred pounds?

'Come on, buddy, let's go for a walk,' Dennis said, trying to appease his friend. 'Or I could take you to the pub for a drink.'

I hoped he didn't mean that. Craig had clearly had quite enough although I somehow felt that he would still be a total twat even if he hadn't got alcohol inside him. What a vile little man he was. I was surprised Dennie would even be friends with someone like this. He didn't strike me as the sort of person he would want to spend time with. Maybe they were just colleagues. I was sure he would tell me as soon as he could get rid of him.

Though I wasn't sure where he would go. The last train back to London would have gone by now. Maybe Lucy and James would still have a vacant room for the night – he definitely looked like he needed to sleep this off – although I didn't think they should have to put up with someone in his state.

'I don't want to go to the pub. I want to have a look round this lovely bookshop that's been keeping you away from the office for so long.'

He wandered over to the shelves, picked up a special edition of a Dickens novel, a gorgeous specimen with sprayed edges and one that would have sold for quite a tidy penny to a collector. He flicked through the pages with his clumsy fingers, and then dropped it on the floor. I scooted over to retrieve it, trying to limit the damage, and at the same time I tried to block off the shelf that held all the most valuable stock.

Dennie came to my side immediately.

'Ah, so maybe you're what's keeping our Dennis here then. You're a pretty little thing, aren't you?' He sneered at me and laughed right in my face. 'It's making more and more sense now.'

'Come on, mate, let's go.'

'Ah, but, Dennie, I wanted to come and see it for myself and see if you really did make this "poxy little bookshop"—' he made the universal sign for speech quotes '—isn't that what you called it, into a thriving profitable business. It looks like you have, mate. Well done. And found yourself a sexy little shag too. Top marks. Top marks.' He reached into his back pocket and threw some folded-up notes at Dennis. 'Here's your winnings. And congratulations. Not only will you now get the promotion you've been desperate for. You also won the bet.'

30

'What the hell, Dennie?'

His head turned sharply to me. 'This is not what it sounds like, Nancy. Craig, just do one, will you? You moron.'

'What's up, Dennie?' His voice was clearly taking the mickey. 'Don't want your little lady to find out why you've really been helping her? Nice pet name, by the way. Suits you.'

'Just go, Craig, before I knock you out.'

Craig sneered.

My brother took a step towards him.

'It's OK, mate. I've got this.' Dennis moved closer to Craig.

Dennie put his hand out to stop him and he and Dan stood in a face-off.

'Don't, mate me, Dennis. Sort it now or else.' I'd never heard Dan more assertive.

'Dan. Nance. Let me explain. It's not what you think it is.'

My brother stood with his hands on his hips. 'It had better fucking not be.'

This time my mother didn't reprimand him for his language. Instead, she came over and put her arm around my shoulders. I didn't realise it until she was holding me still, but I must have been shivering.

What I did know was that it had felt like a knife had cut right through the middle of my heart. I knew it. I bloody knew it. So Dennie wasn't helping me for nothing. He was helping me because of a bet. A lousy hundred quid bet. I'd never been so insulted in my life.

Laughing, Craig sauntered over to the door. 'Coming to the pub, mate? We can celebrate by spending your winnings.'

Dennis grabbed him by the jacket and manhandled him out of the door. I could hear Craig going off up the street laughing. God knows where to. And I didn't care one iota.

'So that was what this was all about then? A lousy bet. You screwed me over – literally – for just a hundred pounds? If you'd have told me you were that desperate for the money, I'd have given it you myself.'

'It's not like that. I've told you.'

'So, it's not true then? You didn't have a bet with Craig that you could turn the business around?'

'Well, yes... But, not in that way.'

'Well what other possible way is there?' I spat the words out.

'Give me chance to explain please?'

'Get out. Just leave me alone.'

I walked to the back of the shop. I didn't want him to see the tears streaming down my cheeks, and the turmoil that he was putting me through. I needed to show dignity and grace. I could hear Dan telling him to leave and Dennis trying to get to me, before the door slammed.

When Dan came through into the back, I fell into his arms and wept into his chest. He kissed the top of my head while I uttered a muffled, snotty apology for getting mascara all over his clean white sweatshirt.

'It's OK, Nance. He's gone. Let it out, I've got you.'

He rocked me gently from side to side trying to soothe my sobs. When they had finally subsided, we went back outside where Mum was sitting staring out of the window. Dad had taken Vi home. She had apparently apologised on Dennis' behalf, mortified for the tale that had come out, and Dad had told her it wasn't her fault that her grandson was a weaselly wanker. For some unknown reason, despite it being quite funny, that made me burst into tears again. How could my Dennie, the man who had changed so much over the last few weeks, the kind, fun, loving man that I felt I'd known all my life, even though it had only been a few short weeks, be the same man who had just admitted that he'd taken a bet on me and my bookshop? I hated him and I would never ever forgive him for allowing me to give him my heart, then ripping it out and stomping all over it.

'Come on, darling.' Mum came over and switched the lights off behind me. 'I've got the day's takings with me. Let's go home.'

As I grabbed my handbag, my phone signified that I'd just received a text. I dug deep and pulled it out.

Dennie.

> Please give me a chance to explain, Nancy. I would like to tell you all the details so you fully understand the situation. Please. I beg you x

My heart felt like it had been replaced by a piece of lead. The man who I thought was so right for me had turned out to be so wrong. How on earth did I manage to bugger this up in such epic proportions? Was I such a bad judge of character? Did I just not see the truth when it was right in front of me? Why on earth would someone who earned hundreds of thousands of pounds each year, who lived in a swanky penthouse apartment in the City of London, be interested in little old me? Numpty Nancy strikes again.

'Why don't you just listen to what he has to say?' Mum suggested. 'Give him a chance to explain?'

'Seriously, Mum! Seriously?'

'Maybe Craig got the wrong end of the stick. All I'm saying is hear him out.'

I quickly bashed out a return message.

> I have nothing to say to you. Do not contact me again. Take your twatty mate and fuck off back to London. You don't belong here, Dennis. We're way too good for the likes of you. Go to hell.

And then I blocked his number from my phone.

31

I didn't know how I was going to afford it, but I was going to have to shut the shop while I cleared my head. I didn't know how long it was going to take but I needed to get away and the only place I could think of was the cabin in the woods that Dan was staying in. It was the perfect escape. Dennis had no idea where it was and I had sworn Mum, Dad and Dan to secrecy. Under no circumstances whatsoever did I want Dennis to know where to find me.

My poor bruised and battered heart needed to heal and I couldn't do that with the eyes of Driftwood Bay upon me. I knew I'd get over Dennis in time. Everyone did get over heartbreak, I wasn't naive enough to know that I'd be broken forever, but he'd done a very good job of damaging it. What better place to be than with my brother. Us looking after each other like old times.

When I arrived home on the night of the launch, the indent of Dennie's head and his scent were still on my pillow. That upset me more than I ever thought possible. Mum sat with me and stroked my head to try to get me to nod off and eventually I did, although my sleep was so very restless that night.

Dan took me over to the lodge early the next morning.

For the first two days, I finally surrendered to sleep, only getting up to go into my en suite or to accept the food Dan had left me. My appetite had gone, I didn't fancy anything at all, and quite ungratefully, only picked at what he made me. I just felt constantly nauseous.

On day three, there was a loud knock on my bedroom door.

'Right, sis. What would you say to me if I was lying in my pit wallowing over Sabrina?'

He plonked himself down on the bed and I could feel it go down with his weight. I buried myself under the covers but he swiped them away and I felt arms scoop me up.

He carried me into the lounge area despite my protestations.

'Put me down, you dickhead.'

'Nope!'

He opened the door to the decking area while still manoeuvring me around. The cold wind whipped around my ears and he put me down on the wet floor.

As he closed the door behind me, he winked and grinned.

'You git!'

'Language, Nancy!'

And then he closed the curtains so he couldn't see me any more.

I'd forgotten what an idiot my brother could be. In our youth, he'd done several stupid stunts like this. He used to sometimes come into my room and tell me it was snowing. I'd jump out of bed to look and it wasn't at all. It was just his daft sense of humour. I remembered how much fun we'd had as teenagers. He may well have teased me constantly and wound me up but we were as thick as thieves and as well as being my brother, he was also my best friend and I adored him. That's why the way Sabrina treated him affected me so much and I hated to see her taking him for a mug. I realised also that this was the first time in the last few days that I'd thought of someone else apart from Dennis. Maybe this short sharp shock was exactly what I needed.

Banging on the door and shouting 'I'm cold' only resulted in the door being opened and a throw being thrust at me. The door closed again as quickly as it opened. I noticed that someone, presumably my brother, had wiped the furniture down, put the cushions out and had placed a cup of tea in a thermal mug on the table. There was a parcel wrapped up in tin foil too. My curiosity got the better of me and I sat and unwrapped it, smiling from ear to ear when I saw the bacon sandwich inside. He knew me so well.

As I draped the throw around me and devoured the sandwich – made just as I liked it; well done on crusty freshly made tiger bread with red sauce – my heart swelled with love for my brother. Maybe he knew me better than I knew myself. Maybe this was just what I needed.

Around me, I noticed that there was a coating of frost on the ground, yet the sun was shining high in the sky, giving it a slight heat, and the blue sky above was such a contrast to the lush green grass and the trees which surrounded the cabin. Squirrels scampered along the balustrade around the decking, brave and hoping that I might drop a crumb. I know people always said they were vermin and no better than rats but with their cute faces and bushy tails they were far cuter and more acceptable.

The last bite of the sandwich was amazing. I hadn't realised how very hungry I was.

I knocked on the door.

'Thank you,' I said when he opened it.

'You're welcome.'

'Can I come in now please, Dan?'

'Are you going to stop moping?'

'That's rich coming from you. Moper of the year award. Every year!'

'OK, so clearly you are feeling better. But for every insult you throw my way, that's another half-hour on the decking. It's for your own good.'

'Dan, let me in!'

Silence.

'*Let me in!*'

'In a bit!'

Yes, I loved my brother, but God he was annoying.

An idea sprung into my mind and I left the throw on the rattan settee and climbed over the balustrade. The grass was cold and wet on my bare feet, but I ran around the lodge to the front and tried the front door. Ha! It was open.

I ran inside, jumping from one foot to the other. Dan was sat watching the TV.

'Hey, sis.' His super-friendly tone did not reflect the fact that he had just shut me out of the lodge.

'You forgot to lock the front door. Loser!'

'Or maybe I never intended to keep you out there all day. You could have walked around at any time and let yourself in. I never locked you out. I just *put* you out. Very different.'

'So kind!'

'Anyway, I've run you a bubble bath. Get your arse in it. You stink!'

'I do not.' Despite my counterclaim, I sniffed my own armpit and admitted to myself that maybe I did smell a bit.

'You do, Nance! You haven't been near a shower for days. And you might want to wash your hair too. Just a suggestion.'

I walked over to my brother and gave him a hug, then breathed hard right into his face.

'Jaysus, Nancy. Shrek breath or what?'

'I think you mean Princess Fiona.'

He raised his eyebrows.

'I think when you look in the mirror, you'll realise that you look more like Shrek than her.'

I grinned as I headed off to the bathroom. I'd never been able to stay in a mood with Dan for long. He was kind and considerate and he was loving and wonderful. Sabrina didn't deserve him and it broke my heart to think he knew no better or thought that behaviour like that was acceptable. Although now I'd had a taste of what love could be, maybe I understood him a bit more: perhaps he just lived for the good times and easily forgot the bad. Was that the secret of life? Or did we all deserve more?

Pondering this major philosophical question, I looked in the mirror, realising that it probably was best I washed my hair and got myself sorted out. A good soak in the bath was always good for my soul.

I had a little cry as the memories flooded my mind: of how it felt to fall asleep in Dennie's arms and wake up to what I thought was the start of something special. But then I took a deep breath and washed that man right out of my hair.

As I walked back into the lodge lounge, which was cosy and warm, I knew that I not only looked better but felt better too.

'Much improved! Well done.'

'Kack off.'

The insult that we'd used to give each other when we were children made us both laugh. I flung myself on the settee next to Dan and gave him a proper big sloppy kiss on the cheek.

'Thank you!'

He screwed up his face in a fake throwing-up way and wiped the kiss away with the back of his hand – again, like he used to when we were kids. It was amazing how quickly we'd stepped back into our childhood lives. We both laughed as we locked eyes.

'I love you, sis.'

'I love you too.'

'Good, because we're going for a walk in the fresh air. It's good for the soul.'

* * *

He was so very right. Walking amongst the trees, the sun casting its magic spell as it weaved its way through the trunks, making sure we knew that it was always there, was pure bliss – Mother Nature doing her thing – and it filled my heart with joy. I didn't do this enough. Living by the sea had kind of made me forget that I loved to be in the woods too. Nature was amazing. The sound of silence and only the clearest shrill of birdsong was balm to the soul and my spirits were lifting with every minute.

'It's OK to have a pity party, you know, Nance, but you've had it now and you need to get some normality back in your life.'

'That's rich coming from you.'

'Yeah, I've realised that. But since I've been here, I've been doing a lot of thinking and I'm ready to make some changes. Yeah, so I do love Sabrina, but she's not good for me and I've realised now that I do want more. I do want to be treated properly – all the time. I don't want cling on to those nice moments while I'm being treated like shit. I know you've been influenced negatively by our relationship, but I've been influenced positively by you and Dennis and what you had. I could see in his eyes every time he looked at you, the love shining through. The way he helped you. The way that you were, well, you know, a team. Working at the shop together was like you'd always been that way and that you were meant to be. That's why I was so surprised when we found out what we did. It just doesn't fit with what we know of him.'

'Me too. I can't believe it to be honest. I've done nothing but think about it over the last few days.'

'Yeah, I got that.'

I smacked him on the arm and he slung his arm around my shoulder and pulled me close while we continued to walk, the leaves crunching underneath our boots.

'Do you not want to hear what he's got to say?' Dan asked eventually.

'No, I can't right now.'

'Maybe it would help.'

'Nah, I don't think so. It's done now. I could never trust him again.'

'But you haven't heard his side.'

'Why are you sticking up for him all of a sudden?'

He handed me an envelope.

'Vi gave Mum a letter to give to you.'

Coming to a halt, I stared at the envelope in my hand. I could tell it had been written with shaky hands.

'You don't have to read it now but maybe when you're feeling a little stronger, you should. Vi apparently said that she wanted to explain a few things to you.'

'Oh!' It was the only word that I could find. After a few seconds, I put the envelope into the back pocket of my jeans and linked my arm with Dan. The letter felt like it was burning a hole in my pocket but I was determined that I wasn't going to read it until I went to bed that night. Today, I just needed some time to be me.

32

My brother had always been great company and I loved spending time with him. After a lovely morning together pottering in the woods, we went out for lunch and then headed back to the lodge and because he'd had a couple of beers with lunch, he decided he was going for a snooze.

I retrieved the envelope from my pocket and sat and looked at it for five whole minutes before going to make a mug of hot chocolate. Dan had decided that these few days were for totally indulging ourselves. He was fed up of being controlled by Sabrina, to the stage where she even told him what he could and couldn't eat and drink, so he'd thoroughly enjoyed the lunch of massive pastry-topped pie and creamy mashed potato with a good helping of broccoli, carrots, peas and beans.

I squirted some cream on the top of my drink and sprinkled it with chocolate shavings and mini-marshmallows. Lush.

The envelope was propped up against the fruit bowl which was sat on the coffee table in the middle of the room. The letter needed to not be calling out to me, so I went and put it under my pillow. I put the TV on low, and watched a couple of quiz shows – I always felt that they were great to get your brain going and the hosts were always good fun, making them really entertaining. I also had a huge crush on Ben Shepherd and he certainly cheered me up. When Dan came back from his power nap, we continued to watch them, shouting out the answers and laughing at some of the random things that came out of our brains when put under pressure.

'It's good to see you laugh again, kid.'

'You too, bro.'

'It feels good too. I feel like I've been existing in my life and not really living it the way I want to.'

A flash of inspiration suddenly hit me and I gasped out loud.

'Ooh! I've had an idea.'

'You and your ideas. What madcap plan have you come up with now?'

'Why don't we write a list of all the things we want to do? Like a vision for our future?'

'Like those old vision boards you always used to do?'

'Yeah, the same sort of thing. Only we write them down.'

'God, I never write down the things I think. Someone might read them.'

'OK, so write like no one is ever going to read them. In fact, you don't even have to tell me what's on the paper. You can throw it in the fire if you like. This is about you and exploring your innermost hopes and dreams.'

'We could, and I really like the sound of that, but I don't think there's any paper or pens around.'

'I'm the owner of a bookshop that sells stationery. Like I go anywhere without pads and paper.'

He laughed at me and messed up my hair.

I grinned as I went into my room and grabbed what we needed.

'OK, so let's set a timer for twenty minutes and see what we can come up with when we put our brains under pressure. No interruptions. Write down anything, even if it's completely mad. In fact, the madder the better. Then we can share anything we want at the end, but no pressure. That sound OK? Ready?'

He nodded his affirmation.

'Go...'

For the next twenty minutes, we both alternated between staring into the forest and frantically writing down our thoughts, and when the timer on my phone went off, we both breathed out loudly at exactly the same time and laughed at the similarity between us. Like peas in a pod as Mum and Dad have always said.

'Right, let's get a bottle of wine open and share away,' Dan said, a smile on his face. 'I'm actually excited and *would* like to share what I've written with you. Shit, sis, that was liberating to write with the freedom of not worrying about what Sabrina would think.'

I had a feeling it might be. It was something I did from time to time. I did journal every day, but normally about my daily feelings rather than my hopes and dreams: all the plans for the shop for the unforeseeable future with Dennie – I had the shop parts nailed down, but I needed to do more in the rest of my life – thinking about how, if I was going to save the planet, I was going to do that, but also, thinking about what I wanted in my personal life. I'd had a taste of love and I needed to consider whether I wanted to risk having my heart broken again or whether I would continue on my own forever, not trusting anyone to keep it safe.

It turned out that Dan's first item on his list was to do more water-based hobbies. After all, what was the point in living by the sea if you never went in it? He'd always loved it as a kid. It probably wasn't the wisest time of year to start this as a new hobby, with the sea getting colder by the day, but he said that he'd be happy to buy himself a wetsuit and risk it for the rush he felt when he was younger.

The second thing was that he wanted to start his own business. He'd always been brilliant with his hands, excelling at all of those practical lessons at school, like woodwork and design and technology. The furniture he'd made for me at the shop was always getting compliments and I was pretty sure that he'd have a really successful business. And now that I'd learned so much from Dennie, I knew I could help him. He said that he'd mooted the idea to Sabrina in the past and she'd insisted that he stayed in his job, because it paid him a regular wage and she didn't want him to take any risks. But now that I was loving what I was doing so much, he said he was inspired to do the same.

I was absolutely delighted for him and proud of him for making such a momentous decision. He'd make it awesome. There was a little bit of me wishing that Dennie and he could work on this together, but maybe he could ask for his help. Just because Dennie and I weren't going to have a future together, it didn't mean that my brother and he couldn't be friends.

The third thing was that he wanted a dog. He's always wanted one but Sabrina said that she wouldn't have dog hairs in her house or her house stinking of smelly mutt. I'd only been to their place a couple of times, but you had to take your shoes off outside because she wouldn't let a shoe that had been outside over the threshold, and she insisted on everyone washing their hands before they touched anything. She was never a person to relax. Dan said she was always dressed in her designer clothes even if she was just lounging around the house and insisted on having the most expensive of everything. He felt like he'd been working to pay for her luxuries.

But now, he'd decided to find himself a doggy mate and go for long wonderful walks in the woods and play catch on the beach.

I was loving his list and, more than that, his lust for life. I think the last few days had got him finally doing things he wanted to do, rather than things that he was *told* he wanted to do, and experiencing life for himself. I loved this new version of my brother. He was fun and was finally excited about what the future for him might hold.

'So, what's on your list, Nance?'

'Nothing as exciting as yours, I have to say. I've got that I want to make part of the shop a recycling centre and that I want to do more locally in educating the people of Driftwood Bay about recycling, reusing and repurposing. It's something I've always wanted to do and I'd like to go into local nurseries and schools and get the children on board right from a very early age. They're the future and we need everyone to think differently.'

'You'd be great at that.'

'I want to make more jams and chutneys,' I continued, scanning my list. 'Maybe I could sell them in the shop.'

'Your chutney is divine too. You'd sell that by the bucketload.'

'You think so?'

'I know so. I know I don't normally have any but that's because Sabrina used to throw it away when I got it home and it seemed really unfair.'

'Why did she do that?'

'Never trusts anyone to cook for her. She's a germ freak and says she never knows where anyone's hands have been.'

'Bitchbag!'

He laughed.

'That's the perfect word for her.'

I looked back at my list. 'Something else that might seem a bit mad, but I'd love to make things out of recycled materials from the beach.'

'Such as?'

'Maybe things like table mats and coasters. I don't know, but I'd love to figure something out. Items made literally from our own beach and then sell them in our village.'

'I could make you some more display shelves to sit on the countertop. You're going to run out of shelf space soon and you are supposed to be a bookshop, you know.' He laughed.

'Yeah, I know, but Dennis did teach me that you have to diversify and if people who come in to buy books purchase other things too, then that's fabulous. There may also be people that come for the recycled stuff, who then go on to buy books too.'

'Then more shelves I shall build, milady!' He took a bow and I threw the pen I'd been holding at him, which he luckily dodged before it caught his nose.

'You're an ace brother, you know.'

'Yeah, I know.' He winked.

We were still stuffed from our humungous lunch but did manage to squeeze in some cheese and biscuits, accompanied by some gorgeous grapes and home-made chutney, which I'd batch-made recently and brought some along with me.

'We've got a lot to give, you know, me and you,' I said.

'You think?'

'I know so. I'm proud to have you as my brother. I wouldn't want anyone else.'

'Good, because you're stuck with me now. Anyway, do you fancy a quick game of Scrabble before we head off to bed? I'm sure it's my turn to thrash you.'

'Ha, I'd like to see you try. I've got a degree, you know.'

'Yeah, in art not English and even though you have one, you work in a shop.'

Brother banter could sometimes be a little cruel and he liked to insult me. We both laughed and then I smacked him over the head with a pillow.

After he won only one game out of the five we played, I think I'd made my point.

'Right then. I'm off to bed. I'll see you in the morning. And I'm glad you are not Mopey Nancy any more.'

'Yeah, me too!'

33

The time had come. The letter stared at me from the dressing room table. I couldn't put off reading Vi's letter for any longer.

My darling Nancy,

My heart reaches out to you. I hope you are managing to work through all of your feelings. I cannot imagine what you are going through right now.

I can only apologise for my Dennis. He's a fuckwit. I have told him this about three billion times since Saturday evening. He sat on the step of your shop on Sunday morning after he tried to see you again at your parents' house and was sent packing by your mother. And I really don't blame her.

I'm not saying that I blame you either, Nancy. But hopefully what I tell you now might help the situation.

When Dennis was a child, his parents treated him very badly, and when he was eighteen, they did something that was unforgivable. That's his story to tell, not mine. And I'm sure he'd want to tell you everything, if you gave him the chance, but let's just say he was left to fend for himself. I'm ashamed to call Dennis's father my son, especially when they left him to move to Spain.

Dennis had to grow up very quickly and had to survive. His dream to go to university no longer an option, he had to get himself a job, which he did, and since that day he has made money his ultimate goal in life. He always had here to come to, of course – he had (and will always have) a home here with me – but he made a life for himself in London. Where he felt he could be the most successful. Because success was the other thing he needed. To show them that he didn't need them, or anyone in fact.

I won't be here forever, Nancy. I'm an old woman and I don't mean to be dramatic or use this as a way of making you change your mind (although if you'd like to I'd really love that). There is nothing on this earth more that would make me happier than to go to heaven knowing that he has someone here that loves him and will look after him for me. And maybe even someone with whom he would go on to have his own family with. He's always said that he doesn't need anyone in his life, Nancy, but these last few weeks I've seen a change in him. It's been so nice to spend so much time in his company. I know he had an issue at work and wanted to get away for a bit, but you've made his life here happy and even if this is the end of the road for you both, then it's been a pleasure to see.

However, I do hope you give him the chance to explain more to you. You and he, in my opinion, are absolutely perfect for each other and I believe you are destined to be together. Dennis will tell you that he doesn't believe in destiny but I think he should. My husband and I were together for many happy years. Some shit ones too, I have to tell you, but mostly fabulous ones.

Vi was a true diamond and I had to wipe my snotty tears away with the sleeve of my pyjamas. *Stay classy, Nancy.* I was glad I was alone as I could only imagine how very attractive I was looking at this point.

I grabbed some toilet roll from the en suite, noisily blew my nose and picked up the paper once more.

> *Dennis is a proud boy. He's a fighter. He had to be. And he's never needed anyone in his life. But there's a huge difference between needing someone and wanting them. And I can see that my boy truly does adore you. He's always been a good lad and as a child had the hugest of hearts, and I'll never forgive his mother and father for breaking it. He felt like he had to spend his life protecting his heart from further harm and the only way he knew how to do that was to distance himself from everyone and everything. But then he met you and everything changed.*
>
> *Please give him a chance to explain, Nancy. What happened with his so-called friend isn't quite what you think, although I can totally understand why you reacted the way you did. The friend is a total cockwomble (a new word I learned recently) and think Dennis is probably being one right now too. But I hope that you can find it in your heart, which I believe loves Dennis as much as much as he loves you, to find a way through.*
>
> *Much love to you, my darling.*
>
> *Vi*
>
> *xxx*

It was another restless night where dreams invaded my sleep. In one, Dennie and I walked on the beach for ages and ages, our hands tightly welded together; in another I was reaching out to him and he was holding a big red heart in his arms, but he was holding it away from me, not letting me near it. In the final one, which woke me at 5.30 a.m., we were in bed together and he was holding me in his arms. I couldn't get back off after that, as I was so gutted when I woke up to realise that it wasn't reality and it broke my heart all over again.

I crept into the lounge where Dan had made me leave my phone each night and unlocked it to see if I had any messages. I felt a huge urge to message Dennis. Tell him I was missing him. Then I remembered that I'd deleted and blocked his number so there was no way that I could contact him.

The scene from the shop kept replaying in my head. The look on Dennie's face when he thought Craig was going to say something and how quickly he tried to get rid of him. The shame of what he'd done. And then I became angry with him again.

Dan wandered into the lounge, rubbing his head with one hand and scratching something down his pants which I didn't really want to think about with the other. Quite a skill.

'You shit the bed or something?' I asked.

But he ignored my jibe and began to talk animatedly. 'Know what, kid? I'm quite excited about the thought of what's ahead for me. I'm so determined that I'm going to go through with everything we talked about yesterday.'

'But what about Sabrina? What happens when she clicks her fingers this time, like all the other times and expects you to go running back?'

'Dunno why, but this time it's different. I feel completely different. Can't explain it but it's just the way it is. I feel strong enough now to tell her that it's over. Once and for all. And to be the one that calls the shots in my own life. I don't know what you've done to me, sis, but you've made me realise that life is too short to be unhappy.'

I punched the air – literally. Hallelujah! He'd got it. My brother was back.

'Now, we just have to sort out your life.'

'Ha!' I huffed. 'I've been thinking about that and have a short-term plan. Wanna hear it?'

'You can bet your life I do.'

'Good, because I need your help.'

34

Night-time in Driftwood Bay could go one of two ways. You could have the most glorious display of stars, lighting up the sky and casting a silvery spell across the bay, which along with the street-lamps, made it look like a stage waiting for a play to start, or, if it was cloudy or rainy, you couldn't see a bloody thing. Luckily tonight was the first.

Mum had popped over to the lodge that morning and had said that she'd passed Dennie who was sitting on the steps of the book-shop waiting for me to open up.

She relayed the tale of how she told him I was keeping the shop closed for the moment and that I hadn't decided when I was coming back. He begged her to tell him where I was staying because he wanted to come and find me but she refused flatly, saying that she couldn't possibly give away that information without checking with me first. I was glad she hadn't. I wasn't ready to see him. She did say that she was going to go into the shop to collect the post and would bring it to me, and at that point, his eyes lit up.

Up until that point, apparently, he'd looked washed out, pale, despondent and dishevelled; the polar opposite of how he normally looked and acted. I sighed at this and she gave me a great big hug.

She didn't stop for long, and before she left, she told Dan to look after me, gave me my post and went on her way to work.

But today was not one for wallowing. I finally had a new plan, and today I was going to put it into place. Dan thought I was a lunatic but if he wanted me to humour his wishes and dreams for the future, then he had better do the same for mine.

It was in the light of the silver moonlight that I unlocked the shop door and the loudness of the bell jingling against the silence of the night made me jump out of my skin.

Dan went out back and checked for parcels – Karl the postman always left anything that was too big for the letter box in a rattan box in the porch area by the back door – and came back with just one thing. On closer inspection, it was a small red box tied up with pretty ribbon with a big bow on top, with a gold envelope inside. I used the letter opener on the counter to prise the envelope apart and clutched my hand to my chest when I realised that the letter was from Dennie.

I looked over to Dan, who had grabbed a blanket from the back of the wing-backed chair and, within an instant of sitting down in it, was gently snoring away. Mum always said he could sleep on a clothes line if he had to.

My heart pounded as I began to read.

Nancy,

I can only presume you have blocked my number, because I am unable to connect with you, so as you are the biggest lover of words I know, I thought that the only way I could tell you how much you mean to me was by writing you a letter and using my own words. I do hope you don't mind.

Nan has told me, on numerous occasions over the last few days, that I've been a total fuckwit and that I had a lot of work to do to make up for my behaviour. So I'm going to try my hardest to do that and hope that by communicating in this way you might find it in your heart to forgive me. If you are dead set on not doing that, at least maybe you might humour me and soften your heart towards me enough for me to explain a few things to you.

I'm truly sorry that I have bruised your heart, Nancy. I never ever meant to do that and you are the last person in the world that I would ever wish to hurt.

While Craig was wrong in the way that it came across, he was right, and I did accept a bet from him to turn your bookshop around.

I gasped out loud. The bastard. I looked up to the ceiling, trying to blink back the tears that were threatening to spill at any point. I looked down again.

I reckon that right about now, you are probably looking up at the ceiling trying not to cry.

How did he know that I'd be doing this? He hadn't known me long. He couldn't know me that well surely. I looked around me. Was he somewhere nearby? Then I realised that it was a letter and I had no idea when he would have written it. I continued to read.

I know that we haven't known each other long but believe me when I say that I feel like I've known you all my life. Right now, I feel like I've had my arm chopped off and I have an ache in my heart that just won't go away.

I never thought it would be possible to ever feel like this about someone and I probably should tell you why I've shut myself off for so many years if you could bear to read on, to hear my reasons. They are not excuses but they are explanations. Above all else, I feel that I owe you that.

My parents have never been the most loving parents in the world. When I was eleven years old, they sent me off to boarding school. I was petrified. They used to tell me that they would come and collect me for the holidays but they never did. There was always something more fun for them to do and a child wasn't someone they wanted hanging around them hindering them. I left that school, hoping they would then see me as an adult and we would all live together as adults. I was looking forward to it so much. It was really the only thing that kept me going while I was away at school. But instead of that, my whole life was blown apart.

It happened on my eighteenth birthday when we were sat eating a meal around their dining room table. I'd like to have said, in our home, but I never saw it as my home. The meal was nice, the company was, I suppose, stilted. They didn't know me; I didn't know them.

I'd been dreaming of where I'd been brought up for the last year. How when I left school, it would eventually become my home too, how we'd all learn to know each other and become the family that we hadn't been up till then. I'd been excited of what lay ahead and what the future held for us.

I should not have expected more. Instead of getting a normal present, they gave me £5,000 and told me that they were selling the house and going to live in Spain. It was their dream when they met and apparently when I came along their dream was somewhat scuppered. They'd been holding back for so long, while I grew up, and now it was their time to live their lives their way.

I tried to process what they were telling me and couldn't have been more mortified when I said that I was OK with that decision and that I would look forward to learning about a new culture and a new home in Spain. My parents looked at each other, before my father turned to me and told me that a child didn't feature in their plans. Even when I argued that I was an adult now, they were adamant that it was a future for just the two of them and I had to make my own way in life.

Needless to say, I've never been so shocked in all my years. They made me feel like I'd been a mistake since birth and it probably explained the way they'd treated me all my life. Their absent parenting.

They sent me off into the world to fend for myself.

I'd never felt so alone.

I'd love you to call me so we can talk and I can explain more.

And I suppose what I'm trying to say, Nancy, in a ridiculously roundabout way, is that quite simply, I am an idiot and I miss you.

Dennie

X

Wow! Coming from a loving, close family, I could not imagine how that must have felt. Poor Dennie. However, while what happens to you in life does shape your future, it still didn't give him permission to walk all over people and not have to deal with the consequences.

As the hours ticked by, I tried to concentrate on my shell painting but I couldn't stop thinking about what Dennie had written. After I'd finished a couple of the commissions I'd committed to, and tidied everything away, I gently shook Dan awake.

Once we were back at the lodge, I fell into bed, so weary, but once again my sleep was restless, this time dreams of a sweet little boy on the steps of a grey, daunting-looking building, waving at a car that drove away, the occupants laughing as they fled, taunting me.

35

I woke the following morning to the aroma of freshly brewed coffee and the sizzling of bacon frying in a pan. I rubbed my eyes, grabbed my dressing gown, and was trying to tie the belt on it as I walked into the lounge area. I couldn't believe that Dan was already up and dressed, looking bright eyed and bushy tailed.

I peered at the clock. It was eleven o'clock. My heart gave a little skip as I realised that it was so late, but then calmed again when I realised that I had nowhere I needed to be. Dan handed me a mug of coffee and a plate with a bacon sandwich and then flung himself on the sofa next to me, the movement spilling scalding hot coffee in my lap and all over the food.

'Watch it, Dan. You are such a twat!'

'Yeah, but I'm your twat!'

I screwed up my face.

'Ew! That sounds very wrong.'

'Yeah, it definitely sounded better in my head.'

'Anyway, why are you looking so bloody pleased with yourself this morning?'

'Nancy, just because you are a miserable old bitch at the moment it doesn't mean we all have to be miserable, you know.'

'Jeez, thanks. And you said I wasn't moping around any more.'

'Yeah, that was just to make you feel better, sister dear.'

I laughed.

'It worked.'

'Yeah, I knew it would. Well... guess who I got a text from.'

'Mum?'

'Sabrina.'

'You could have at least given me three guesses, you dope. So I suppose she's forgiven then. You're now back together. You'll move back in with her as always and then in six months' time, we'll just go through it all over again. You're so selfish. You don't think about how your relationship affects all of us, you know.'

I took a bite of coffee-tasting bacon sandwich and raised my eyebrows. It was actually quite nice.

'For your information, sister dear, I told her to leave me alone and not contact me again. I said that I'll be in touch with her when I'm ready to pick my stuff up from the house.'

I sat up straight. That definitely grabbed my attention.

'Shit. You're joking, right?'

'Does this look like a face that's joking?'

'No, it looks like the face of a baboon's bum. Specially that little dimple there.'

I poked him in the chin. Why on earth did we resort to this daft behaviour whenever we were together?

He pushed my arm away with his. 'Geroff! This is serious.'

I backed down. 'Sorry, bud.'

'S'OK. I suppose.'

'So what happened then?'

'Well, look at my phone.'

I reached over. Twenty-two missed calls and a string of text messages, getting more abusive.

'Blimey. How do you feel?'

He took a deep breath and then let out a huge sigh.

'Actually, I feel pretty good. It's different this time. Normally, I back down and apologise for whatever started it all off, even if it wasn't my fault. I've spent my whole time with her making sure she's happy, and I think somewhere along the way, I lost myself. I've realised that I have to think about my own well-being and my own mental health. It's almost relief I feel, to be honest. Like a weight has been lifted from my shoulders.'

I smiled. Thank goodness he'd realised what he'd been going through.

'It's all thanks to you. Dennie too.'

'How do you mean?'

'When you and Dennie were together, it just felt, I don't know. Different, I suppose. Like he really saw you. Like he really liked you. I'm not sure Sabrina has ever looked at me the way that Dennie looked at you.'

'Yeah, well, he might have looked at me like that but he still fucked up in the end.'

'Maybe he didn't. Maybe you do owe him the chance to explain some more. What he said in that letter was pretty awful. He must be so damaged, Nance.'

'How do you know what he said in the letter?'

'Err, I read it while you were in the loo.'

'Is nothing private around you?' I huffed.

'Should have taken it with you then.' He laughed, then his face got serious. 'Perhaps he does deserve a chance.'

'Nah.' I swigged the remains of my coffee quickly and banged the mug down on the table, harder than I intended. 'He had his chance and he blew it.'

'You're a hard woman, sis.'

'Yeah, well they do say that if you let someone upset you when you're first seeing them, and then take them back, it paves the way for the rest of your relationship. If they're hurtful at a time when they should be on their best behaviour and trying to be nice, then your future is going to be bleak. Look at yours. No offence.'

'None taken, but who says that?'

'Me!'

He laughed.

'Dick!'

'Yeah, well I'm your dick.'

I overexaggerated a mock heave.

'I hate you, Nancy.'

'I think you'll find that you absolutely don't. You love me. Who wouldn't love this?' I waved my hands down my body – my coffee-stained dressing gown and pyjamas that hadn't been washed for days. I brushed the breadcrumbs from around my mouth and wiped away the dried tomato ketchup from my chin, then leaned across and pinned him down to the sofa, giving him a big slobbery wet kiss.

Just as I thought he was going to push me away again, he pulled me close into the crook of his arm and held me tight.

'We're going to be all right, you know, sis. Both of us. We'll laugh about this one day.' He kissed the top of my head.

'You think so?' I looked up, searching his face. I could see that tears were pooling in his eyes and I could feel myself holding back a lump in my throat.

'I know so.'

We didn't move for the next ten minutes, both deep in our own thoughts, snuggling in close to each other until the door flung open and Mum appeared.

'God, are you two actually being nice to each other for a change?'

We both laughed, got up and stood either side of her, wedging her in the middle in what we'd always called a Mum sandwich as kids.

She kissed us in turn, squeezing us tightly, her turn to well up with tears.

'I couldn't love you two more if I tried. It's OK, my babies. It's all going to be OK. Life is hard sometimes. But we've got each other and together we can do hard things.'

* * *

A long walk in the woods for the three of us, kicking up the crisp crunchy leaves and splashing in muddy puddles, definitely soothed all of our souls, as we reminisced about our childhood holidays spent on this lodge park. Dan and I had definitely become so much closer since spending all this time together over the last few days. It was funny how families were so close, but you didn't actually spend that much time together. Not quality time. It was more snatched time, while busy lives were being lived. Obviously, I'd always loved Dan, but over the last few years he'd changed beyond recognition and it had made me feel a little bit sad.

Getting to know him all over again, while we were both nursing our tender hearts, meant that a special bond had begun to form between us and I realised what a blooming fine young man he really was. He was way too good for Sabrina, and I knew it wouldn't be on his radar now, but I hoped that in time, he would find someone who genuinely loved him and treated him the way he should be treated. He deserved the love of a good woman. He would make a wonderful father and I knew it was something he'd always wanted. I hoped he would find the person who would let him find joy in all that he did.

As Mum was leaving, she asked me to walk with her out to the car, and before she got in, she reached into her coat pocket and handed me an envelope.

'He was there again this morning, darling. Sitting on your step. He looked so sad. Do you feel up to speaking to him yet?'

I shook my head.

'OK.' She kissed my cheek. 'See you soon. Love you.'

36

Dan and I spent a lovely evening cooking together and drinking wine. I didn't think I'd ever drunk as much as I did than in those few days. It really needed to stop. I managed to avoid the envelope until I went to bed and snuggled under the duvet before I was brave enough to open it.

Nancy,

I hope that being away is helping you to heal. I feel so responsible and still want to explain what happened. Apparently, I'm still a fuckwit, sometimes a cockwomble. Nan manages somehow to smack me round the head most days while calling me one of her new affectionate names and telling me that I have to fight for the things I want in life. I feel like I've been fighting for things I've wanted all my life. So once again, let a battle commence.

I wish you didn't feel that you have to be away from the place that you love so much. Driftwood Bay suits you and you suit it. You are perfect for each other and I know how much you are part of this community – this community that I've grown to love more over the last couple of months than anywhere I've ever lived. I also think you are perfect for me, but I know that right now you don't even want to think about that, and that you might not ever give me the chance to speak to you in person. But while I still think there's a chance, I won't stop trying to change your mind.

I never thought that missing you would be as hard as it is. I know that we've not known each other long, and I'm sorry if I'm repeating myself from another letter but I really, really miss you.

I miss the way you flick your hair out of your eyes when you are painting. I miss the way that you poke your tongue out when you are concentrating on something. I miss the way you soften your r's (or is it rs – I'm no English teacher, you know) when you speak, the way you walk, the way you swing your hips, the way you lick your lips, the way you lick my lips. God, my lips miss you! My whole body misses you. I miss you like the trees miss the leaves, like the desert misses the rain (think that might be a line from a song, but it's still true).

The thing I miss about you the most (have I mentioned your lips, by the way?) is that I can talk to you for hours about anything and also about nothing. And yes, the irony of that is quite unbelievable, considering what has happened and the fact that I didn't tell you something really important that was going on in my life and the fact that we are now not talking.

I'm not someone who is used to opening up to people, I've put barriers up all my life. But you, Nancy, are so warm and lovely and make me feel so comfortable, and so safe, that I felt like those barriers were coming down. I do feel like I've changed a lot since we met. I feel like you've shown me a part of myself that I'd shut away for so long that I'd forgotten it was there. The part that used to be full of hope.

Please, please, please, give me the opportunity to explain.

There's still so much I'd like to say and I'm not sure I can capture it all in a letter. I'm not great with words (you may have noticed). Numbers, they're more my thing. Numbers are my life. Well, they were until I walked through the door of Books In The Bay. Also, writing by hand is really time consuming and makes my hand ache.

I miss you, Nancy. Please call me.
Dennie
X

In my mind's eye, I could see him sitting on the step of the shop, waiting for me. Perhaps I *should* call him. But what would I say? The longer the silence went on, the worse it would feel to fill the void. I had no idea how to even start the conversation. I knew that I wasn't quite ready. Maybe a text would be OK though, just to let him know that I'd read and received his letters and that I was thinking of him. But then would that give him the wrong idea? Would it matter?

He'd made the effort to write, so maybe I should be the one to text.

I picked up my phone and scrolled through the numbers, stopping when I got to his name. I took a deep breath then quickly typed the words.

> Dennie. I'm not ready to talk to you yet. You see, I'm still quite furious with you and I think that needs to die down before I'm ready or I don't think our conversation would be a very constructive one. Please let me take some more time and hopefully soon I might feel like talking. I do, however, want you to know that I miss you too. More than I ever thought possible to miss another person. Who knew that I could feel like this over someone who I hardly know? I suppose what I'm trying to say is that I'm thinking of you. A lot.

When I read it back, it sounded snatched and stilted and didn't make any sense and I was the one who wrote it. I hastily deleted everything and turned my phone over, not wanting to look at the wallpaper photograph on the home page. It was a selfie of me and Dennie on the beach, blue sky and sea behind us, both in woolly hats and grinning madly at the camera. We'd been litter picking a week ago and I'd only changed it to that photo on the morning after the night he'd stayed over. When everything seemed to be perfect. Before a fabulous day and an end to it when my world imploded.

Sadness seemed to seep through my every pore. It wasn't insurmountable. Everyone suffers heartbreak at some time in their life, whether it be a pet, a relative, a lover, a spouse. Love was what apparently made the world go round. But right then I wanted to wallow in my sadness and feel really flipping sorry for myself. I'd get over it, but I was going to be a martyr and let my pity party go on for a little bit longer.

37

When Dan and I arrived at the shop that evening as the church clock struck midnight, I could picture Dennie sat on the steps of the shop passing the time of day with Mum. I knew that she would be kind to him. Would probably have told him to shuffle over and then sat beside him. Listened to him. She probably knew much more than I did at this stage, but I just wasn't able to hear what he had to say right now. Once more, I pottered around the shop, painted a few more shells, processed the orders that had been left to one side for me and then before we left, popped my head out of the back door, looking in the box to see if any parcels had been left. Another small, wrapped box with a big blue bow on the top this time. When I opened it up, once more there was a gold envelope and underneath it a stunning large shell. This time I couldn't wait until I got back to the lodge before I devoured the letter.

> *Nancy,*
>
> *Today when I walked on the beach, I stumbled across this shell. Obviously, it had been sent by the universe for me to send*

on to you. (Maybe I'm getting this whole universe vibe after all. What on earth have you done to me?!)

The message that you don't want to speak to me is getting through loud and clear but I still have things that I want you to know. I don't want us to leave things this way. You are far too important a person in my life for that to happen. I never, ever meant to hurt you. I would never intentionally hurt you. I do want you to know that. By omitting something, which I didn't feel you needed to know, I have made things worse and I can't even forgive myself for that, so I certainly don't expect you to.

Driftwood Bay isn't the same without you. It's like the heart and soul has not only gone from my life, but from the village too. I'm not the only one who misses you. Lots of people are stopping me in the street to ask when you will be back. I keep saying soon, but I honestly don't know the answer. I hope and pray that my words have been the truth.

I hope you'll indulge me and allow me to tell you a story. I know you love a good tale. This one is based upon on a true story. My words are not as eloquent as Charles Dickens or Charlotte Brontë but apparently God loves a trier.

Here goes!

Once upon a time there was a young boy called Dennis. He was a quiet child, good as gold. He knew that if he was a good boy, then he wouldn't get shouted at by his mummy and daddy who always seemed annoyed with him.

Dennis did well at school, studied hard, wanting to be the student that his mum and dad would be proud of. But he was also the boy whose Mum and Dad never had time to come to parents' evenings. They never had time to come to the Christmas nativity play. Not even the year that Dennis got to be

Joseph. And not the time that he played the part of Romeo in the school play. That time, he was so sure they'd come he'd told the headteacher to leave two seats in the front row for them, but they never showed. He was heartbroken. Luckily for Dennis, he had a wonderful grandmother called Violet who even though she swore like a trooper, loved him to his very bones, and when his parents didn't step up, she did. She loved Dennis like he should have been loved. She spoilt him rotten and she did all that she could to turn him into a wonderful young man.

Despite this, Dennis still felt the need to prove himself, so he stayed on at school and worked hard to achieve his results so that he could impress his parents further with the next stage of his life which would be at university. He'd hope that while he'd been away from them, they would have missed him terribly and looked forward to the times that he returned. So he researched a university close by so he could live at home and commute. He couldn't wait to tell them his plan.

Sadly, on Dennis's eighteenth birthday, the present he got was not the one he had been expecting. His mother and father's present to him was independence and instead of giving him something wonderful, they showed him their plane tickets and told him that they'd put some money into an account and that it was time he went on to fend for himself. This was their time to finally do the thing they'd wanted to do before they found out they were expecting him, and they would therefore be moving to Spain. When Dennis had a little time to think about this, he plucked up some courage and asked if he could go with them. They said that sadly that wouldn't be possible, they wanted a different life and that he had to make his own life now. (I know that you already knew this part, but it felt strange not going over this and it seems important to say again where it all started.)

Dennis's heart was smashed into smithereens but he didn't

want to let them know how much his heart was broken, so he waved them off and wished them well.

Weeks of worry and depression followed. Dennis had no clue of what to do. He had to find himself somewhere to live, somewhere to work, his dream of going to university not possible without the financial backing of his parents. His lovely nan, Vi, offered for him to come and live with her in Driftwood Bay, but he knew it wasn't a place he could earn big money. Big money was what he thought he'd have to earn to prove to his parents that he didn't need them. To prove to the world that he didn't need anyone. He told his nan that he would be fine, that he loved her very much and would be in touch and he headed off to London.

After weeks of applying for every job he could, his money was dwindling fast and the job market felt like it was getting smaller every day. But luck was on his side when Dennis was offered a job in a hotel as a porter. It wasn't what he'd envisaged doing. His dream was to work in finance, but no one would hire him without any experience. How people were meant to get that experience was something he needed to figure out. He always offered to do both the late shift and the early shift. It was the only way he could find a bed for the night and somewhere to shower. His only possessions, he carried around in a rucksack which he clung on to, as if it were a bag of diamonds. But one day he returned to his locker at work, and the lock had been smashed and his bag had been stolen, all his worldly possessions gone. Even his most prized item – a photo of him, his mother and father, which had been taken when he was a young boy. Even though neither of his parents were smiling in it, he had kept it with him to help him through his dark days. Dennis had never felt so low in his life.

To be continued...

Nancy, I know that this doesn't excuse my behaviour and I'm coming to that. It's just a little about my background. Also, by writing to you, I feel like I'm really talking to you, even though you're not answering me back. It feels soothing in a way. Perhaps I'm going a little insane. Forgive me for that.

I miss you.

Dennie

xxx

I didn't realise that I'd been clutching my hand to my heart and tears were streaming down my cheeks. Dennis had put his story into words, for me, more eloquently than he could ever have envisaged. He'd made me feel so emotional and sorry for him. For everything he'd gone through. It must have been a really awful time. He was just a young man on a roller-coaster ride that he never asked for.

I wanted to reach out and hug him. To pull him tightly to my chest and never let him go. To show him that he was worthy of love. Christ, it was no wonder the man was totally and utterly messed up. But did it excuse him treating me the way he had? I honestly didn't know. I needed some time to process.

Whilst it wasn't time to go back to Driftwood Bay properly, I was wavering. Softening towards him maybe. But there was still a bloody good explanation needed for why he'd taken a bet on me and my shop.

That night, my dreams were so vivid; full of Dennie and Craig laughing at me, as they agreed a bet on me. Whether he could bed me. Whether I'd fall under his charms. Whether because he'd made me fall in love with him, I'd hang on his every word and do everything he said. Just so that he could win a bet. When I woke, I was having palpitations and the last thing I remembered was them sitting laughing and clinking their beer bottles together. It took me ages to get back to sleep.

38

I was in a foul mood when I got up the next day. Tired, cranky and even another of Dan's bacon butties wasn't hitting the mark. Our walk through the woods was more of a stomp, me trying to get the rage out, and answering Dan's questions in one-word sentences, while Dan was chattering away totally oblivious to my mood. The unusual hours we were keeping were clearly taking their toll on me though I did feel slightly better after my afternoon nap, which followed our three-mile hike – longer than usual due to me refusing to go back every time Dan suggested we should.

Yet my brother was more understanding and lovelier than ever, sensing what I needed and just going along with it. He sympathised with me when I walked back in the lodge lounge, rubbing my eyes and still trying to wake my body up fully.

'It's OK, mate. Sabrina used to be like this all the time. I'm used to it.'

Horrified that I was behaving in exactly the way that I deplored in her, and very probably exactly the reason why he said it, I soon snapped out of my funk and the subsequent three games of Scrabble, which had started off quite tame and ended up in us including all the swear words we could find, certainly put me in better spirits. We watched an action movie, both of us not in the mood for a cheesy romcom, and then grabbed a couple of hours' sleep again before we headed back out to Driftwood Bay.

This time as soon as we arrived, just after midnight, I headed out to the box at the back, feeling quite forlorn when it was empty.

My chores in the shop done, we were just pulling the door to as the church clock chimed 3 a.m., when Dan yelled, 'Wait!'

He pulled back the doormat, saying he'd noticed something gold poking out from underneath.

Dennie's now familiar handwriting stared out at me and I waited until we got back to the lodge again before reading the next letter.

39

Nancy,

I hope that the story I started yesterday about Dennis helped you to understand a little of his childhood and his early adult years.

Please find below the next chapter.

While Dennis was at his lowest, Ron, the hotel manager, took pity on him and helped him to get back on his feet. Dennis had never been so grateful for help and support. The only thing he had to his name was his mobile phone which his nan had bought him. He couldn't make many calls, he hardly had any money, but she called him from time to time. He did, however, tell her that he had a swanky flat in London and was doing well. What she didn't realise was that he was still scratching around to pay his bills and was living in a shitty bedsit that you wouldn't let a dog live in.

He still had a passion for learning and the kind hotel manager taught him lots about running a hotel. Dennis had now been promoted to the position of concierge. He had a fancy black uniform with shiny buttons that he loved, but he yearned for something more. He wasn't engaging his brain as much as he would have liked, and had too much time on his hands to think about the past. He needed to silence his thoughts, keep his mind active and he wanted to learn more. Sadly, the hotel manager, who had now become a friend, had a heart attack and was signed off work, being replaced by someone younger and fitter, who was nowhere near as nice and Dennis went back to being the same as everyone else, fighting for his job and still fighting for his life.

His thirst for knowledge took him to night school. He was shattered. Working his backside off all day long and then slogging away at night school on a business course. When Ron passed away, Dennis was devastated. He was the only true friend he'd ever had. Ron had had a feeling he wasn't going to be in the world much longer, and when his wife came to see Dennis, to his surprise, he discovered that in Ron's will, some money had been left for him. Ron's wife said that Ron had thought the world of Dennis; he was like the son he never had. Ron was furious with Dennis's parents apparently, wanting to kill them with his bare hands for what they'd put that young child through – and then as a young adult.

She left after a very tearful farewell, and Dennis carried out some research and found an Open University degree course in business management, knowing the only way he could repay the kindness of his friend was to do the best he could do and pass his exams. He worked hard and studied hard – some days a struggle through the exhaustion – but he pushed himself to the limit. Failing was not an option.

Dennis qualified with flying colours, his grades the highest his tutors had ever known and that night as he raised a glass to

Ron, he felt that the world was now finally going to be his oyster.

To be continued…

Nancy, I was so lucky to meet Ron and to be able to use the money he left me so wisely. Us talking and you teaching me about the universe and the way in which it works has made me wonder whether Ron was my guardian angel. Sent to me at the right time, when I needed someone. If it wasn't for the kindness he showed me, I honestly don't think I would have survived. There were times when I thought that maybe the world would be better off without me, but with his friendship and support, I learned that there would always be a way through everything that's thrown at you. That's why I wanted to make sure that the legacy that your Aunty Theresa had left was being spent well. That it would go towards a sustainable business for years to come. And that's why I was hard on you at first. I suppose I was projecting my past onto your future and it was unfair of me to do that. It's your money and you can do with it what you want.

I'm truly sorry.

I wish I knew how you feel while you read my letters. It's quite cathartic to write. As if you're listening to me. I hope beyond words that you are. Maybe you were right about journaling every day. You've taught me so much, Nancy. You taught me how to laugh again. How to live again. And whatever happens between us now, I will always be truly grateful for the time that we've spent together and for all you've made me feel.

I miss you.

Dennie

xxx

People don't realise just how lucky they are. I certainly hadn't realised how lucky *I* was. I had a wonderful family who loved and supported me, whatever I chose to do. A prime example was when I decided I was going to stop teaching and open a bookshop instead. And it was nice to know that me living my dream had inspired my brother to do the same. To go through life without any of that, having to fend for yourself, maybe lucky enough to meet a friend on the way who might give you a helping hand, must have been truly awful.

I was a big believer that people came into your life when you needed them to. I also believed that books found their way into your hands when you needed them. That night I slept sounder than I had for days.

40

I woke the following day to Mum's voice. She and Dan were talking in the lounge.

They both hushed when I appeared.

'Aha. Sleeping Beauty awakes!' she called over to me. 'I can't stop. I've been here for ages but we didn't want to wake you. I just wanted to bring you this.'

She handed me a metallic green box with a familiar big bow on the top. This time I could feel the corners of my mouth turning up and I saw Mum and Dan catch each other's eye.

'Your brother has been telling me some of his plans.' She grinned and he bobbed his tongue out at me without her seeing.

I laughed.

'Yeah, exciting times ahead for him. Finally seeing sense, thank God.'

He mouthed 'fuck off' at me behind her back, at which we both laughed.

'Right, I'd best be off now I know both of my children are perfectly fine.'

'Well, that's a matter of opinion,' I replied as I bobbed my tongue out at my brother.

It was her turn to laugh.

I thanked her, gave her a kiss and she left.

This time, I headed straight back into my room and opened the box. Inside was a beautiful, huge, tumbled rose quartz crystal, the classic crystal that symbolises love. My face broke into a full smile and I ripped open the envelope, trying not to damage the beautiful paper in my haste.

Nancy,

Please excuse my terrible attempt at shell painting. I have learned something else about myself this week and that's that creativity is not my strongest suit. Give me a spreadsheet and I'm your man (I wish!) but give me some paints and a shell and I'm probably worse than most of the kids that you used to teach. However, if you can find your way to even decipher what the image is, it's you and me being beach angels. I thought you might like to look at it from time to time and smile at the fact that I will go through the rest of my life recycling all my rubbish and encouraging people to do the same and also to use less plastic. I've already spoken to the HR department at work about how there needs to be more bins around. God, woman! What have you done to me?

Anyhow, we're finally getting to the end of the story so I won't leave you hanging. You might have actually given up on my story already and marked it up as a 'do not finish'. I do hope not, though, because we're just getting to the good bit.

So here goes!

Newly qualified Dennis felt like he'd won the lottery when he secured an internship at a finance company in London. He gave everything he'd got and worked his way up from an assistant to an executive (posh, eh?) and then he was promoted to become a fully-fledged business analyst. There was only one job going and it was Dennis who got it, much to the displeasure of colleague – and friend – Craig, who had started at the same time as Dennis, and up until that point had mirrored his career progression. To make matters even worse, Craig ended up working for Dennis. He hated this fact and tried to trip Dennis up at every opportunity, making it look as if Dennis wasn't doing his job properly. Yet Dennis tried hard to cover things up. Whilst Craig wasn't the best friend in the world, he was the only friend Dennis had and he didn't want to go back to being all alone again.

Dennis met a young lady at this point. She was a nice girl, and ticked all the boxes – tall, slim, pretty – and she batted her eyelashes at Dennis and he was flattered. What Dennis didn't realise was that she was batting her eyelashes at Craig too and when he caught them 'in flagrante' one evening on his office desk, he was gutted. Once more, people who he'd put his trust into had let him down. He'd done all he could to be kind to Craig and while he didn't exactly think that they had major chemistry, they had had a nice time and he enjoyed her company.

Eventually, and due to all the bickering at work, things reached a head. Craig and Dennis were hauled into their boss's office and asked if what all the staff were talking about was true. Craig confessed all and asked to be moved to another team. Dennis got a bollocking for covering up for Craig, but, worse still, he was told that they'd been planning on making him a director of the company, but in the light of what had happened, they didn't feel it would now be appropriate. When Dennis asked if this decision might ever be reversed, he was told there was a possibility dependent upon how he performed from that moment on.

So Dennis worked even harder on his accounts, made sure he kept his nose clean, and made millions for both the companies he worked on behalf of, as well as the one who employed him.

To be continued...

I hope you haven't nodded off reading this story. It might not be a gripping thriller, an unputdownable page-turner, or one of those romantic uplifting stories that you normally read, but there's not much left now, I promise.

Even the weather has changed in the few days that you've been gone, Nance. The sea is a murky grey and the beach is full of washed-up seaweed and there is literally no sunshine, in all ways!

I'd still have loved to have told you all this in person. The front doorstep of your shop is getting colder and colder each day. Nan keeps telling me I'll get piles and insists that I bring a cushion to sit on. She still says I'm a fuckwit. I don't think she'll ever forgive me, although she doesn't seem to slap me round the head quite as much now.

I miss you, Nancy.
Dennie
xxx

The last part made me laugh. I didn't think I'd laugh again at one point, but life goes on. Things felt a little easier than they did before. Spending time with Dan had helped enormously. It had been so nice getting to know him and to plan his future. He said that he felt he'd be strong enough soon to go and get his things from his house, face Sabrina and put the past behind him. The distance from her had made him stronger each day he was away and he was finally ready to get back into the real world. He said that he was excited about what the future held for him and his business, for which we'd done a plan, the way Dennie had taught me. If only Dennie could see what I'd done, I knew he'd be super proud of me. I'd listened and I'd learned from him. He was wrong when he said I'd been the only one teaching him things. We'd taught each other. That was what partnerships were about and we, for a very short while, had made a really good one.

I still couldn't imagine anything that he could say that could shine a light on why he had accepted a bet from Craig. And why Craig thought it was necessary to come all the way to Driftwood Bay to drop Dennie in it. He must really hate him.

Maybe I should message him, I thought. See if he was OK and find out the rest of the story for myself. I still wasn't sure if I could face him. I wanted to. More than anything. But I needed to make sure that I was strong enough to listen rationally and then deal with what he was going to say. My head was still all over the place. Being away in the lodge was supposed to help me get my mind clear and then either go back or move on, but I was as confused as ever.

41

Our walk that day was helpful. Dan gave me some great intel into how stupid he thought men were. It was interesting to say the least. He felt that men had to have things pointed out to them. He laughed when he remembered that Sabrina used to shout at him when he would walk over the washing basket she'd left on the stairs rather than take it upstairs with him. His argument was always that if she had asked him to take it, he would have, but his brain didn't register what she wanted, so he didn't bother. He also remembered another instance where it was his job to sort out the bins. Way too messy a job for Sabrina. She might break a nail. When the kitchen bin was full, she expected him to take it out. Rather than asking, she would start to pile rubbish on top of the full bin. He remembered the night that she hinted that the kitchen was starting to smell because of all the rubbish, but instead of taking it out, his brain told him that the probably needed a bigger bin and then he spent hours googling bin storage, which led to a huge argument where she yelled at him and told him he was absolutely useless.

These were the small things, that she got at every single day.

There were other huge things that I'd discovered recently. The frequent times when she'd shut him out in the garden late at night because she didn't like the way he'd spoken to her. The times when she'd ridiculed him in front of her friends, making him feel completely stupid when he didn't know the answer to something or when he didn't give her constant adoration and she sent him back to Mum and Dad's telling him that he could come back when he'd learned how to treat his woman much better. He'd even admitted to me recently that he'd always made sure his car keys were in his pocket, so that when she did kick him out, he could sleep in his car, as on several occasions when she didn't feel that he'd spent the right amount of money on her for Christmas and birthdays.

Years of someone telling him that he was absolutely useless had convinced him that that was exactly what he was. He couldn't see what we could all see. The wonderful, kind, clever, creative man before me today. He had become a shadow of his former self and it was lovely to now see him take back his control and look forward to a life he loved.

His take on the whole women and men coming from different planets was that they absolutely were and that their brains were wired up differently. He went on to say that he thought Dennis wouldn't have even thought about the consequences of me ever finding out about the bet, because his two worlds would never have collided.

It was useful to have this insight, but I just had to figure out what I wanted, whether this was enough for me to forgive him.

I did know that I was getting restless and was itching to get back to Driftwood Bay and the bookshop properly, and it be my life once more. I missed it, but wasn't sure how it would feel going back. Would I ever be able to forgive Dennie? Could we ever go back to how we were? Or did I cut my losses and break all ties with him? I didn't think we could ever just be friends again, so maybe that was the best thing to do. A bruised heart was not one that could make sensible decisions. But whatever I decided, I did know that life would go on. I could wallow with my wounds, but the only person suffering from that would be me. The world would keep on turning and I had to jump back on the merry-go-round of life.

My brain hurt from overthinking everything. Tomorrow was another day and I would try to make some decisions about it then. I'd been away long enough and skulking around in the middle of the night was playing havoc with my circadian rhythms. It was time to take back my life just like my brother was taking back his.

42

The next day, Mum was busy at work but said that she'd pop in for post when she'd finished, and Dan and I were so tired we decided we wouldn't go to the shop that night. When Mum phoned to say she couldn't get round because her car had broken down, Dan and I had both drunk the contents of a bottle and a half of wine so there was no way either of us could drive.

Mum came round early the next morning instead and this time there were two gold envelopes, both of which I practically snatched out of her hands. I opened the first one immediately, sloping off to my bedroom where I sat on the edge of my bed and read it.

Nancy,

It's time for the final part of the story. But before you read that, there is something else I want you to know.

I'm not one for showing my vulnerability. I've kept it buried for years to protect myself. But with you it was different. Once I held you in my arms, and kissed your lips, I felt like it was the start of something huge. It was like you'd claimed the missing piece of my heart and made it complete once more. I pictured a future that we could have together. I clung on and didn't ever want to let go. I saw us together for years to come, growing old together, being an old couple sat in bed, discussing our children and our grandchildren. Reminiscing over our life and how fabulous it had been. Me still watching you like I watched you that morning when I stayed over at yours. I couldn't tear my eyes away from you. You were so beautiful that day, the light so bright in your eyes with everything that lay ahead. I hoped that we would love each other forever. When you were in my arms that night, it was everything to me. You were everything to me, Nancy. You gave me hope.

I will be eternally sorry that I messed that up.

The Final Chapter

When the company was sold a few months later, Craig was promoted over Dennis's head and it soon came to light that the person who bought the company was Craig's uncle. And so he'd had to hand the reins over to Craig. Dennis had always dreamed of being made a director and now he felt that it was never going to happen.

One day, Dennis came to visit his nan in Driftwood Bay. He'd been many times before but this time was different. When he collided with another body in the harbour, his eyes fell upon the most beautiful girl he'd ever seen and he couldn't drag his eyes away from her. He'd never been a huge reader, but his nan had invited him to go along to the launch of the girl's new bookshop that was opening up. He was desperate to see this girl again and when he walked through her shop door and she turned and smiled at him, he felt like he'd known her all his life. This feeling was new to him and if he was honest, it scared the crap out of him, but he spent a little time with her and they got on like a house on fire. He tried really hard not to show off, but the experience he'd gained over the years told him that he could help her have a much more successful business than she currently had.

They couldn't have been more opposite. He was fact and evidence based, and she left everything to the universe to decide. He was into designer gear because it was his way of showing people how successful he was, whereas she wore vintage clothes and those she'd found in charity shops, wanting to save the world with her strong values on recycling. He was guarded and closed off. She wore her heart on her sleeve. He had to be financially stable; it was his only way to feel safe and protected. She already felt safe and protected by the people and the environment that she lived in. He wanted to make money. She wanted to make the world a better place.

When they finally worked out that opposites could indeed attract, they began to bond. They learned from each other and they began to fall in love.

Dennis returned to London to sort things out for work. His feelings for the bookshop owner were stronger than anything he'd ever experienced before. He knew that their worlds were very different and that she could never work in London, but he knew that if he did things right, he could work from Driftwood Bay, travelling back to the city if and when he was needed. It was a perfect solution. But first he had to get Craig to agree to his plan.

Dennis channelled his inner Nancy and put his vulnerability on the line and told Craig the truth. That he'd fallen in love and wanted to give it a chance to bloom and flourish. Craig agreed that it was definitely a solution but the only way that he would agree for him to have the time off was if Dennis and he had a wager. That Dennis couldn't turn around the little bookshop in the little seaside town into a booming business. If Dennis refused to take the bet, then Craig would refuse to let his plan come to fruition and would send him all over the country on assignments just to make his life as awkward as he could. Craig really was an arsehole.

But sadly, Dennis needed Craig to agree, for him and Nancy to stand a chance of being together. He wanted this more than anything else in the world, and so he accepted the bet, hoping and praying that Nancy would never find out.

Epilogue

Unbeknown to Dennis, Craig's uncle who had previously owned the business had told Craig when a deal had turned sour that he wished he was more like Dennis. That he wished he'd made Dennis the CEO instead of Craig because he would have been a better choice. Craig obviously saw red, jumped on the first train to Truro, got in a cab to Driftwood Bay with a bottle of whisky and blurted out the whole story.

Dennis loves Nancy. Nancy doesn't like Dennis any more.

The End

I'd been trying to fight my feelings since I met you, Nancy. But it was hard. My feelings for you grew by the day until you became my everything. The person I looked forward to seeing each day. The person who made – makes – my heart happy.

Thank you for letting me feel that. I shall be forever grateful.

Right now, there's a Nancy-shaped hole in my life. And my heart hurts. Like hell!

I miss you, Nancy, and I love you.

Dennie

xxx

I knew now. What I needed to do was to go back to Driftwood Bay. Dennis would be waiting for me, and while I wouldn't make it easy for him, I would in time forgive him and we could move on with our lives. Together.

Like Dennis, I had also made myself vulnerable. I'd let my mind run away with me to a future with him. Maybe even a family and there were times when my daydreams would show me the two of us strolling hand in hand along the beach, our children running ahead, splashing in the waves and squealing with joy. When Craig smashed into our lives, he also smashed my hopes and dreams, but now I'd had some time to think, and I'd realised that maybe they could still come true.

I started to frantically throw things into my case. I needed to go back to Driftwood Bay. I would find Dennis and tell him I loved him. Tell him that we did have a future together.

'Dan!' I yelled. 'Dan! We have to go. Now!'

There was no response. He must have gone out.

I was mumbling away to myself. 'Why didn't I just hang around and listen to what he had to say? You're a fool, Nancy. Come on, get yourself sorted out and get back out there and go get your man!'

As I shoved everything into my case, the other gold envelope somehow flipped off the bedside table and landed right in my eyeline. It felt like someone was telling me I had to read it right then. The universe was sending me a message for sure.

I ripped open the envelope and my heart sank as I read it.

Nancy,

I've tried to get you to speak to me. God knows I've tried. With you being such a lover of words, I hoped that these letters would be enough to bring you back to me but sadly it seems that I was wrong. I've tracked down a beautiful edition of Romeo and Juliet *and I've left it at Nan's house for you to collect as soon as you are ready to return. I hope you like it. I hope that one day you'll find it in your heart to forgive me but that every time you look at this book, you might think of me and a little bit of your heart will remind you of what we had, which, to me, was very special.*

I'm going back to London tomorrow. I wanted you to know. At least this way, you can return to the bay and get on with your life, which you clearly don't want to do while I'm still around. I hope that if I return at some point to see Nan, and we bump into each other, that you will speak to me. That we can eventually be friends. I can't imagine being here without you and being here with you ignoring me is even worse. This week has been awful. I'm constantly looking for you, around every corner, in every shop. I've sat on the doorstep of the bookshop every morning, for hours on end, in the hope that you'll come back, but sadly, as your mum keeps on telling me, you have chosen to stay away.

It's not fair of me to keep you away so I'm going to go instead. Take myself out of the equation. And let you be free to return.

I'm truly sorry that things have worked out this way. I've never regretted anything more in my life.

Please know, Nancy, that you have meant more to me than anyone else ever in my life. I've never found it easy to love, but you made it easy for me. You took me with all my flaws and accepted me for who I am. You allowed me to be just me and I finally worked out that I was enough for someone. You never wanted me to be anything more. And for the first time in my life, I liked who I was. And I felt free from the past.

You showed me the things that had been missing from my

life that I didn't even know were missing. You showed me how it feels to be truly loved.

I have loved being with you here in Driftwood Bay. You've taught me more about life and about myself in the last few weeks than I ever thought possible and for that I am truly grateful.

My life will never be the same.

I hope that in time, the memories you have of our time together are not awful. I hope that eventually you remember them as I do. Amazing. Fabulous. Enjoyable. Fun. Joyful. Funny. Hilarious. Sexy. Incredible. Beautiful. Special. Memorable. There are some more words for you. I know you love them but they clearly just weren't enough for me to find the way back into your heart.

I will never forget you, Nancy. You are the most special person I've ever met. I was never looking for love yet I found it.

A huge, massive, incredible love that made anything seem possible.

But then I was a massive fuckwit and threw it all away.

I'm sorry.

I LOVE YOU!

It's time for you to go home now.

Yours forever, Dennie xxx

I ran into the lounge. There was a note on the coffee table to say that Mum and Dan had gone for a walk in the woods. I was still in my pyjamas but stuck my coat and wellies on and headed out to try to find them. They could be anywhere. I shouted their names as loud as I could, and my heart soared when I heard their voices shouting back.

'Mum, when did you pick these letters up?'

'Erm, let me think. Well, I was at work all day and I'd been to Driftwood Manor and got chatting to lovely Samantha...'

'Mum, quick! When?'

'All right, Nancy. There's no need to shout. I picked them up late last night. Your dad fixed the car this morning because it wouldn't start. Bloody flat battery. You can tell winter is here.'

'So this last one's only a day old then?'

'Yep, only a day!'

'Shit! Bollocks! Bugger!'

'Language, Nancy!' Mum and Dan answered me in unison.

I plonked myself directly downwards in the pile of wet leaves at my feet and burst into snivelling tears.

'What one earth is the matter?' Mum crouched down next to me, wise enough not to get her own backside wet.

Through my sobs and hiccups, I managed to croak the words.

'He's gone!'

43
___

My heart felt as heavy as lead as we arrived back into Driftwood Bay and pulled up in the harbour outside our house. The lousy weather matched my mood. It was starting to sleet, the sky was grey and full of plenty more to come and it was cold. Miserable. I looked across at where Dennie's car was usually parked but there was no sign of it.

As I got out of the car, Mum tried to lift my spirits.

'Just because his car isn't there, doesn't mean that he might not be.' Always a glass-half-full person, my mum. 'Go on! Go and knock and see.'

Sadly, I felt like a glass-with-just-the-slops-left-at-the-bottom type of person right now as I trudged along the harbour wall to Vi's cottage, full of doom and gloom, wondering what the point was.

I called out to her as I knocked and opened the door and she called me through.

'You're back. Thank goodness for that.'

'Nice to see I've been missed.'

Vi wasn't someone you could be grumpy around for too long.

'Yes, there was a book that I wanted to get and didn't want to order it on that Amazonian thing. Not when we have a perfectly good bookshop in the square.' She grinned at me and then suddenly caught herself. 'Sorry, love, I didn't know I was having visitors or I'd have put my teeth in.'

She literally took her teeth out of a glass by her side and slid them into her mouth, immediately looking ten years younger.

'I, err. Well, I don't suppose he's here, is he?'

She shook her head. I knew it.

'He's gone back to London. He left last night. I'm sorry, love.'

I put my head in my hands.

'Honestly, you pair! I could bang your bloody heads together.'

'Do you think he'll be coming back at all?'

'Not for a while, my darling. He spoke to someone at work and they've sent him over to somewhere in Canada for a few weeks. Not sure where. Special project or something. He said he was setting off early this morning so he'll probably be...' She peered down at her watch. 'Somewhere over the Atlantic right about now. He didn't see the point in sticking around after you ignored his letters. He wanted to get away from it all. Start afresh. And bury himself in work again, no doubt, knowing Dennis the way I do.'

The sigh that left my body seemed to never stop. Canada was so very far away.

'I wish he hadn't already gone. I've messed up, Vi. Didn't give him chance to explain.'

'So I hear. Fuckwits, the pair of you.' She smiled as Mum walked in behind me. 'Pop the kettle on, me darlin', and we can all have a little chat.'

I sat on the footstool at Vi's feet and she sat with her hand on my shoulder, while Mum sat opposite.

'I think I thought he'd come to the lodge. Maybe I've been reading too many love stories. I suppose I was after my own fairy-tale ending. I think I was waiting for him to come and whisk me away. To tell me everything was going to be OK. But he never came.'

'He didn't know where you were, my love.'

'Mum could have told him.'

'You told me not to.'

'Just because I told you not to, didn't mean that you couldn't have.'

'Hang on, lady. You can't pin this on me. I asked you many times to talk to him, but no, Little Miss High-and-Mighty knew better when all the while Vi and I were saying that you should just speak to each other and sort things out. Love doesn't always run smoothly, daughter dear. Sometimes you have to work at it. Sometimes you have to compromise. Give or take. Like me and your dad. He gives, I take.'

We all laughed. It was just what we needed to lighten the mood.

'I wish I'd have let him explain, Vi.'

'And I'm sure he wishes he hadn't given up so easily.'

'Why don't you just take this time that he's away to see how you feel with him out of the picture? Maybe it'll all be OK. Sometimes things have a habit of working themselves out in the end.'

I hoped she was right, more than anything in the whole wide world.

44

We had decided as a family that it would be better for Dan to go and get his things from his old house as soon as possible. Easier for all concerned if he just got it over and done with. I know he was dreading it and originally he said he wanted to go alone but this morning, he crept into my room around seven and said he was dreading it. When I offered again to go with him, he said he'd love me to be there as his backup in case he weakened.

'You won't though, will you?'

'God, I hope not. She's just so bloody manipulative. You know that.'

I did and it was one of the many things that I hated about her.

When we arrived at Dan's house, I agreed to wait in the car, and had the window open so I could hear if everything was OK.

'Stay strong, buddy. You've got this!'

He blew air out of his cheeks and nodded, bravely steeling himself as he walked towards the house.

I could see he was in trouble the moment the front door opened. Sabrina flung her arms around him and started to wail. I could hear her begging him not to leave her. And her empty promises of changing, which we'd all heard a million times before. He unravelled her arms from around his neck and turned towards me, not really knowing what to do.

Within seconds I was by his side.

'Hi, Sabrina. I hear you've already put things into boxes for him. Can we come in and get them please?'

'Oh, Danny, you didn't need to bring backup surely.' Her true colours would be coming out any time now. We just had to wait. 'Little Miss Do-Gooder come with you to do your dirty work for you, has she?'

And there it was.

'Don't call her that please. She's my sister and she's come to help me.'

She rubbed at her eyes and made a fake baby crying noise. 'Oh, Sabrina,' she began. 'I love you, can I come back? I can't believe you just asked me that. No, you fucking can't, Dan. Oh wait, maybe you can. I can't quite decide. Give me a moment.'

She put her finger on her lip and looked up to the sky, pretending to consider it.

Dan turned to me, not quite believing that she'd turned so quickly. The penny was finally starting to drop with him and he was seeing her for the absolute horror that she was. He'd never really seen her ability to switch personalities so quickly even though we'd tried to point it out to him time and time again.

'I've tried so hard over the years to like you, Sabrina, and I promised Dan that I'd come with him here today and not say a thing. But...' I turned to Dan. 'Sorry, bro, but I have to have my say. You...' I prodded Sabrina in the arm '...are a narcissistic controlling cow. And it's gone on for long enough. He...' I pointed to Dan '... isn't going to take it from you any longer.'

Her face changed, the penny finally dropping. Dan had finally seen sense and was moving out.

She pouted. 'You won't get better than me, Dan.'

He went to speak but I cut across him.

'He'd get better than you every day of the week. You've never been and never will be good enough for him. He's worth a million of you and we're all just so delighted that he's finally realised it. Are these his?' I tilted my head towards some boxes in the hall.

She nodded, stunned into silence.

I pushed past her and Dan and headed to the boxes, strength I didn't even know I had taking over my body. Dan stood with his mouth open, staring at me.

'Come on, Dan. Help me put these in the car.'

Sabrina finally found her voice again. 'Go on, Dan, do as your sister tells you. You're nothing, you know, without a strong woman behind you, telling you what to do. You haven't got the bottle to make decisions yourself.'

Dan brought himself up to full height and approached her. I hoped to God he wasn't going to do anything stupid. His face was as close to hers as he could get and she had nowhere to go because the wall was right behind her.

'I'd rather be on my own than with you, Sabrina. You can find someone else to play your little games with. I'm done.'

'Fuck you!' She spat in his face and spittle from her mouth landed on his nose.

He was totally dignified when he grabbed the rest of his belongings from the hallway and took them to the car.

'I'll take these for now and I'll be back at twelve tomorrow for the rest. Make sure you're out. I'll leave the key behind me.'

'Keep the key,' she said, in a quieter voice, beginning to plead with him now. 'You never know when you might want to come back.'

'I said I'll leave it tomorrow. I'm done.'

He held his head high and walked back to the car. Sabrina was leaning on the door frame. I didn't know whether her tears were real or fake. I did know that Dan's hands were shaking as he tried to put the key into the ignition and turn it. He put his hand on the gear knob ready to put the car into reverse, and I covered his hand with mine.

'I'm so fucking proud of you.'

'Come on, let's go. I can't quite believe I just did that. I need a stiff one.'

'Don't we all,' I replied flippantly.

He threw his head back and laughed. My brother was back. My job here was done.

'You should be so lucky,' he said. 'God, look at us pair. Both single—'

'And ready to mingle,' I finished for him. We both laughed again.

'It is Christmas, after all. Maybe we can jingle too.'

'Come on, let's go and drop the car off and go to the pub. I need me a drink. I'm not intending to get shit-faced but a beer or two with my little sis is just what's needed right now.'

45

Unlocking the door at Books In The Bay the following morning felt very different. Opening my little bookshop really had been a dream come true, but now it felt like there was something missing. Or should I say *someone* missing. In the short space of time that Dennie had been in my life, he'd carved out a position for himself. But now, instead of us sitting together planning and plotting, I felt like I was just passing time. Days seemed longer without him in them and the nights seemed to go on forever. I hadn't realised what a routine we'd got ourselves into, quiz nights at the pub, walks on the beach, fish and chips in the harbour. Just being with each other was enjoyable. And I'd gone and thrown it all away because I was too stubborn to see someone else's point of view; too quick to pass judgement and think badly of someone. If I'd just let him explain at the time, we wouldn't have spent the last week apart and Dennis now would not be over five and a half thousand miles away, not just in another country but a whole flipping other continent.

Dad was constantly wearing his I-told-you-so expression. He had spent most of my childhood years telling me that all is not always as it seems.

'Reasonable people listen to explanations, Nancy. Give people the chance to tell the whole story.'

He was saying that I'd been unreasonable. I should have known he'd be on Dennie's side.

The one good thing in my life was that Dan had given in his notice at work and was sowing the seeds for his own business, working on pieces that he thought he'd be able to sell easily and quickly for a decent profit. He'd been making some lovely book boxes for me, which I was selling in the shop. I had my own by my bedside table and a little wooden box with handles, which was just the right size to hold about six books when they were upright. We called them our TBR boxes. I put a picture of mine on the shop's social media page and the response was incredible. I was selling and shipping them as quickly as he was making them. I'd even been asked whether I'd hold a workshop for a book club in Truro who wanted to come and decorate their own.

As I planned it in the diary, along with two others for the following year, I thought how proud Dennie would have been of me for thinking ahead and getting these exciting projects off the ground as well. Christmas was looming and the orders were coming in thick and fast so I suppose everything was keeping me busy even though he was never far from my thoughts.

Canada seemed a million miles away. Dennie seemed so very far away from me. I still felt this constant ache in my tummy, which I presumed was loss, and even though I was functioning, I felt totally numb and wandered around in a cloud of sadness. I had allowed myself to get carried away thinking about a future with him. About us maybe moving in together, eventually getting married, even the possibility of having a family and like he said in his letter, growing old together. But it clearly wasn't meant to be. Maybe I wasn't cut out for a relationship. Perhaps I was better on my own.

It didn't stop me spending all the free time that I did have googling Canada. Looking at the weather and the nightlife and thinking that he was probably out there having the time of his life and might have forgotten me already.

It was so hard not to ask Mum if Vi had said anything about him or ask where exactly in Canada he was, but I was determined that if he didn't think enough of me to stick around, then he couldn't have wanted us to be together that much.

While I was in a total daydream, the door to the shop barged open and Vi burst in.

'It's no wonder he's a fuckwit, is it, with me for a grandmother? I'm so sorry, Nancy. I came as quickly as I could.'

I led Vi over to one of the chairs and sat her down. She was trying hard to catch her breath.

'It's OK, Vi. Whatever it is can wait. Just get yourself feeling right again.'

'Oh, Nancy, I'm such a silly old goose. People have been telling me for years that I should be using my hearing aid more.'

'What on earth are you on about, Vi?'

'He's not in Canada at all, Nancy. He's in Canada Square in London. In Canary Wharf.'

46
———

'London? How? What? Why?' Random words were coming out of my mouth, making no sense at all.

'I clearly didn't hear him right when he told me where he was going. He's not in Canada after all.'

Even though it was great news that he wasn't hundreds of thousands of miles away, he was still not in Driftwood Bay, although at least London was on the same island as me.

Rash thoughts entered my head. Could I? Would I? No. It would be ridiculous. Wouldn't it?

'I know you won't ask me how he is, because you're both as shitting stubborn as each other, but he's sad, Nancy. I can tell. My boy is sad and he won't bloody do anything about it.'

'Do you think he'll come back?'

'Well, I asked him to come home for Christmas but he said he didn't think he should. Thought it would be best if he stayed away.'

* * *

For the next week, I could think of nothing else. Truro was the furthest I'd been for years and even going there gave me severe anxiety. The thought of travelling to London literally gave me palpitations, but the idea would not go away. I dreamt of trains coming off tracks. I read articles about the threat of terrorists, which gave me the heebie-jeebies. But there was still a tiny little bit of me that felt like I had to go. Owed it to myself and to us.

A knock at the shop door was unusual. If we were open, people normally came straight in. I went to the door and opened it but the street was empty, however on the step was a bag full of second-hand books. I'd started to get more and more of them recently and it was getting harder to find somewhere to display or store them. I'd have to speak to Dan about building me some more shelves.

As I put the bag into the storage cupboard, I noticed the book on the top was described as an uplifting second chance romance. Sounded just what I needed right now to take my mind off things, and as the weather had turned colder and the shop had gone quieter, I decided to grab myself a cup of coffee and settle down in the armchair and have five minutes reading time.

Reading did two things. Firstly, it was helping me to push all the thoughts of Dennis and London from my mind, and secondly, it was giving me a place to escape to. Books as they said, really were portable magic and could transport you away from the world as you knew it to a place where you'd rather be.

Five minutes turned into hours as the pages turned themselves and the book ended before I'd realised that I hadn't done a thing apart from sit and read. I smiled for what felt like the first time in a while. There was still a part of me who was like the little girl I once was, who wanted her own bookshop and thought that you just got to sit and read books all day long. Another dream come true. Sadly, that was not the case and owning a bookshop is not about reading books day in, day out. Although with my Dennis hat on, I could just hear him saying, 'A shop full of customers would have been more profitable, Nancy.'

I thought about the plot of the book. The description had promised a feel-good read and it definitely delivered. I thought about the protagonist who, instead of waiting for a man to come and fix things for her, took the bull by the horns and went out there and did everything herself. It was nice to read something that reflected the world we lived in. These days women were more forthright and just cracked on with stuff.

It was that book that gave me the inspiration for what I knew I was about to do. Maybe in this day and age, a girl didn't have to wait for the hero to come and rescue her. This girl knew then exactly what she was going to do. She was going to go and get her man!

47

The journey from Truro to London reminded me why train travel was not my favourite mode of transport. Just the eleven station stops, with passengers getting on and off, was enough to stress out the most seasoned traveller. But sitting cooped up in a packed carriage for four and a half hours, trying to keep my eye on my overnight case and wondering whether I should leave it to go to the loo or not, had not helped my anxiety. I couldn't remember the last time I'd had to go further than Truro but I did remember why I liked to stay in my part of the world. Just imagine if I did manage to fix things between me and Dennis, and had to do this regularly! Could I cope? Would I want to? It surely would test our commitment to each other and show us whether true love really does conquer all.

As the train pulled into Paddington Station, my heart was pounding and I started to feel stressed again when all the bodies stood up, racing each other to alight onto the platform. I was already totally fed up with travelling and worrying about my case not bashing into anyone and was desperate for a decent cup of tea. As the flow of passengers went from one way to all ways, I felt like a duck out of water. People were crossing my path without any notice or apology; my ankles had been rammed several times with other people's luggage and one man swung his rucksack round without even checking there was anyone behind him, very nearly smacking me in the face. Being quite short, I already felt quite claustrophobic, with everyone else taller than me and being in a packed station was really pushing me out of my comfort zone.

I decided that instead of trying to navigate the tubes and then the streets to the hotel I'd booked myself into, not too far from Canada Square, I would treat myself to a cab and made my way towards where the signs were indicating, to find a queue of about forty people in front of me.

'Excuse me?' I tapped the shoulder of the man in front. 'Does the queue go down quite quickly, do you know?'

He looked at me and babbled quick frantic words in a foreign language, possibly French.

I smiled, not having a clue of what he said and for some reason muttered my thanks.

Twenty minutes later, I was finally at the front of the queue and peered in through the window of the cab, citing the address to the driver.

'Hop in, love. Won't take too long.'

I heaved a sigh of relief knowing that the end of my journey for today was not too far away and glad that I decided to stop overnight and then go to find Dennis tomorrow. We'd waited this long, another day wouldn't matter, and it might be better for me to turn up looking fresh-faced anyway, and not like I'd been dragged through a hedge backwards.

'First time in London, love?' the driver asked.

'That obvious, hey?' I laughed.

'It's that rabbit in the headlights look. Here on business or pleasure?'

I sighed.

'Pleasure hopefully. I'm hoping to surprise someone. If it all works out.'

'Ah, that's nice. Not enough surprises in life. My wife now, she's constantly surprising me. Says it's the way to keep a marriage alive.' His eyes connected with mine through the mirror.

'I'll bear that in mind.'

'Yeah, just as I think we're getting into a bit of a rut, she does something mad.'

'Have you been married long?'

'Thirty-five years.'

'Wow. That's an achievement.'

'It is these days. She's wonderful and I wouldn't swap her for the world. I don't deserve her really. Punching way above my weight, my friends said when we first got together, and that it would never last. But I love her just as much now as I did the moment I saw her in the school playground. It's now four children and seven grandchildren later.'

'Wow. What a lovely story.'

'True love for you. And I tell her I love her and appreciate her every single day. I hope the person you've come to surprise appreciates you, darlin'. Don't be wasting time now on someone who doesn't love you equally as much as you love them. Sorry, I'm wittering on. My wife is always telling me not to dish out advice unless I'm asked. I'll shut up now. Leave you to your thoughts.'

'It's lovely to talk to someone, to be honest. I feel like I've landed in a very anonymous city.'

'Yeah, that's London for you. Not everyone, but most keep themselves very much to themselves. Have you come far?'

We chatted about my journey and life in Driftwood Bay and he told me that he proposed to his wife in Cornwall and had wonderful memories there.

The journey took no time at all and before long we arrived at my hotel.

'Good luck with everything, darlin'. Just be brave and I hope everything turns out well for you.'

I thanked him and gave him a huge tip. The receptionist at the hotel was equally as lovely and explained how to get to my room. She offered to reserve me a table in the restaurant that night, but I didn't fancy dining alone somewhere I didn't know and said I'd grab some room service instead. As I kicked off my shoes and walked across to look out from the window of my room, the lights of high-rise office blocks reflected in the vast expanse of water as raindrops started to fall. It still looked incredibly pretty though, even if I felt like a very small person in the midst of a massive city.

Maybe London wasn't so bad after all. Meeting that nice friendly taxi driver had given me hope that things might turn out well. But all after a burger and fries from room service, a big glass of wine and a good night's sleep. It had been quite a day.

* * *

I took a deep breath as I closed my hotel room door behind me, double-checking it was locked properly. Hopefully, the next time I was in the room, I would have found Dennis and he would be with me. I grinned at the thought. This room might have cost me an arm and a leg, more than a week's holiday to Spain in Dan's opinion, but I hoped it would be worth every penny. I felt that I deserved to stay in a nice place and not a run-down motel. I was worth investing in, Dennis had always said. Also, if he did come back with me, I wanted it to be somewhere nice. He was used to luxurious hotels in swanky places, so I didn't want to give him less than he was used to.

Dressed in a new-to-me floral dress that I'd not worn before, in mid-height long boots and a fake fur coat, I felt glamorous for the first time in a long time. I had made extra effort with my make-up and had straightened my hair, wanting it to look different to the normal surfer shaggy look that I wore.

The sun came out just as I stepped out onto the pavement outside the hotel. I hoped it was a good sign. I was clutching the instructions from the concierge of how to get to the address on the business card I was holding in the other hand.

Just ten minutes later, I arrived at the large glass-fronted building where Dennis worked. I started to run various scenarios through my head. He'd left and didn't work there any more. He'd gone on holiday. He was off sick. He'd refuse to see me. In none of them did I see him standing with open arms welcoming me to him.

Remembering the taxi driver's last words to me from the day before, I took a deep breath, pushed on the revolving door and walked towards the reception desk, which was manned by a very glamorous young woman who was talking into a headset. She just stared at me as I approached and I wasn't sure whether she was talking to me or someone on the other end of her headset when she tutted and said, 'Yes?', looking me in the eye questioningly.

This was my moment. I just had to be brave. I could either back out now or I could do something that could change mine and Dennis's lives.

I gave Dennis's name and asked if he was free.

'Gosh, not another woman here to see Dennis.' She rolled her eyes. 'Take a seat and I'll try and get hold of him for you.'

As I sat on the very low and quite uncomfortable reception chair, I wondered what she meant.

I was surprised that she hadn't even asked my name and when she sashayed across the foyer to me in heels and a very tight short pencil skirt that were both more apt for a nightclub than an office, in my humble opinion, I smiled, trying not to judge.

'He's in a meeting. It's not long started so he'll probably be a while. Do you want to come back later?'

I quickly thought about what might be best, feeling very on the spot.

'Would it be OK if I wait?'

'Suit yourself.'

Gosh. Talk about an attitude.

I was trying not to keep glancing at the clock above the desk but failing miserably. I kept locking eyes with Miss Prim and Proper; the more I tried not to, the more I failed. When I noticed that an hour had passed, suddenly desperate for the loo, I asked her if I could use the ladies'. She pointed a long-manicured finger in the direction of the corridor and I headed that way.

Checking that I still looked reasonably put together in the bathroom toilets, I took a deep breath and opened the door back into the corridor.

A familiar voice drifted towards me although I couldn't work out the words until the person speaking was much closer. There was a male and a female voice, and I pulled the door to, peering out through the gap that I'd left open, my heart beginning to thump so loud, I thought they might be able to hear.

The woman who stood with her back to me, just about three metres away, was tall and elegant with her platinum blonde hair pulled back into a swingy high ponytail. In cream tailored trousers, bronze high-heeled shoes and a heavy giraffe-print coat, her style radiated glamour, and the heavy gold bracelet dangling from her wrist seemed to ooze class and money.

I took a sharp intake of breath when she raised her hand and cupped Dennis's face which he, to my horror, seemed to be enjoying.

'Don't take too long to make your mind up, Dennis. There's a place on my yacht with your name on it, just waiting for you to say yes. Just imagine what a fabulous time we could have. Just like the last time. You know it makes sense.' She made the shape of a telephone with her hand and simply purred, 'Call me!'

As she turned to walk away, I could see that she was beautifully groomed, with perfect make-up, and ruby-red glossy lipstick. She was simply stunning and, looking down at my second-hand outfit, I felt like a frumpy old country bumpkin compared to her. Why would Dennis ever look at me when he could have a woman who looked like that?

I turned and locked myself in one of the cubicles and banged on the door in frustration.

I couldn't believe how ridiculously stupid I could possibly be. I'd come all the way here, assuming that Dennis would be waiting for me, ready to fall into my arms. When all along, he'd got other women just waiting in the wings. Keeping his options open no doubt. My only saving grace was that he hadn't known I'd been here at all.

When the tears stopped, I took another deep breath and bravely opened the door into the corridor, checking that there was no one around. A glance towards the reception desk told me that Miss Prim and Proper was talking on the phone and I walked as quickly as I possibly could past the desk and out through the revolving door, leaving the shouts of her yelling 'excuse me' behind.

As I stepped out onto the street, the tears fell and this time I didn't even bother to let them stop as I started to run.

Maybe I *did* read too many romance novels. Not everything tied up nicely at the end and the happy couple lived happily ever after. I was a fool. An absolute idiot. Happy-ever-afters obviously never happened in the real world. Life was not a fairy tale after all.

48

When I arrived in the foyer back my hotel, I asked if I could check out early and get a refund, but sadly, they wouldn't refund the extra night. It was the night before Christmas Eve but their Christmas spirit was clearly not at the forefront of their customer service. My heart and my soul was completely deflated and I didn't care how much money it would cost me now, but I just wanted to go home and lick my wounds in my familiar surroundings. But fate had other ideas because when I checked the train time app to change my tickets, there were no more trains until the following day anyway.

I left the hotel, not knowing where I was going but knowing I didn't want to go and sit in my room alone.

All my visions of spending time with Dennis in London were now long gone. When he'd talked about how fabulous the Oxford Street lights were at this time of year, and how beautiful Covent Garden was, I had envisaged us wandering around hand in hand, taking in the sights and then coming back to the hotel and spending the night together, truly being with the one I loved.

I wandered for miles before I realised I hadn't a clue where I was. Being lost in London made me realise just how out of my depth I was and how I should never have come. My battery had run out on my phone so I couldn't even use Google Maps and if I stopped to ask someone, I probably would have scared them to death. I was pretty sure I looked like Alice Cooper. I was sat on a stone bench somewhere in London, with a cold backside, not knowing where the hell I was and not knowing a soul apart from someone who didn't want to see me.

A beep of a horn startled me, and bizarrely the taxi driver from yesterday was dropping off a fare.

'Small world, eh? What's the chances of seeing you here?' He laughed out of his window before he saw that I was clearly not happy. I'd spent the day looking at faces that I didn't know, yet when I saw this man's friendly face, I burst out into tears again.

He pulled over a little further up the road and was suddenly beside me on the bench.

'What on earth has happened?'

It all came tumbling out before I had time to think. How I'd very nearly made a total fool of myself and how instead of doing those touristy things that people did in London at Christmas, I wouldn't be doing any of them, least of all with the man I loved.

'Don't be hard on yourself, lovely. I just want to ask if you're sure of what you saw and heard.'

'Yep! He's just a complete bastard. It's my own fault. I should have known better. Why would someone like that ever be interested in someone like me?' I wailed loudly and he handed me a crisp white cotton handkerchief.

'People still use these?' I hiccuped through my tears.

'Every day my lovely wife gives me a freshly ironed one as I leave the house. Says you never know when it might come in handy.'

I scoffed. 'She won't like it much if you return it full of snot and mascara.'

'She wouldn't mind at all. Salt of the earth, my Emma. And I know that if it was one of my girls, who was sat on a stone bench crying over a man, in the middle of London in December, getting a cold arse, she'd hope that someone would do the same for them. She'd also give me a huge bollocking if I didn't get you into my warm cab and take you back to where you're staying.'

I laughed through my tears.

'Sounds like my mum.'

'She sounds like a good mum.'

'And so does your Emma!'

'She'd also tell me that if I didn't take you to see the sights you wanted to see I'd be in big trouble too. Look, I know this just sounds weird, but that last person I dropped off is my last call for the day. How about I take you to Covent Garden and we have a nice cup of tea somewhere?'

I had no idea who this man was, and if I read more psychological thrillers, I probably wouldn't ever have given him the time of day, but he seemed so lovely and genuine, and I felt like he was honest and good.

I dithered. Should I go or not?

'I promise you I'm not a serial killer.' He winked.

'Yeah, that's what they all say!' I laughed.

I remembered his kind words from the day before. And his great advice. *Be brave.*

'A cup of tea, you say?'

He nodded his head.

'If you make it a gin and tonic and I buy, you're on!'

He grinned back at me.

'Only if you sit up front though. I do this with my daughters and they get really annoyed with me for pointing out all the landmarks.'

'It's a deal. I haven't a clue where all the landmarks are anyway. I'd love you to point them out to me.'

'In that case, you can consider me your personal tour guide. This way, milady.' He hooked his arm for me to grab on to and then opened the passenger side door to the cab. 'He's a fool, you know. A real fool.'

* * *

Sitting with a total stranger in an outside bar in Covent Garden, under a patio heater and wrapped up in my fake fur coat, should have seemed really bizarre but it wasn't at all. Ralph was a total gentleman and told me all about his children and grandchildren, clearly a wonderful man with family at the heart of everything he did. We even called his wife from the bar so I could speak to her. She was so lovely and said that he was just a big old softie who wanted to help everyone and that he'd never been any different. It was one of the many reasons why she loved him so much.

We went back to my hotel via Harrods, Trafalgar Square, the Houses of Parliament, Oxford Street and even Buckingham Palace, with Ralph pointing out all the landmarks.

'I just wanted to make sure that your trip to London wasn't a total waste of time, darlin',' he said as he pulled up outside my hotel.

'Considering what happened earlier, I've had a really lovely end of the day. Thank you, Ralph.' I leaned across and kissed his cheek.

'You take care, girl. And remember, you're too good for him anyway.'

He dropped me off at the hotel entrance and I waved as he

drove away. Going back into my hotel room that evening should have felt a million times worse than it did and I thanked God for genuinely wonderful people in this world we live in.

* * *

'Have you enjoyed your stay, madam?' the receptionist's sing-song voice asked me as I checked out the next morning.

I hesitated before answering. 'It wasn't quite what I was expecting but yes, in the end I did.'

'Well, that's good to hear. I hope to see you again soon.'

As I walked away, dragging my case behind me, I realised that I would probably never return to this hotel again. And possibly never again to London. I had mixed memories. Ralph had somehow turned a shitty day into a really pleasant experience, but I just wanted to be back at home now, sat around the table in our kitchen with my mum, Dad and bickering with our Dan. Maybe it was OK if that was what my happy-ever-after was meant to look like. Times change after all. Maybe fairy tales do too.

49

I'd texted Mum and said I didn't want to talk about it but would be on the first train out of Paddington at 6 a.m. Dad picked me up from Truro and I arrived back in the bay just before twelve and decided to go straight to the shop for a few hours. When I arrived, it turned out Mum and Dan were already there, as well as a steady stream of customers. I got to work straight away, trying to welcome the distraction and avoid the pitying glances that Mum and Dan were giving me.

I knew we were a funny bunch in Driftwood Bay and we were properly stuck in our ways and when Mum said we'd be having tea at the bistro before going to the pub, I said that I didn't feel like going after my long day of travelling.

'Well, I'm not taking no for an answer. Otherwise you'll just sit at home and mope. And we don't do that in our family. So we're going and that's that! It's the Christmas pub quiz tonight, so we have to go.'

I felt the huge loss of not having Dennie in our team. There were a handful of questions that we all knew that he would have been able to answer but thankfully no one mentioned it. I'd hoped that Vi would have come along but Mum said she wasn't feeling great and didn't fancy a night out.

It was cold on our walk back to the house, crisp with a frost forming but a clear inky sky, lit up by a million twinkly stars.

'I'll be in shortly, Mum. I'm just going to have five minutes down in the harbour.'

She kissed my temple. 'OK, darling. Don't be long though. It's cold.'

I sat on a bench in the harbour, watching the boats sway on the water, a feeling of heaviness within that wouldn't lift. The halyards clinking was a sound that I didn't normally notice that much after living here for so long but tonight it was the only sound in the air. In my fairy tale, my film star boyfriend would come and sit next to me on the bench and after a few moments of silence just say hi. Then he would declare his undying love for me, take me in his arms and kiss me passionately before taking me home, throwing me on the bed and, as Vi would say, roger me senseless.

I looked across at the empty space beside me on the bench and sighed loudly, wondering what Dennie would be doing right then. Was he with her? Were they planning to spend Christmas Day together? On her yacht? Had he forgotten about me already? Were all those words of his lies? Did he mean any of it?

Heavy footsteps interrupted my thoughts and a shadow fell across my lap, blocking out the light from the street lamp. The bench dipped as someone sat next to me and snaked their arm around my shoulder and I found myself folding into them, crying quietly into their parka jacket.

'It's OK, sis. I've got you.'

And my brother rocked me until, sniffing loudly and wiping at my nose with my sleeve, I suggested that we went home. I fell into bed and slept like a log.

50

'Today doesn't feel the same without you,' I said, leaning forward over the grave. 'I have such amazing memories of you coming over every Christmas Eve and as kids it was nearly as exciting as Christmas Day because we were always allowed to open our present from you. I loved those times. We were always allowed to stop up late and had such fun playing board games together.'

Kneeling down on the gardening pad I'd brought with me, I removed all the dead flowers that were lying around. I placed them, along with a few stray leaves, in a cloth bag, replacing them with the beautiful poinsettia I'd brought with me. Dan and I had always bought one of these plants for Mum and one for Aunty Theresa at Christmas. Just another little family tradition that made things feel extra special.

'You'd have made a wonderful mum, Aunty T. You have been a second mum to me all my life and I can't tell you how much I miss you. I know you told us not to come to your graveside, because you wouldn't be here, but I just wanted to come by today. It's been quite a funny few months. I don't know if you know everything that goes on down here, and if anyone is listening to me they probably think

I'm stark raving mad for talking to you, but I'm not entirely sure how all this works.'

I adjusted my position.

'I've always been able to talk to you about anything. Your advice has been invaluable to me over the years and I could really do with it now. I met someone, you see. I thought he was... you know... the one. I feel so stupid now for thinking it. I've made a fool of myself in front of everyone. You always did say I had a trusting nature, but this time I think it got the better of me. I trusted someone who I thought loved me as much as I loved them, but it turned out not to be quite what I thought. I know I'll get over it given time. But right now, I'm just really, really sad.'

A stray tear rolled down my cheek and I brushed it away with the back of my hand.

'Some days, I forget you're not here any more. I do something at the shop and think, I must tell Aunty T about that, but then it hits me all over again that I can't. Mum lets on that she's OK, but I've heard her crying and talking to Dad about you. She tries really hard to put on a brave face and says that we have to live our lives to the full, because not everyone has that privilege. She talks about how she hated you when she first met you but how she gave your friendship a chance and what firm friends you became.'

Their friendship was something so special. I'd watched them over the years and longed for a friendship like theirs, but there wasn't really anyone in my life like that. As a child, I always had my nose in a book and then I moved away to go uni and was soon back again. With Driftwood Bay being such a small place, I suppose those that never moved away had made their friends by then. I'd just never found that person for me. I think that's why I fell so hard for Dennie. I'd felt like we really were becoming the best of friends. And I missed my friend.

'I really wish with all my heart that you were able to see my gorgeous little bookshop and know how grateful I am to you for giving me the money to realise my dream. I know I had a bit of a rocky start, but the last thing I would ever have wanted would be to let you down and I hope that now I've had some great help, you are proud of what I've achieved. I would never want to disappoint you. You mean – meant – the world to me and you always will, and I feel like a little bit of you lives on in the bookshop. I hope you are always around me, watching over me, protecting me. I'll never forget you.'

I closed my eyes, picturing Aunty T. sat in the wing-back armchair in the bay window of my shop overlooking her beloved Driftwood Bay. I did know that she'd have been the biggest supporter I could have had and would be telling all her friends about the shop. She was a huge bookworm herself and I remembered vividly the weekends when I used to go and stay with her and we used to have quiet time where we'd both sit and read. She really was the one that made me realise it was OK to be a book nerd. Book nerds were – and are – cool.

'I could sit here talking to you all day, Aunty T., but my backside is starting to go numb. I hope you like your plant. I might not have Dennis with me for Christmas, but I have everything else in my life that I need: a fabulous family, a gorgeous bookshop and some wonderful memories. Thanks for the chat. Merry Christmas.'

I blew a kiss to the grave and read the inscription which I already knew off by heart.

Theresa Matthews
Beloved daughter, friend and aunty
Forever in our hearts

Life was cruel at times, taking our loved ones way too soon, when they still had so much life ahead of them. It makes you realise – we think we have all the time in the world when we don't. If we're lucky enough to have hopes and dreams, it's up to us to go and grab them while we have the chance. Aunty T. might have been gone from our lives but the lessons she left behind would live on forever in Books In The Bay, but more than that, in my heart.

51

'He's been!'

Dad tapped on my bedroom door gently and I put my head back under the covers. Surely it wasn't time to get up yet.

'He's been, darling.'

This time I could hear Mum's voice but I chose to ignore her too.

'Fucking hell, Nancy. Santa's been all round the world last night, including here and you can't even be arsed to get out of bed.'

My brother suddenly landed on top of me, rocking me not so gently.

'Ooof!'

'Get up, get up, Nancy!'

'Kack off, Dan.'

'Language, children.' Mum laughed.

'Kack isn't even swearing, Mum.' Dan always argued this point.

'I don't care, Daniel. I don't like it so stop using it. You're not too big for a clip round the ear, you know.'

Dan climbed over the top of me and landed heavily on the other side, digging me in the ribs.

'You'd have to catch me first,' he laughed.

Mum squidged in next to me, the bed dipping, and she reached across, slapping Dan playfully. At the same time, Dad shuffled in on the other side. I grinned. It had been years since we'd done this. It was nice to have the family all together. I knew this would be a very different day for Dan to his last few Christmases, where he wasn't permitted to come out at all, not even to see his family. And we weren't allowed to visit either. Mum had always tried not to show she was bothered that he went to Sabrina's family instead but every year I could see the hurt in her eyes.

This year, she looked deliriously happy as she pulled us all in tight for a hug.

'My family,' she muttered under her breath and sighed loudly. 'Merry Christmas.'

* * *

'Right, the turkey is in, there are forty pigs-in-blankets ready to go in the oven, the veggies are all peeled and there's just time to have a quick cuppa before we head down to the beach to watch those total nutters do their Christmas Day swim.'

Every year at midday on Christmas Day, the Driftwood Babes braved the cold water and did a swim, encouraging the locals to join in. There were never many people who joined them, despite them all saying that they would, but always loads who stood by and watched. Gemma always brought down her mobile catering unit, and hot drinks were available and very much needed, and there was even the odd Baileys in coffee, or brandy in hot chocolate to warm up the swimmers.

Dan had been behaving quite shiftily in the last hour, and when the door went, he grabbed his coat.

'Where are you going?'

'Mind your own beeswax, missy. You should never ask questions around Christmas.'

My brows furrowed. I hoped he wasn't planning something as a surprise. I'd gone off surprises. In fact, recently, I'd gone off most things.

'Nothing for you to worry about, sis. Just need to see a man about a dog.' He grinned and slammed the door behind him as Mum yelled, 'Daniel, don't slam the door!' as she headed through with mugs of tea for me, her and Dad. Maybe today was going to be all right.

* * *

This year, it was a cold but bright sunny day. No white Christmas for us, but a sunny day at the beach as long as you were wrapped up.

A kerfuffle behind us made us all spin around, and we saw Dan being yanked along by two very energetic reddish-brown small Border collies.

'Oh my God, Dan. What the hell?'

'Well, if you can't give yourself a Christmas present, what can you do? I'd like to introduce you to Dexter and Meg. My new pals.'

'You said you wanted a dog but I didn't expect you to get them *today*. Or have two.'

'Well, I thought they'd be good company for each other. And I suppose if you have the commitment of one, you may as well have two. It's a good job Driftwood Bay is a dog friendly community, isn't it?'

Mum and Dad joined us and soon most of the villagers came over to see the new additions.

'You've met your brother's two new pups then?' Mum grinned

at me as she leaned down and tickled one of them behind the ears. Would I ever be able to tell them apart, I wondered.

'You knew?' I turned to them both.

'We all thought it might be a nice surprise. And obviously with Dan now moving back in with us again, he had to ask us whether he could have them in the house. He had the sense to not just turn up with them. Even he's not that stupid.' Dad ruffled his son's hair. 'Although the sooner he finds himself somewhere else to live, the better. I never thought at our age in life, we'd still have our two kids living at home. This should be the time your mother and I are enjoying our lives without you lot hanging around.'

'Ah, be off with you. You know I love to have my babies home. It's like my world is complete.'

'And there's me thinking that I was your world.' Dad laughed.

'Absolutely not. I never gave birth to you, did I? I grew these two and they are my special ones and they can stay at home as long as they want.'

'I did have something to do with making them, you know.'

'Yeah, not that much though. You just provided the sperm. That could have been anyone you know.'

'God you're harsh.' He laughed.

'You know I'm only joking. You *are* the love of my life. Our family are the loves of both our lives. And we both know how much you love having our kids at home too.'

Dad nodded. 'You're absolutely right. Two kids and now two dogs. God help me.'

You see, this was the type of relationship I wanted. Someone to laugh with, to love with. To know that I was loved unconditionally and never doubt the strength of that love. It was no wonder I found it hard to find someone to live up to that. I thought I had that with Dennie, but obviously not.

I fell to my knees on the sand and both dogs came tumbling

over, dragging Dan behind. They both turned a full circle and sat, nestling their bums into me.

'That's a sign they trust you. Did you know that?'

'Aw, that's nice.'

'I'm glad you like them, Nancy, because you might have to have them at the shop with you from time to time if I have to go out on a job.'

'Now, that will not be a problem at all. They're both gorgeous. I love them already.' I buried my face in Dexter's soft fluffy neck and he snuggled into me. It felt like he and I were going to be the best of friends. Meg too. She was such a pretty girl and soon bumped her brother out of the way to get to me. I think we were kindred spirits.

'Phew! Glad you said that because I've already booked some work in that might need Aunty Nancy to be their Fairy Dogmother.'

We all laughed at my new nickname. They really were little bundles of fluff, although I'm not sure I'd get any work done with them around in the shop. However, Dennis was due to launch his business properly in the new year and I would do everything I could to help him make it work. The dogs would be lovely company for me at the shop too. I couldn't wait to be their dog aunty. What an honour.

* * *

'Here come the girls,' Mum announced as she and Rachel from the bistro, who was helping out Gemma that morning, came over with a large tray of hot chocolates for the swimmers to warm them up. When her hands were empty, Rachel came over to see the dogs.

Dan lit up like a Belisha beacon as she fawned over them. And she said that she'd love to join Dan on a walk if he ever fancied any company or needed an extra pair of hands. At that, he became a little tongue-tied. Mum and I shared a look. Rachel was nice. She'd really changed her life around since moving to Driftwood Bay to be near her daughter Occy who was now Gemma's stepdaughter. Maybe they'd become friends. It would be good for Dan to finally have some friends that he'd chosen for himself.

When all of the Driftwood Babes were wrapped back up again and their hands warmed through the heat of their mugs, Dan yelled, 'Look, is that a dolphin? Or a seal?'

We all looked out to sea.

In the distance there was definitely something bobbing around in the water, which we couldn't quite work out. But then when the blob raised a bare arm and waved, we realised that it was a person.

'Well I never...' Vi exclaimed loudly. 'The silly daft boy.'

'Who is it, Vi?' Dan asked. 'Who's stupid enough to swim in the sea on Christmas Day?'

Realising what he'd just said rather loudly, he turned sheepishly towards the group of women stood behind him draped with towels thinking that they might be offended, but luckily they didn't appear to have heard him.

Those strong forearms looked mighty familiar to me, even from this distance. I started to wander nearer to the shoreline, frowning to make sure I was right.

I snorted as the voice that shouted out confirmed it was Dennie, who was now waving at me from the sea.

'Are you coming in?' he yelled.

'The hell I am.' I laughed.

'Well, if you don't come in then I'll have to come out and embarrass myself in front of the whole of Driftwood Bay and I have to tell you that I am totally naked and it's not a pretty sight. You wouldn't do that to me, now, would you?' He was shouting from his position and started to wade towards me, his shoulders now above the water level.

'I am *not* coming in, Dennie.'

'Well, in that case, I'll just shout to you from here.'

He waded a little further towards the shore, the water level now just above his belly button. I threw back my head and laughed.

'What are you doing?' I asked.

'You once told me that a boy at school wouldn't prove his love to you by swimming in the sea on Christmas Day.'

I remembered telling him about my schoolboy crush.

'It's true! He wouldn't.'

The water was now just above his hips. He was close enough for me to see the line of dark hair which trailed downwards.

'Well, I will. I love you, Nancy. And I don't care who hears this. The whole of Driftwood Bay can hear for all I care. The whole of Cornwall even. I love you, I love you, I love you.'

I threw my head back and laughed.

'Dennie, you are mental.'

'Am I? I honestly can't feel my brain right now, let alone anything else. I think my whole body is numb with cold. I'm trying to work out if I'm a boy or a girl right now because I think something might have dropped off in there.'

I looked back towards the beach where it seemed like the whole of Driftwood Bay was watching and waiting for me to say the right thing.

I grinned and started to take off my trainers and roll up my trouser legs.

Then, throwing my coat off onto the sand behind me, I ran full pelt into the sea.

'I must be bloody mad!' I mumbled to myself.

The smile on Dennie's face as I approached was as wide as the sea itself. When I got to around two metres away, I slowed down, finally coming to a halt. He stepped towards me and closed the gap, and when I could feel his breath on my face, he reached up to tuck a wayward strand of my hair behind my ear. He ran his finger down my cheek.

'Is this really you?' he asked.

I nodded and shivered, not sure whether it was from the temperature of the water or the fact that I was stood in front of the man that I now knew, without a shadow of a doubt, was the person I wanted to share the rest of my life with. I tilted my head up until there wasn't a millimetre between us and finally our lips met. I ran my hands all over his torso and finally lowered them under the water.

I felt my eyebrows nearly leave my face.

'Oh hello! You really *are* naked.'

'I did tell you I was.'

'I can confirm that you are most definitely *not* a girl.'

'I was hoping not. Now can put your hand back down there again and kiss me like that again, please?'

I stood away from him, and frowned, a memory flooding back into my mind.

'I came to London.'

'I know.' He tried to pull me against him but I pulled away.

'How do you know?'

'The girl on reception. She described you to me and there was no doubt that it was you.'

I thought back to how frumpy I'd felt that day next to the gorgeous woman that I'd seen Dennie with.

'But I saw you with someone.'

'Did you?'

'Yes, she was stunning.'

'That would have been Craig's wife.'

'Oh!' I was starting to tremble, the cold creeping into my bones and he rubbed my arms with his hands. I was struggling to keep up with what he was saying. All I could think about was how icy cold the water was.

'She'd asked me to take over the company. To be the CEO. Her uncle had asked her to ask me. We'd all spent some time in the summer on his uncle's yacht and she wanted me to join them again this year in Dubai for Christmas.'

'So you're taking over then? Is that what you've come back to tell me?' I tried to get away from him.

'No, you idiot. I've come back to tell you that I love you and that I've handed in my notice and that I'm moving to Driftwood Bay. If you'll have me that is. I've heard that there's a flat that needs doing up above a really pretty little bookshop and I was thinking about putting an offer in on it.'

'Oh!'

'Is that all you've got to say, Nancy?'

'No! It's not. I do have something else to say.'

'Go on.'

'I love you too.'

'Thank fuck for that. Does that mean we can get out of this water now then, if you believe me? I'm freezing my nuts off!'

We both laughed and headed for the shore, holding hands so tightly that I thought my blood circulation would be cut off, although it could just be the cold. My mother walked towards us, handing a towel to Dennis.

'Cover yourself up, dear.' She winked at him. 'You are making every male in Driftwood Bay feel extremely inferior.'

Dennie had the good nature to blush.

'*Now* I can see why you love him, Nancy.'

It was my turn to blush. 'Muuuummmm!'

She walked away, waving over her shoulder. 'Only saying what everyone else is thinking.'

We both giggled as Dennie wrapped the towel around his waist, tucking in the end part. I could hear Mum's voice as she made a concerted effort to round everyone up to give us some privacy.

'Come along, everyone, nothing to see here.'

Dennie grinned and turned to face me again, cupping my face in his hands and staring deeply into my eyes.

'God I love you, Nancy.'

'I love you too.'

Our lips met once more. I would never tire of kissing that mouth. Tasting Dennie.

'Look!' someone yelled out from the top of the beach and pointed out to sea. When we looked up, a pod of dolphins was arcing through the water, a truly beautiful and special sight. So rare, as dolphins normally migrated to warmer waters at that time of year.

'You don't see that every day in London, do you?'

'In the Thames you don't see an awful lot to be honest.'

'Maybe you should stay in Driftwood Bay after all then.'

'Is that a yes, Nancy? Are you happy for me to stay?'

I hesitated, and laughed out loud at his mortified face, which was an absolute picture as his towel seemed to unravel itself and dropped to the sand and my eyes flicked down and back up again, before he grabbed it to cover himself up again.

'Oh yes, I definitely think you should stay.'

We closed the distance between us and he took me in his arms once more and dipped me backwards, kissing me.

'Thank goodness for that. I don't think I could ever write letters like that again.'

'You're an excellent writer and I will expect beautiful love letters like that every day we are together.'

He laughed.

'No, I mean it. Now shut up and kiss me.'

Despite the audience, it felt like we were the only people in the world as I explored every tiny part of his mouth, while running my hands all over his body.

'Seriously, Nancy, if you do that again, I'm not sure I can be responsible for my next actions.'

So, I did it again...

ACKNOWLEDGEMENTS

The biggest thank you goes to my readers and the book reviewing community. If it wasn't for you wonderful people who read my books I wouldn't be writing them. I appreciate that you choose and love my books when there are so many fabulous authors in the world for you to pick from.

To my writing retreat buddies Sue Watson, Emma Robinson and Susie Lynes. Thank you for filling my joyometer when we meet.

To my lovely friend and fabulous author Beth Rain. Thank you for always being at the end of a message for a whinge, a whine, a reality check, writing sprint, motivational chats and virtual hugs.

To Ian Wilfred. Thank you for being an amazing beacon of light in the writing world. For always having the time to share a promo, retweet a tweet, comment on a Facebook post and generally being one of the most supportive people around.

To the wonderful author community, thank you for all the love and support you give to me. Special thanks to Jessica Redland, Helen Rolfe and Jo Bartlett.

To the Boldwood Team, those behind the scenes and front of house. I appreciate your hard work so very much. Thank you for everything you do to bring my books into the hands of readers.

To my editor Emily Yau, thank you for loving this book and for your supportive editorial comments.

To wonderful Sandra Ferguson, for your eagle eye and for spotting how repetitive I am, and how repetitive that can be (winky face! LOL). Also, I'd like to give a huge thank you to the fabulous Shirley Khan. Whatever would I do without you?

To my cover designer Alex Allden for doing such a fabulous job of bringing the village of Driftwood Bay and the characters alive.

Last but one to the Jenkins family. My darling sister Lisa, my favourite brother-in-law Peter and my lovely nephew Marcus. It's been a tough old start to the year, but we'll get through it. Together.

And finally to my son Ollie. I'm so proud to be your mother. I love you to the moon and back and thank you for your hugs, support and encouragement and for reminding me of what I've achieved when I'm being a mardy cow. This has been a huge year for you with GCSEs, college searches and trials and you have been amazing. You are an absolute joy to be a Mum to and I'm so incredibly proud of you.

ABOUT THE AUTHOR

Kim Nash is the author of uplifting, romantic fiction and an energetic blogger alongside her day job as Digital Publicity Director at Bookouture.

Sign up to Kim Nash's mailing list for news, competitions and updates on future books.

Visit Kim's website: www.kimthebookworm.co.uk

Follow Kim on social media here:

- facebook.com/KimTheBookWorm
- x.com/KimTheBookworm
- instagram.com/kim_the_bookworm
- bookbub.com/authors/kim-nash
- goodreads.com/kimnash

ALSO BY KIM NASH

The Cornish Cove Series

Hopeful Hearts at the Cornish Cove

Finding Family at the Cornish Cove

Making Memories at the Cornish Cove

The Bookshop at the Cornish Cove

Standalone

Amazing Grace

Escape to the Country

BECOME A MEMBER OF

THE SHELF CARE CLUB

The home of Boldwood's book club reads.

Find uplifting reads, sunny escapes, cosy romances, family dramas and more!

Sign up to the newsletter
https://bit.ly/theshelfcareclub

Boldwood

Boldwood Books is an award-winning fiction publishing company seeking out the best stories from around the world.

Find out more at www.boldwoodbooks.com

Join our reader community for brilliant books, competitions and offers!

Follow us

@BoldwoodBooks

@TheBoldBookClub

Sign up to our weekly deals newsletter

https://bit.ly/BoldwoodBNewsletter

Printed in Dunstable, United Kingdom